THE MIRACLE WORKER
OF MINGO COUNTY

DAN SCOTT

EDITED BY
ELICIA HYDER

INKWELL & QUILL, LLC

CONTENTS

ALSO BY DAN SCOTT

FAITH IN THE AGE OF AI

Artificial Intelligence, decoding the human genome, links between mind and computer... All these things that were once science fiction, are now quickly—and *absolutely*—becoming science *fact*.

The world is understandably worried. Fortunately, this isn't the first time humanity has faced such uncertainty.

In Faith in the Age of AI, pastor, scholar, and counselor Dan Scott invites you to learn what revered early writers—from Plato to St. Paul, and Laozi to C.S. Lewis—have already said about faith in the age of Artificial Intelligence.

1

DESPAIRING CRIES

MICHAEL COOPER

I didn't figure God was smilin' down on Logan County that night of the flood. I just couldn't figure out for the life of me where he was when all hell broke loose on Buffalo Creek.

That boy hangin' on a porch swing, fightin' to keep his head above water and disappearin' neath the cold waters of Buffalo Creek . . . Lord, that's something I wish I'd never seen!

You can't unsee something like that. You blot it out for a while, but it comes roarin' back, at the darndest times and for no particular reason.

When I recall it, I think of Granny's song about a soul sinkin' in sin, far from the peaceful shore. In her song, the soul is just about to sink to rise no more when the Master of the Sea swoops in to save it.

The problem is, there weren't no Master of the Sea anywhere near Buffalo Creek that February. If he had of been, he would have heard plenty of despairing cries.

Me? Well, the good Holiness kid that I was, I kept

commandin' the waters to stop, pacin' up and down the edge of the creek yellin' out the name of God, like Moses. It didn't work, but I kept right on a beseechin' and a commandin' anyhow. Them houses, cars, and stuff just kept pilin up against the bridges, just like they was bein' pushed by invisible snowplows.

Finally, the blasted bridges broke up, and all the furniture, toys, and bodies from up Buffalo Creek started flowin' down together in a muddy heap, all the way down to the Guyandotte.

Course, the Pittston Coal people were all safe up in New York—them who weren't at the Riviera or the Bahamas—busy investin' all the money they had saved from not payin' engineers to design drainage systems for their blasted dams.

What they said was that all them dead babies and destroyed houses was an act of God! In the opinion of Pittston Coal, it was the Lord God Almighty hisself who sent that two-hour scourge of toxic sludge gushin' down the mountain to bury the bodies of the dead and the spirits of the living.

The honorable Governor Arch Moore said the lost reputation of the state was even worse than the flood!

We had more sense than that down in Logan County. We knew it was the owners of Pittston Coal who had set loose the hounds of hell. I don't recall anybody on Buffalo Creek havin' an ounce of concern about how the flood damaged the state's reputation. We knew that although Governor Moore's mouth was open, the words comin' out of it weren't his. He was talkin' like a ventrilo-quist dummy on the knee of his owners. We couldn't see the coal company owners' mouths a movin' but we recognized the voice comin' out of the governor's mouth.

So, no. I didn't blame God exactly.

I just wanted to know why He watched those fat-assed vultures up North pocket the money they had made from the bones of miners and kids. I wanted to know why he allowed them to go on about their business, like swollen ticks on a hound dog's leg, suckin' up the last drop of its victim's life . . . Why the God who's got the whole world in his hands kept watchin' 'em up there in New York City a wallowin' around in blood money while poverty-stricken, God-fearin' coal miners' children kept bowin' their heads and givin' thanks for gravy and biscuits, nary a one of 'em knowin' that a wall of darkness was already gushin' off the top of mountain, comin' t' wash 'em away.

Pappy used to sing about an All Seeing Eye. Lordy! When he sang, the blood in a man would just stop and stir inside 'im. You ever hear singin' like that? I'll tell you what, when Pappy sang that song, you could almost see that big eye a hangin up there in the air, starin' down at everybody on earth!

After the flood, I started askin' myself why that All Seeing Eye seemed mostly interested in catchin' people drinkin' moonshine or fornicatin'—crap like that—but didn't notice that little kid hangin' on a porch swing, callin' out the name of God at the top of his little lungs.

I never made sense of it. I just know there weren't no flood up there in New York City. When nighttime tip-toed into town up there, the Pittston Coal Company owners were comin' back from fancy dinners over at the club. They tucked their babies in safe, warm beds and then lay their worry-free heads on silk pillows. Meanwhile, the children of Buffalo Creek—the ones who lived anyway—kept on cryin' for their dolls and tricycles. Even them who had lost moms and dads were screamin' for the toys they'd lost. The world was just too mean and big that night to worry about much else.

So, what did God think that night as them kids were a sayin' their prayers? I heard two of them prayin' together, "If I should die before I wake, I pray the Lord my soul to take."

But hellfire, the flood had already taken all kinds of souls up to God—in broad daylight!

To keep from hearin' their prayers, I started sayin' the words of a poem I learned out one of Daddy's old books.

"*When the stars threw down their spears,*
    And watered heaven with their tears,
        Did he smile his work to see?"

I can't imagine he did.

2

GATHERING FRAGMENTS
SAMUEL CANTERBURY

I first heard Brother Michael saying those words from an old cassette while driving to Beckley.

I didn't know much more about him then than you do. Oh, I had met him once, at his drug rehab place down in Logan. I was working on a piece about black lung compensation for the Charleston Gazette at the time, and I interviewed him about the disabled miners of Logan and Mingo Counties.

I wasn't aware of nor quite frankly concerned with, having made any impression on him. He did make an impression on me, though.

We were in the middle of that interview when he suddenly looked into my eyes and blurted out, "Sam Canterbury, what will you do with your life?"

Stunned, I muttered about trying to be a journalist.

"Well, early in our lives we were not to blame for being asleep," he said. "After all, the world puts us all to sleep—just like it did to the disciples in the garden. But there comes a time when it takes a lot of deliberate work to stay asleep. If you get to that stage, your sleeping soul corrupts and can even die. You don't want that."

"No," I replied. "I don't." Though I wasn't really sure what he was talking about.

"You have important things to do," he insisted. Then, he abruptly returned to the discussion about poverty and illness in Southern West Virginia.

That was the extent of our relationship. That's why I was so naturally shocked when his lawyer called to tell me Brother Michael had died. Then he informed me that the so-called miracle-man had willed me his papers—journals, diaries, academic papers—that sort of thing.

It didn't make sense. Brother Michael had to have known I was an obscure, wannabe writer. The part-time work I did for the Gazette barely supported my family. I was forty-three years old and hadn't completed a single book or even written a widely-distributed article of any kind. I now knew I wouldn't likely achieve any great success in my chosen profession, and I knew it was my own fault.

I went into debt studying journalism against the advice of my father and uncles and everybody I knew back in Cabin Creek. They all predicted I would never make enough to "buy a pot to pee in." That went on for years, kind folk telling me to get my head out of the clouds and make peace with the mines.

I still heard the voices in my head nearly every day.

So, why had led Brother Michael to will his papers to me? And what the heck did he want me to do with them?

It was another fool's errand, I thought; a seductive

voice wooing me to dream again, daring me to think I could ever be more than a third-rate copy writer.

My wife, Lois, would say it more gently and diplomatically than that, but I dreaded for her to know about this all the same. I wanted to be done with dreaming. Having already experienced several grand adventures that didn't pan out, I wasn't ready to run after another one. Once you eat enough sand, you become rather leery of mirages.

Unfortunately, this mirage would prove to be as insistent about being noticed as I was about ignoring it.

Anyway, I drove to Williamson the following Friday.

When I left that morning, I knew Lois would assume I was driving to work in Charleston. She already knew I would be coming home late. I had told her the night before that I would be going to Beckley later in the day. Of course, I didn't go to Charleston at all. I headed up Route 119 for Williamson.

It took me two and a half hours to get there because of the rain and the road work around Madison. I found the office easily enough though. It was near the river on Harvey Street. A lawyer named Josiah Cummings met me at the door, offered me a cup of coffee, and unlocked a large walk-in closet, where he retrieved five medium-sized boxes. Three of them were filled with old spiral notebooks, but on top of one of them was a large envelope. The old cassette tape envelope was all I found inside it. Two of the boxes contained formal-looking papers, college stuff I decided.

After signing the forms, I saw the notebooks were Brother Michael's personal journals. The other papers were his college and seminary class work. After saying my goodbyes to Mr. Cummings, I loaded the boxes in the back seat of my car and headed for Beckley.

Now, driving from Williamson to Beckley takes about an hour and a half. I figured that would put me into Beckley a couple of hours before I had promised to meet Buddy McCafferty, my old high school friend.

Buddy was originally from up Cabin Creek, near the mouth of Dawes Hollow. Shortly after graduating from East Bank, he'd moved to Roanoke. Most of my classmates had moved to Ohio to find work, though as many as could returned home after a while. The joke back then was that at East Bank, graduates were handed a map of Ohio along with their diploma. Buddy was always a bit different that way. He'd headed east.

A couple of weeks before, Buddy had called. He said he was planning to drive over to Huntington to see his sister. He wondered if I could meet him in Beckley and offer my opinion on a property he was thinking about buying.

I thought about telling him I was a poor judge of real estate, but in our part of the world people don't really ask their friends for advice because they actually think the advice will be worth anything. One just asks for advice because it shows you're not too big for your britches, that you haven't outgrown your raising. That's why we ask for advice we don't intend to heed and offer advice we don't expect to be taken seriously.

I figured I would arrive in Beckley a couple of hours before Buddy. I was glad about that. I was ready to see what this was all about.

Fortunately, my '87 Cougar happened to have a cassette player. That's how I heard Brother Michael talk about the flood. The tape wasn't easy to understand, and so I listened to it three or four times on my way to Beckley.

After I arrived at the Burger King where Buddy and I had agreed to meet—the one over on Harper Road—I took a journal from one of the boxes and went inside. I ordered a medium coffee with four little cups of cream, found a table near a window, and wiped a bit of water off the plastic blue seat. I then sat down, took a sip of the coffee, opened the notebook, and started to read.

There are a few times in life when a wondrous terror lets you know that you have crossed some sort of line that separates your "before" from "after." That's what I felt when I read the first few pages of that notebook. One moment, I had been casually flipping through the journal of a person I judged to be a kind but confused man.

The next moment, I was seized by something beyond myself and made to know I would be writing the story of the man that folk in Southern West Virginia (either in derision or awe) had called the Miracle Worker of Mingo County.

I hardly recall the visit with Buddy. I visited the property he wanted me to see and told him I thought it looked like a good deal. I then drove to the turnpike and headed for home.

The next morning, I got the boxes out of my car and carried them to the makeshift office I had built from what was once a back porch. The office wasn't much to look at. It was my personal space though, and I was proud of it.

I put the two boxes of college papers in the closet. After a perfunctory look at the titles, I decided I would not be reading any of them for a while. The journals however, I decided to read as soon as possible. I set all three boxes of spiral notebooks on my desk, announcing what I was doing in an official-sounding voice.

"Mystery Box Number One!

"Mystery Box Number Two!

"Mystery Box Number Three!"

After going into the kitchen and making a pot of coffee, I started reading through the contents of Mystery Box Number One.

That afternoon, I took a break to mow the grass. Just as I was finishing, Lois's brother Freddy came over with his family. We made hot dogs and talked on and on into the evening about not much.Sunday, we went to church, over in Cabin Creek. Monday, I edited a piece for the Gazette.

It was Tuesday before I had time to read any more in the journals.

Wednesday morning about 9:30, a UPS truck pulled up in front of my house. A man stepped out into the drizzling rain carrying a large box, which he set down near my front door. He then handed me a clipboard and asked me to sign. According to that form, the box had been sent from a clinic in Pittsburgh.

More befuddlement!

I didn't know anybody up in Pittsburgh. As far as I knew, there was nothing up there but a zoo some people around home talked about. But after opening the box, I read a letter laying on top of the other contents. It explained that a former patient, one Michael Journeyman Cooper, had made a legal request by certified mail for the clinic to release all copies of his files to:

Mr. Samuel Canterbury
411 Riggs Street
Montgomery, West Virginia.

Underneath that letter, in individually wrapped envelops, were pages of medical notes and a few cassette tapes. Each envelope was labeled, *Cooper, M. J. #1*, *Cooper, M. J. #2*, and so forth.

I didn't know then and haven't figured out since how Brother Michael got my address.

Furthermore, what did Pittsburgh have to do with this story? What I had been pulled into? And why had Brother Michael been a patient in a mental health facility? I had no idea.

One thing for sure, I wasn't ready to tackle another collection of papers just yet.

I had already been working through Mystery Box Number Three by that time. So, I decided to keep reading through the old journals. About halfway through that box, I picked up a small, grey stenographer's notebook, opened it, and saw a list of names, addresses, and phone numbers neatly arranged under the heading:

FOR INTERVIEWS WITH SAM CANTERBURY.

Every hair on my head stood on end. What in the name of everything sane and rational did any of this mean? Why had Brother Michael imagined I would come across this notebook and, even if I did, that I would be doing any interviews.

With whom? For what?

Lois was away with the boys, visiting her sister up in Clarksburg. I had been glad for a few days alone. It would allow me to catch up on stuff, I had thought. At that moment though, I would have been delighted for all three of them, and the dog too for that matter, to burst into the house. Anything to break the spell! But I kept staring at the list of names, including my own, compiled, according to the date written on the front of the notebook, two years before.

My eyes fixed on a name Brother Michael had underlined in red ink:

<u>Frieda McDaniels</u>
56 Bostic Road
Man, West Virginia

Followed by a phone number.

My stomach churning and my skin crawling, I picked up the phone and made a call.

A sweet and well-used voice soon answered.

"Hello?"

"Hello," I said. "Mrs. McDaniels?"

"Yes?"

"This is Sam Canterbury. I'm a reporter in Montgomery, over in Fayette County. I have recently come into possession of a collection of papers that once belonged to Michael Cooper. I hoped that you could help me make some sense of them. Did you know him?"

"Oh yes!" she said. "I'm not sure that I want to talk about him over the phone though. What exactly is your purpose for learning about Michael?"

"I'm not entirely sure," I said. "To tell you the truth, I am somewhat weirded out by everything connected to him. He willed me his papers—I have no idea why. One of them has your name and contact information, underlined in red. That's the reason I called."

After a long silence, Mrs. Frieda McDaniels chuckled. "Well, Mr. Canterbury, Michael seemed to have had that effect on people. Why don't you drive over here to Man so we can talk face to face?"

I asked whether the following day might work for her.

"Certainly," she replied. "I have been retired for years now. I don't keep what you would call a full schedule."

The following morning, I was wide awake by 6:00. I dressed, picked up the stenographer's notebook and a couple of the journals, and drove to Logan County. I stopped in Marmet only long enough to get a cup of coffee and a sausage biscuit to go.

The drive was uneventful. I listened to the radio but I don't recall much else about the drive. I just know that I arrived in Man without incident and quickly found Mrs. McDaniel's house.

It was a well-kept, Jim Walker prefab home, surrounded by flowers. Driving into the driveway I saw a woman standing on the porch under a couple of dozen pots filled with flowers hanging from the roof. She looked to be in her late 70s, of medium build, with white hair pulled back in a tight bun. She waited for me to get out of the car. When I did, she came to meet me.

"You're Sam," she said confidently.

"I confess," I replied.

"Do you have any conviction against eating apple pie at 9:00 in the morning?" She asked.

"Can't say that I do," I shot back.

"Then come on in. Let's talk about our dear Michael over some apple pie. It was his favorite."

The house smelled of apples, unsurprisingly. There was something else too though, something different than I had ever smelled before but which seemed attached to a memory I had lost sometime in the distant past. It made me sad and joyful at the same time.

I was glad Mrs. McDaniels was preparing the pie because by the time she had placed a plate in front of me and sat down at the table, I had conquered my unwelcome emotions.

She waited for me to comment on her pie, which fortunately was not difficult. It felt trite to say the pie was "heavenly," but what better word did I have?

As we ate, I explained how I had received Brother Michael's papers, including the ones from Pittsburgh. She listened intently, obviously evaluating my intentions as I talked. She seemed unsurprised by everything I said, including the part about the clinic.

"I was Michael's high school English teacher," she said. "Beginning in 1973.

"He was a mess, Michael was. He claimed he had

stopped smoking dope and drinking—and I do think he had—but he still wasn't right. The flood, you know.

"In the first months I knew him, Michael's words didn't come out right. Often, he would stare out into space. Then one day, I was introducing the life and work of William Blake. As soon as I mentioned Blake, Michael looked up was like someone had slapped him.

'Blake was the greatest writer ever!' Michael blurted out.

"Well, everyone in the class just looked at each other. High school boys aren't often interested in old authors like Blake anyway, but after a disaster like they'd all been through there didn't seem to be much point in studying anything connected to a subject like English Literature. Besides that, Michael hadn't made so much as a grunt in class before. Now he couldn't stop asking questions about everything related to Blake: Blake's poems, Blake's life, everything about William Blake."

Mrs. McDaniels smiled and shook her head.

"What was that about?" I asked. "It's been years since I studied English literature but wasn't William Blake kind of crazy?"

"Well, Sam," Mrs. McDaniel's replied, "that may be part of what you need to discover!

"The important thing for me was that Michael was awake. He suddenly cared about something. Teachers live for moments like that!

"I even drove over to Huntington to get a book of Blake's poems because I thought Michael might find it interesting. Didn't that turn out to be an understatement! Michael acted as though I had brought him an original Gutenberg Bible. For weeks, he worked at memorizing those poems. He wouldn't stop talking about them. His obsession began disrupting my class though.

"That's why I asked him to meet with me one day a week after school. I was determined to do my best to help him, you see. I thought if he could discover whatever it was he was trying to find, his life might take a turn for the better."

I had been writing on a legal pad as she talked. I stopped her from time to time only to ask questions about Michael's late teenage years. I was especially interested in his obsession with William Blake. I didn't know if Blake had anything to do with the adventure I had stepped into, but for the moment, the crazy poet was about all I had to go on.

A couple of hours had gone by before I knew it, and so I began to wrap things up.

As I walked down the steps of her porch, Frieda McDaniels, retired high school teacher of English literature, stood in the doorway looking me over.

"Sam?" she blurted out.

"Yes?"

"Wait just a minute, please," she said, darting back inside.

She quickly returned, holding several bulging manila envelopes in her hand.

"These are copies of Michael's high school papers," she said. "We discussed them in those after-school sessions I told you about. These papers are mostly about his early life in Mingo County. Some of them aren't pretty. I promised him I would not show them to anyone, especially the ones about drugs and snake handling. But I have been sitting here thinking that Michael has obviously trusted you with the most intimate details of his life. So, the more I thought about it—especially considering how he underlined my name and address in that notebook—well, I think he has been sending me a message: that I should to give you these papers."

I walked back up the steps to take the envelopes from her hands. However, she maintained her grip on them as she looked in my eyes and added, in a kind but stern voice, "Sam, don't make fun of him. And don't make fun of the people he loved. You're a West Virginian. You ought to know that we get enough of that from outsiders."

"Yes ma'am," I promised.

"OK then." She watched as I walked to my car, shut the door, and then drove away.

———

That is how most of the written information that made this book possible came into my hands. I have tried to weave the pieces of the story together in a way that allows it to unfold in Brother Michael's own voice, at least when that has been possible. When it has not been possible, I have used the voices of those who knew him. Like most of you, I heard his story from others. I wasn't there.

One final thing: Michael Cooper had some passionate convictions about Appalachian English.

As a young adult, he experimented with writing in what he regarded as "the unique grammar and vocabulary of our authentic and respectable dialect." His linguistic experiments made it challenging to use his own words in some places. Nonetheless, I did not think it right to edit passages that he wrote as experiments in dialect.

Fortunately, he moved away from this youthful idealism as he got older. As a result, his writings from (or about) the latter periods of his life reflect the standards of the educated man he had become.

Michael Cooper's college and theology papers were written at a level expected for academic life. Although I drew on these writings sparingly, the difference of style is evident and you may notice a shift from informal to formal, or from dialect to standard English from time to time.

Including different writing styles, whether from a single writer—as in the case of Michael Cooper himself, or from people from such different backgrounds—as in the case of the interviews and letters of those who knew him, has given this book a somewhat uneven and even inconsistent voice.

However, it will make your reading easier if you keep in mind that although I have lifted portions of Brother Michael's writings from the different eras of his life, I have also tried to arrange them in ways that made chronological sense.

Given the weirdness, terror, and grandeur of the story you're about to read, I doubt much of this will matter. I'm not sure why it matters enough to me anymore to even explain it.

The story begins with Michael Cooper's own reflections about the geography and the people of his early life. He wrote most of these pieces for English Composition, in high school, though I have added material written by him later in life where it seemed to help explain the context of the unfolding story.

At any rate, these early writings offer a valuable snapshot of the world from which he emerged and, in a real sense, the world to which he returned.

I'll have more to say later. For the moment, you have had heard enough from me. It's time to hear from Brother Michael in his own words.

3
MORNING IN MINGO COUNTY
MICHAEL COOPER

When you wake up in Southern West Virginia, the first thing you see is the mist hoverin' over the streams and rivers, formin' a meeting place between earth and sky. Sometimes it becomes a ghostly tide, movin' through the valleys, leavin' behind a watery film on the grass and the trees as it retreats from the midmorning sun.

You're never far from a railroad track; that's why a train whistle pierces the air from time to time, soundin' like a spirit conjurin' the dead and the living. Course, if you live by a river, you'll hear tugboats too. Them are all the sounds of mountain coal, makin' its way downriver to fuel America's factories and electric plants.

My first memory of wakin' up in the mountains was the smell of apples a cookin' and knowin' there was probably trout to eat with 'em. Ain't nothin' much better'n 'at, as we say back home. People in other places think that's strange, but fresh trout for breakfast is the best. If you get up early and are lucky enough, you can have it cleaned and ready to fry by the time anyone's ready to eat.

In the summertime, we eat tomatoes and apples.

In the fall, we eat corn and apples.

In the wintertime and spring, we eat canned tomatoes and dried apples.

There's always gravy too, which we make from flour and from whatever meat we can get our hands on.

Wildlife is everywhere, even in the cities. Skunks, coons, possum, deer, rabbits, and squirrels are always running around trying to escape human consumption. We eat all those things, except for the skunks, which we sometimes call pole cats. I would guess that getting hungry enough, some mountain man somewhere has served pole cat to his kids. Course, he kept his mouth shut about it. That ain't pleasant for some folks, but that's just the way it is, at least in Verner.

Verner ain't much, and we lived out a ways even from there. But its the only place you might still find on a map remotely connected to the first part of my life. Verner's right on the county line separating Mingo from Logan County. We had kin in both places and so Verner was a good place to live. We were constantly goin' back and forth between both places, which wasn't no big deal. But back then, if we were goin' over to Logan or Man, we acted like we were starting out on some long journey. Momma usually made sandwiches for us to eat on the way.

I'm getting ahead of m'self, but all of that came to me, which is why I said it.

You may not know that Mingo County used to be

part of Logan County. Course, for that matter Logan used to be a part of Tazwell, which was once part of Giles, which was once connected somehow to Kanawha. Mingo was kind of what got left over after all of that was over.

It's still rugged country, Mingo, but in the old days, people could hardly move through it, especially the government. That's why it took the law a long time to sort out things in Mingo, and they ain't quite sorted it out yet.

Mingo County is named after the Mingo Indians, Chief Logan being the most famous on account of him leadin' the Indians to attack settlers.

Course, the Indians lost.

We still use the words the Mingos gave to the rivers and creeks. We have also made statues of them for our parks. Other than that, they're long gone, except for generous amounts of genetic material they left behind, which shows up in our relatives.

That biological heritage proves that colonists and Indians weren't always fightin', that indeed sometimes they got along rather well.

But I was explaining to you about why there's a Mingo County. The people of Mingo didn't have anything against Logan County. It's just that in 1895, Logan County authorities arrested one of our inhabitants for practicing chemistry without a license, if you know what I mean.

In God-honoring parts of our country like Mingo County, only the government is authorized to make or sell whisky. A good-for-nothing moonshiner dishonors the state's righteous heritage and will be punished.

Course, that particular moonshiner proved in court that he lived beyond Logan County's legal jurisdiction.

The government had to do something about that, lest it be said that a hillbilly livin' in the sticks had outwitted the law.

West Virginia legislators, ever the champions of righteousness, had feared that moonshining and other notorious evils would go unchecked unless they acted quickly, so they carved out a brand-new county for us. That made it easier for the guardians of justice to traverse the mountains and root out all the evils a festerin' in our towns and hollers.

In due time, the state government also volunteered to sell most of our land to some rich people up in New York. Those good folks come in and kindly offered us work, which involved diggin' up coal underneath the mountains they had just purchased.

They also explained how we could earn enough money from diggin' that coal to pay rent to our new landlords. They built us special stores where we could buy supplies and even made up special money to help us buy the supplies. And if we happened to run out of money before we got enough supplies? Well, they would supply them anyway, provided we kept on a digging coal and promised not to move away before we had settled our debt. Since our special money wasn't good anywhere else and we kept buying supplies before we got paid, the debt got so high that it didn't make any sense for anyone to do anything else but mine coal.

That has been our arrangement for over a century

and a half now, and it works right well for the folk who own things.

The nasty truth is that our state is a colony, owned and controlled by people who don't live here. We periodically hold elections to decide who gets the privilege of representing our owners to us and us to our owners. For that privilege, our local representatives get paid healthy sums of money.

Every few years though, we throw a governor, a judge, or a legislator in jail, particularly if he gets a little too ambitious with our special arrangement with the coal companies. That's why many a governor has moved directly from the governor's mansion to the state pen. So appointing wardens is a particularly important responsibility for our governors.

Like the Blessed Lord Jesus said, "One must make friends with the unrighteous so they will welcome you into their eternal habitation." We practice that down in West Virginia.

Now, you won't understand either Mingo or Logan County unless you know all this stuff. On the other hand, if you do understand it, you are probably smarter than any of us who actually live here. Because if we really understood it we would probably do something about it. What we do instead is ignore it mostly, living our lives like none of the big stuff matters, which, in the end, it probably don't.

We have moonshine.

We have music.

And some of us have snakes.

Lest I mislead you, I hasten to add that West

Virginians love this land and forgive all its faults. Wherever else we go to find work (or to find sanity, for that matter) we remain loyal children of the mountains. All the days of our life.

You can test that for yourself. Just ask anyone born here about what I'm a sayin' and every one of them will agree with me. But if you keep diggin' deeper, tryin' to find out why we love our mountains as much as we do, you won't get much of an answer.

John Denver wasn't trying to be cute when he called our state, "Mountain Momma." He heard that phrase from West Virginians as he was driving through. He made a good song from what he heard and we thank him for it. But my point is that it's dumb to ask a man why he loves his mother. People just love their mothers 'cause they do.

So yes, people in Southern West Virginia complain everyday about the evils of their state. However, if you're not from here you best not join in.

We are easy goin' folk. We just have that one sore spot: people insulting our home place. It just isn't done. So, I would advise you not to do it. Just listen to the stories and try not to think too hard about how to figure 'em out. Mountain people know that stories are not mostly for thinking; they are for feeling. They also know that the truth is not in the words of the story; it's somewhere between the words. Course, everyone has to discover that for themselves.

Like just about everybody else in West Virginia, we lived up a *holler*, which is a long, narrow valley that people in other places call a hollow. That's also how the word is properly spelled, I reckon. Even newspapers in West Virginia write it that way. But if you say, "hollow," in either Mingo or Logan country, nobody's gonna know what the heck you're talking about.

We have our own way of talkin' you see.

It's not as different as it used to be, but it's still different enough to notice. People keep trying to educate us out of our dialect, but the way we talk has been around for a long, long time, and there's nothing wrong with it. Generations of teachers imported from proper places have tried their best to cure us, but they haven't succeeded.

That's why there's a difference in the way we say things and the way we write them down. It makes spelling and other parts of our education difficult, but that's just the way it is.

I'm tryin' to help you understand how we talk to one another 'cause it won't do to tell mountain stories in words meant to describe things up in Manhattan. We don't tell people up there how to talk about subways and avenues, so we figure they shouldn't tell us how to talk about sassafras and ramps.

I don't mean any harm by it, I just want to make things clear.

A dictionary is a book about the history of words; it's not a part of the legal code. We respect dictionaries in West Virginia, even though people who compile them don't take our opinions into account. But dictionaries don't have any special authority. They just teach people how to write and talk with folks who aren't from here.

If you meet us in Charleston or Huntington, we'll

accommodate you by watchin' over how we talk. But if you want to go on into the mountains, you need to learn how to pay attention so you can understand us. That's the way you do with people anywhere else and it makes sense to do that with us too.

It's not just about paying attention to the way we talk though. It's how we think. There's different things goin' on in our heads than with other folk. People came here a long time ago because they didn't fit in anywhere else, and they still don't, and that causes us to look at the world differently.

The Scotsmen came running after the Battle of Culloden. The English had been takin' their land and giving it to sheep, which didn't sit well with folk. That may be the reason that mountain people don't have much use for mutton, now that I think about it.

The Scots-Irish came because the native Irish didn't want them there and also because they wanted something better for their kids than killin' and gettin' killed.

Germans came from the Palatine to dig coal 'cause that's what they had done over there. They weren't proper Germans anyway. Just more wild Celts like the rest of us.

The runaway slaves came too if they were indecent enough to fall in love with a white man or white woman. That resulted in begettin' children nobody over on the coast could fit into proper categories. Here, they were just more poor folk.

Those were the kind of people who came into the mountains. They fought, married, and either killed or cohabited with Indians, depending on the decade or the circumstance. They worked hard to grow their corn and potatoes up on the hillsides, they hunted and fished, and eventually, they started workin' down in the mines.

Mountain people are the product of all that mess.

So yes, you might say that our ancestors were a bunch of misfits. They made a home for themselves in the mountains though because they were tired of runnin'.

Once they settled down, they made up their own English. They learned how to make whisky out of corn. They made fiddles and dulcimers and created a brand-new kind of music.

They even made up their own religion. Oh, they thought it was just plain old Christianity, just like what was practiced everywheres else. But mountain people needed a religion where people could dance and cry. Lord knows there had to be some way to let out all the hurt.

West Virginia is the only state in the union that fits completely inside the Appalachian Mountains. Over in Virginia, Kentucky, and Tennessee, Appalachian people make do. They learn to fit in with all other folk in their state. But here in West Virginia, we're Appalachian through and through. We don't have to explain ourselves to nobody. If you come here, you're the one who has to do the adjusting.

When the Civil War came, we took our opportunity to say goodbye to Richmond. The people over there owned plantations and all the people working in 'em. The plantation owners got used to calling the shots for everybody, slave or free. So, it wasn't 'cause we loved

Washington so much, but when Richmond rose up against the federal government, we saw that as our chance to file for divorce from the folk over in Richmond.

People always say Lincoln freed the slaves, which he did. They usually don't know that he also freed the western countries of Virginia. Nobody in the mountains had any slaves or wanted any. Truth be told, lots of us were kin to the slaves. Anyhow, we didn't want attached to either side of a chain, 'cause in the end, a chain makes you a prisoner either way.

We don't mean any harm to our neighbors, but nothing makes a Mingo man madder than hearin' someone say he's from Virginia. We'll tolerate that from foreigners because they don't know no better. We'll hold our peace even for an American when he says it the first time. But after being instructed about the matter, a good person will show us more respect.

Our state motto is *Montani Semper Liberi*, and even though I don't know a single soul in Mingo County that speaks Latin, we all know what it means: "mountaineers are always free." And the first people we got free from were the smart asses over on the coast.

Even our capital is a mountain town, just like the rest of the state. We're mountain people, and the mountains is where we want to be. That's why, when I finally got to visit places like Kiev and London, I wasn't a bit more out of place than when I went to Akron that time with my grandpop.

I realize Verner is just a tiny town in the middle of nowheres and that people there don't talk about any of this stuff. Then again, they don't have to.

Everybody in Verner knows things are just the way things are and there's no good reason to change it much.

That's where I was born. I've been to lots of other places but I never intend to grow old anywheres else. When it comes my time, they'll plant me up here up on the mountain, where the mornin' mist will cover my grave.

4

PAPPY MULLINS

MICHAEL COOPER

Pappy Mullins first came to Mingo County in 1910. Couple of years before that, he worked over in Kanawha County with Ezra Pack. That's why he moved to Mingo later, to help Mr. Pack open another sawmill. Pappy's connection to the Pack family is also how Pappy came to meet miners over at Lens Creek, back when the trouble came.

His granddaddy and grandmomma raised him over near Pikeville, Kentucky, on account of his dad and mom dying of the flu when he was little. Said his granddaddy had been on the Union side in the war, which was why his daddy got named Ulysses.

I was still a little boy when I figured out that the Mullinses over in Pikeville didn't care much for Ma. At least they must not have liked it when Pappy married her. I knew that because when Pappy talked about his folks, Ma would make a face. She thought nobody saw her because she kept lookin' down at her sewin'. But I did. She didn't hold the face for long, just long enough

for me to know how Ma felt about things over in
Pikeville.

Momma always said Ma Mullins was some kind of
Indian, which may account for why she was darker than
most people down in Mingo County. I don't know about
any of that. Course, Pappy was pretty dark hisself.

He had a full head of hair up 'til the day he died. It
was as curly as I ever had seen on a white man. That was
on account of him being Portuguese, Pappy said, which
made me wonder how people from Portugal had ever got
over to Mingo County.

I asked him about that once but he just said, "Son,
the ways of the Lord are past findin' out."

That meant Pappy didn't know, and on account of
that, I shouldn't ask the question anymore. Pappy had
the idea that things beyond knowin' should be left alone.

Probably, that's why Ma hung her head down and
made that sour face. Anyway, that's the conclusion I
came to. One thing for sure, back then Pappy set the tone
for everybody.

Maybe that's why when I think about Mingo County,
it's Pappy's voice I always hear first.

"I was the first preacher to have signs following
anywhere in Mingo County," I'd heard Pappy say
hundreds of times. That was, in fact, the first line of his
favorite story.

"I got the Holy Ghost over in Cabell County in 1915,
waist deep in the Ohio River," he'd say. "The man that
preacher put under the water that day was a whisky-
guzzlin', womanizin' sinner, on his way to Hell! But
what came out of the water was a glory-to-

Jesus . . . whew, yessir . . . Holy-Ghost-filled saint O' God!"

When he would get to that part, he would suddenly jerk his head backwards, like someone had waved a sharp knife under his chin. He would pause a minute, shake all over, and then go on telling his story.

"Everybody back then tried to shut me up. Especially in the churches! Can you believe it? Glory to God! You'd think they would've been happy about a no-good hell raisin' man like me gettin right with God. But they weren't. I wasn't even a Mark 16 man back then!

"Well, the Methodists over at Matewan threw me out first, glory to God. Told me not to come back no more. Then the Free Will folks over in Aflex threw me out too, after I spoke the Word O' God with boldness at the homecoming. They're good folk, the Free Wills, but they didn't want nobody actin' up round the mayor and all the other fancy folk a visitin' that day. But the Spirit came mightily upon me, and I had to obey God rather than man.

"Yessir. I did all right with the Holiness people over at Red Jacket for a while 'til they went'n got organized. After that, they started quenchin' the Spirit. I'm tellin' ya saints, the devil don't like it none when God's people get freed! But I'm just not a goin t' shut my mouth if'n the Spirit comes upon me.

"Praise Jesus, we're free around here. Ain't nobody gonna shut you up around here. Ain't nobody gonna take away your liberty around here. Ain't nobody gonna— HAASHA TAKANATA!"

The story always ended with a dance, which Pappy

did backwards; eyes closed, face pointed upward, hands flailing about like washing machine agitators.

He fought at the battle of Blair Mountain back in '21. Folks outside of West Virginia don't know much about that but it was the biggest uprising in American history since the Civil War. Ten thousand miners gathered over at Lens Creek and headed toward Mingo County to avenge the death of Sheriff Sid Hatfield.

Lord knows how many times I heard Pappy tell that story. When he did, I would look back and forth from him to the pictures of John L. Lewis and Franklin Roosevelt hangin' on the wall. Sometimes I thought John L. Lewis, who every kid in West Virginia knew was a modern-day saint, kept smilin' down on us, hopin' we'd pay some attention to all he'd done for us.

"Sid Hatfield stood up for the miners even after the state police came in," Pappy said. "I shook his hand one time, right on the street in broad daylight, over there in Mattawan. Everybody seen it. You can ask 'em fer y'self, bless God.

"Them politicians from Williamson and Logan were everywhere, everyone of 'em crookeder than a hound's back leg. All of them stuck in the watch pocket of the coal companies and the Baldwin-Felts boys. Thems the ones what shot up the women and the children livin' in tents over at Lick Creek. Left them dead, a lyin' there amongst their belongin's. When them crooks and rascals couldn't get their way, they sent for more folks over in Charleston to bring more guns to help 'em.

"But Old Sid wasn't impressed with 'any o'em. That's why they decided to do him in.

"Yessir. Can't have a lawman actually standing up for justice now, can we?

"They shot Sid down while he was unarmed and respectfully goin' into a court of law to answer their questions. Shot him down right in front of 'is wife. Law didn't do nothing 'bout it.

"So, yessir. I was right proud to clean my rifle and head over to Tugg River. By that time they had called in the army, the YEWNITED STATES ARMY! Are you a hearin' me?

"Our own government was a flyin' planes all over Logan and Mingo bombin' miners that was just a tryin' to get a decent wage for their families. Folks nowadays say none of that didn't happen. But they are plumb lyin'. I saw them planes with my own eyes. The federal government a bombin' its own people, them who fought for that government over there across the waters against the Kaiser, all because them who owned the mines were more important than them who actually went down into the ground to get the coal.

"Yessir. A miner spends his life away from his family, livin' underground next to Hell. He does that day in and day out so somebodys up in New York gets t' belong to some fancy club or somethin'. Then all them important people up there act surprised when folks down here in West Virginia get sore about their wickedness. They just laugh when we speak up. If we won't stop talkin', they bring the power of Babylon down upon us and our kin.

"That's why I joined up with the miners at Blair Mountain. Somebody had to listen to what workin' people down here was a sayin'. We had to show 'em Sid

Hatfield wasn't the only man who weren't a scered of 'em. And we weren't. We weren't a scered of the whole YEWNITED States Army and all their planes t' boot if it came to it.

"Everybody dies, boys. You might as well die for somethin'. That's the way we saw things back then."

———

Pappy was nearly fifty when he started the Holiness Church of Jesus with Signs Following.

God told him in a dream one night to form a church. So the next morning he commenced paintin' a sign. He didn't even have anywhere to hang it, but he knew that wouldn't be no problem, 'cause it was God who'd told him to get started.

Anyway, they had their first service up Spice Creek Holler, in the McCafferty store. Old man McCafferty had died already, and his widow had no mind for business. Their son had died years before, over in France. Pappy figured no one else was going to use it, and it turned out he was right.

Most of my oldest memories are rooted in that building. When I think about something that happened there, the first thing that comes to mind is the smell of damp concrete mixed with cedar. I still can smell, even after all these years. Course, it's been torn down for some time.

Widow McCafferty was glad to let Pappy use it for a church, like he thought she would. And even though Ma Mullins didn't care much for Widow McCafferty, most of us were glad she let us use the old store.

The Collines joined in right away and soon brought along their cousins, the Goins. A couple of the Meeks boys came too, all the way from over at Sawmill Holler.

Course, they left a while later on account of the serpents.

I suppose I should say something more about that, since most people make a big fuss of the snakes. I got used to it growing up and it just doesn't strike me like it does most people.

Why our church took up serpents was another story I heard Pappy tell a hundred times.

"It was in October of '34, when I was a workin over near Williamson at Mr. Lawrence's place. His boys had already moved and since he was a gettin' old, he paid a few of us to help him get in the corn. I was workin' out there in that corn when a big timber rattler came a slitherin' betwixt the rows. At first, I was powerfully a feared. Then I recollected the words of Jesus in Mark 16—*they shall take up serpents*—Praise Jesus.

"Them words were just a burnin' in my head—like they was coals of fire!

"I had to decide right then and there if what God said was true or not. So I started praisin' Jesus. That's when God's *par* come down upon me—praise Jesus, hatha ta-ta-ta—and I reched down and picked up that serpent.

"Yessir. I commenced a shoutin' and a runnin' up and down the rows of corn, all the while a holdin' that serpent up in the air. I knowed I was dealin' with the devil his self, and I was determined to do whatever the Lord said do.

"I shouted and praised God like that for a good spell,

'til the par lifted off me. When it did, I laid that serpent down gently as I would a baby. Then I went on my way, and he went on a hissin'.

"Everybody round Mingo County heard about it. And they right away could see something was different in me. For a long time I couldn't preach but what the same par would come upon me that had came upon me in the cornfield. It would leap from me and fall on the people I was a preachin' to.

"They couldn't do nothin' but weep and shake when that happened.

"Yessir. But it wasn't 'til the summer of '35 I started collectin' serpents for the church. I figured that I oughtta give the saints a chance to get what I got out there at Mr. Lawrence's place. The saints over in Jolo recommended that I take my time with people about the Mark 16 message, and I thought they were right.

That was a long time ago! We've been a practicin' the signs for nigh t' thirty years.

"Oh, I know! They make fun of us. But the days are a comin' when they won't make fun of us no more. When the trouble comes upon the earth ... and ... and ... and all the sheep gets separated from the goats—WELL! Everybody's gonna see then what's what when *that* dread and terrible day comes."

By this point, Pappy would be so worked up that he didn't even look human. His eyes would be all shiny, his body lookin' like a balloon ready to raise plumb off the ground.

People who came to make fun of us would just stare at Pappy when he got like that, like they couldn't even move. Sometimes, he would start pointin' them out as they stood there; start revealing things about them nobody could have known.

I think that scared people even more than the serpents.

————

Nearly everybody shouted at one time or another at the Holiness Church of Jesus Christ with Signs Following. It didn't happen in every service or even in most. But it did happen from time to time.

When it did, the Spirit did strange things to people.

Sister Minnie Goins for instance, would start moving her head back and forth until finally it got to jerkin' so fast it was nearly a blur. It would look like her head was goin' a fly plumb off the rest of 'er body. Every bobby pin on her head would start flyin' in every direction, leavin' her hair unraveled and flowin' down her back.

Hershel Doolittle would walk the backs of the pews, his eyes closed, a shoutin' out praises to God.

Others would be a runnin', jerkin', or prancin' around.

Everybody who played an instrument would be playin'; they'd keep on singin' songs to help the saints surrender to the Spirit. Like little David a playin' on his harp to chase that evil spirit off of Saul, the tambourine and guitar players—or whatever kind of instrument they had— would chase away the mockin' and lukewarm spirits off the saints.

Meanwhile, Pappy and Granddaddy would be a

watchin', makin' sure nobody got in the flesh. That's when people just start making up stuff, pretendin' they're in the Spirit when they're really just tryin' to get attention. Most Holiness people know when that's happenin' and they don't like it much.

Once, a man from down at the organized church over at Red Jacket came and started shoutin' around while everyone else was in the Spirit. He fell against the coal stove and burned his self. Everybody knows if you're in the Spirit a coal stove won't burn nobody. Hershel Doolittle laid against that same stove once for fifteen minutes and nothing at all happened to him.

But you can't just go dancin' around and actin' strange and call that "bein' in the Spirit." Like I said, Holiness people know the difference; preachers like my Pappy'll call you out.

5
MOMMA
MICHAEL COOPER

It's might be strange to say, but I don't think Momma was ever really part of our family. She stayed a Mullins her whole life. The reason she was just partially connected to us was because her world revolved around the goings on up at Spice Creek Holler, back at the Mullin's place.

Her brothers—Blizzard and Jep—were always down in the mines. Her sisters, on the other hand, Viola, Bess, and Virginia, kept themselves occupied figuring out what Pappy did or didn't like, what he needed to know and what they ought to keep from him for his own good, on account of him getting old.

Pappy was really my mother's grandfather. I don't think I told you that. Momma's daddy was actually Pappy's eldest son, Issac. He was a kind and peaceful man, my Granddaddy Mullins. His words and deeds didn't make enough of a splash to either please people or upset them.

It's like Pappy had been destined to be the star of the

family drama for as long as he lived. That made everybody around Pappy the supporting cast. When Pappy's time came to leave the stage he just stayed on, which is why Granddaddy never got much of a chance to be much of anybody. That didn't seem to upset Granddaddy though. In fact, I never heard anyone back in Mingo County put things the way I just did. That's just something I figured out later when I was at the hospital.

Momma loved Daddy the best she could. It's just that she had to fit him in somewhere after attending to her folk over at Spice Creek Hollow. Since her children came next, Daddy got what was left. That was the order Momma went by, and it didn't seem wrong back then. It's just the way things were.

Course, it ain't easy growing up in a prophet's family.

It's like Pappy said once, "The Lord God called Abraham to leave his kindred and walk out there into the desert, praise Jesus, without even knowin' where he was a goin'. And he had to do it praise Jesus. Yessir. Praise Jesus. If his wife didn't understand, he still had to do it. If his children got left behind, he still had to do it.

"That's the way it is!

"The Spirit's like a wind. It blows this a way for a while. Then, it turns plumb around and starts a blowin' the other way. Praise Jesus, saints, the prophet has to follow the wind wherever it goes and whatever it cost."

That pretty much summed up Momma's family. Over at Spice Creek Holler, the wind blew first this way and then the other. You never knew what the issue would be tomorrow but that whatever it was, it would be just as important as the issue today. What did not change was that the wind was always goin' to blow and was goin' to blow hard. You just didn't know in which direction.

The Mullins were always nice to Daddy, but everybody knew he wasn't one of 'em. If you married a Mullins, you could get tolerated after a while. You just weren't ever going to be a Mullins unless you were already a Mullins before you married another Mullins.

That's the way it was with Aunt Tina. Tina was a granddaughter of Pappy's cousin but married Momma's brother, Blizzard. That's why she never changed her name.

Daddy was from Man, over in Logan County. So he was in a different category. Nobody thought it out like that back then. It was like you were either born knowin' such stuff or you weren't and there wasn't any need to question any of it.

Unlike Daddy, I was a real Mullins even though my name was Cooper. The Mullinses told me so. They said I looked like Pappy when he was young. Sometimes I liked that. Sometimes I didn't. But they said it to make me feel right about myself.

Momma wanted me to think of myself as a Mullins and would look hurt if I paid too much attention to the Coopers. I figured that was on account of the Coopers not being in the ark of safety.

None of the Coopers believed in signs following, and they all had televisions, even though they claimed to be Christians. I worried about the Coopers, 'cause . . . well, sure they were nice, but they thought nothin' about doin' things like watchin' TV shows.

My uncle Clyde Cooper, for instance. He stayed home

from church one Sunday night to watch Ed Sullivan. Nobody said nothin' about it. I know it was true because he told everyone what he watched. We were all eatin' over at Granny Cooper's house when he told it. I heard it myself.

Pappy always talked about that verse from the Bible. "Not everyone who calls me Lord, Lord will enter the kingdom of Heaven."

I thought of that when uncle Clyde was tellin' us about Ed Sullivan and such. I was pretty sure his kids went to the picture shows too 'cause they seemed to know all about the movies playin' over there in Logan County.

I worried something fierce about all of that because I liked goin' over to Grandpop and Granny Cooper's place. I sure didn't want any of them to be lost and go to Hell. But it was perplexin' because even though they weren't right with God, there were things about bein' at the Cooper's I liked.

For instance, you could just be quiet if that's what you wanted. You could think whatever you cared to think about. It was like the Mullinses were a mountain stream, rushin' down the hill, tryin' its best to get wherever it's a goin'. The Coopers, on the other hand, were like a quiet lake, just sittin' there while an eagle glides above it.

I liked how the Coopers would all sit down together when it was time to eat. Everyone would wait until every person in the house was sittin' down. Then they would all sit there for a minute without sayin' nothin' until Grandpop said grace. Also, people talked one at a time.

Nobody started talkin' when somebody else was already speakin'.

Things like that made things over at the Coopers seem quiet and slow sometimes. I didn't mind it any, even though it was odd. But Momma told her sister Bess on the phone one day that it felt like a tomb over at the Coopers.

"They try and act proper, makin' people think they're important or something," Momma said. "I don't like stuff like that. I think people ought t' be what they are and not put on airs like that."

The next time I went over to Logan County, I began noticin' what she meant.

Once me and my cousins were eatin' dinner with Grandpop and Granny Cooper when I belched out loud. That got me to laughin'. After a while, I noticed nobody else was laughin', except Freddy, who was six.

Granny Cooper smiled a little but asked me, "What do we say when something like that happens, dear?"

Well, I didn't know! Was I supposed to say something? Evidently. At least everyone was waiting for me to say whatever it was I was supposed to say.

Lost for words, I just hung down my head and mumbled, "I don't know."

"We say 'excuse me,' dear. It happens to everybody, but when we are with somebody when we do that, we say excuse me."

"Excuse me," I mumbled, my head still lookin' down at the floor.

"That's good," Granny Cooper said. "You didn't do

nothing wrong, honey. I just want you to know how to act when you are eating with people"

So, I thought, *there's a way to act when you are eatin' with other people that's different than when you're by yourself or with the Mullinses over in Mingo County.*

I remember thinking then that there might be things to learn from the Coopers, even though they weren't Holiness. I kept that to myself, but that's what I thought and learned later how I had been right about it.

I learned how to say "excuse me" like they were words from some foreign tongue. It was like those words didn't really mean anything but were just sounds a person ought to make anyway under certain situations.

It made me think about a third grade teacher who tried to teach us French. She wanted us to say "bonjour" when we came into her room and "au revoir" when we left.

We learned to say them words when she was around, but once when she left the room, Fatty Loudermilk bowed low and said, "BONE CHEER." Everyone laughed, so he bowed again and said, "HAVE WIRE." That set us to laughing so hard we could hardly breathe.

Talking like that just didn't make any sense to any of us, and it was hilarious to think that people across the water would talk like that all the time, on purpose to boot!

That's what it felt like to say "excuse me" over at Granny Cooper's place. I said it because she wanted me to say it, but heck if I knew why. It was just the way people in other places wanted me to talk. So that was something I had to learn if I wanted to fit in anywhere proper. I figured that out by myself early on.

Of course, like I said, Granny Cooper wasn't Holiness. That meant she wasn't going to heaven on account of her not knowin' the truth. But if I lived a good life, her eyes might get opened. It was a heavy burden on me, helpin' her see the light. I feared that on the Day of Doom she would weep and wail, askin' me why I hadn't told her the truth while the devils would be a carryin' her off to Perdition. That was just something I didn't want to contemplate and was one of the reasons I said "excuse me." I was glad doin' it made her happy, but it also helped my witness.

Mostly though, I just liked makin' Granny Cooper happy, which is something I kept to myself.

Momma usually found a reason not to go with the rest of us over to Logan County. The Coopers made her nervous, I guess. But when she went, she was quiet and sat by herself most of the time.

If she had to say something to Granny Cooper, it was about stuff like the crops.

"I think it will be a good year for tomatoes, Mrs. Cooper," Momma might say.

"Well, yes, I think it will be, dear. How are yours a doin'?" Granny would reply.

"Fair," Momma would say.

Encouraged, Granny would try to take the conversation further. "We had an early spring, so we might be in for a hot summer."

"Yeah, I suspect so," Momma would say.

If the topic got too personal, Momma would go stone

cold. And for Momma, that category included nearly everything. Once, Granny Cooper asked about our schoolin'.

"How are the children's education going, dear?" Granny asked.

"All right, I guess. Why?" Momma replied, suspiciously.

"Well, I was just wondering," Granny said quickly. "Nowadays, jobs now require a lot of education. The children need to finish high school."

"I know that!" Momma snapped.

"Well, I'm just saying that because lots of kids here in Logan County drop out of school and then can't get jobs later on," Granny explained.

"School's good for some folk, Mrs. Cooper," Momma shot back. "Don't help none down in the mines though or for drivin' a truck—real work like that. Mostly people just need to learn some common sense."

"Everybody needs to read well, dear," Granny said. "That way they can become good citizens and make a contribution to the world."

Momma, enunciating each word clearly, shot back, "My kids'll do all right."

I could tell Momma was mad. Although Granny seemed not to notice, Momma had just set her straight.

I found out I was right about that because on our way home she went on about it to Daddy.

"I don't intend to tell your momma none of our business, Eddie!" Momma blurted out.

"She wasn't trying to get into our business, Irene,"

Daddy replied softly. "She was just concerned about her grandchildren."

"Just 'cause I don't put on all those airs, she thinks I'm not a fit mother," Momma said in her hurt voice.

Daddy sighed and stopped talkin', which was all he could do, I guess.

Momma didn't say all that much to Daddy either. She saved most of her talkin' for her sisters. Of course, she couldn't talk about the things of the church over there at the Coopers. None of us could.

What were we going to say?

"The power fell over everybody at church last night. Sister Goodie Holbrooke got in the Spirit and drank strychnine?"

No, that wouldn't do. People who ain't Holiness don't understand such things.

But if all you talk about is church and you can't talk about that, then what is there left to talk about? I saw Momma's side of things when it came to Daddy's family, but it still bothered me, her stayin' all quiet like that around the Coopers.

When Momma talked to her sisters, Momma was full of opinions about all sorts of things. Like that time I heard her on the telephone talkin' to Bess about a serious church situation.

"The Collinses were down in Florida visitin' with Big Robert's family," Momma said.

"When they got back, little Bobby told Sheila Lynn they had all gone to the beach down there. Said his mommy went in a swimin'. God knows why Sister Collins would do such a thing! You know full well that people down in Florida walk around half naked, especially on the beach. What's a Holiness woman got to do a goin' to a beach like that?

"Lordy, Lordy, who's gonna tell Pappy? It'll break his heart, poor thing, him getin' s' old and all."

I could see that Momma was frettin' bout the Collinses, which worried me too, something awful. But I also wondered what it would be like down there in Florida, walkin' on the beach with half-naked people, jumpin' around and laughin' in the water and such.

I did think I would like to see that for myself someday. I was sorry to think that, but that's what came to me at the time. I might as well tell it now 'cause someday all the secrets of men's hearts are gonna be laid bare anyhow.

A few days later though, Robert Collins hurt his back down in the mines. He couldn't work for several weeks. So Momma made some food for them and called around to everyone to go help Sister Collins take care of things while Robert was laid up. The church took up a collection and paid their light bill that month too, like Momma asked them to.

After that, nothing more was said about the beach. The whole story just dropped into the sea of forgetfulness, where God puts all our sins when he gets over bein' mad at us.

I guess everyone thought Robert's hurt back was punishment enough. That's why nothin' more needed to be said about them carryin' on in Florida like they did. I thought it was probably something like when your brother gets a whoppin'. You're kind of glad about it at first. Then you decide to treat him better for the rest of the day.

People helped each other like that when somebody got afflicted. That's what I remember the most about life back in Mingo County.

Momma knew when people had had enough. She wanted them to live right but she felt sorry for folks havin' trouble whether they were a livin' right or not. It was like she thought people ought to be happy but not too much. Else they would fall into pride and God knows what else.

I just wished she would have found it in her heart to talk more to Grandpop and Granny Cooper. It worried me back then and sometimes it still does.

————

Everybody thinks their Momma's pretty.

I knew mine was.

Folks said when she was in high school, even the boys out in the world, who weren't Holiness, wanted to take her out on dates. Isn't that something?

I guess you would say she was beautiful. I never saw eyes as black as Momma's or her hair too, as black as Mingo County coal. Her lips were full and red, even without makeup.

Course, that's what led her astray when she got to be a teenager: "The spirit of vanity and the vexation of beauty," Pappy called it. That's what she always talked about in testimony service.

"You all know I went the way of the world for a while," Momma began.

"Amen!" somebody shouted out.

"Bless her Lord," said someone else.

"I done things out there in the world that make me feel ashamed when I think about them, young people."

(There were only five Mullins kids there, so it was us she meant to be listenin'.) She would always start cryin' hard and tell the rest of her testimony through short gasps.

"Oh, young people, don't listen to the devil when he comes a callin'. All it takes is one little dance, one little drink, one little slip to carry you down the road that leads to hell *far*."

Momma's face would start getting red at this point, and her body would begin to sway.

"All the saints warned me but I wouldn't listen," Momma continued.

"A Jezebel spirit got on me. I would leave the house to catch the school bus in the mornin's, and before it got there I would rub a little makeup on my face and puff out my hair. I would fix my clothes in the way girls do to get a boy's attention—you women know what I'm talkin' about."

Some woman would always chuckle and say, "Bless her, Lord!"

"I got ashamed of bein' Holiness," Momma would continue. "I started hangin' out with girls that talked about nasty things. Jesus help me, I soon was a talkin' that way myself.

"Oh, the devil'll fool ye. Little by little, you'll start

behavin' like a heathen, out there in the world, a cussin' and corralin' with everybody else."

Momma would wipe her face with a handkerchief and then continue her testimony.

"I snuck out of the house one night—one night was all it took, saints! Went a ridin' with Eddie Cooper. He was from over Logan, visiting his cousins over at Red Jacket. I ain't a sayin' nothing bad about my husband. He's a good man now. He comes on to church with me nearly all the time. But that's just by the grace O' God. Things don't usually turn out that way.

"Brother Eddie's a good daddy to my youngins and he treats me right, so I ain't talkin' nothing bad about him."

A couple of women would say "amen" at this point

"But when I met him, he wasn't in the truth. He didn't believe in the signs. He made fun of the ways of the Lord. You see, he didn't know no better back then.

"But saints, my heart was already hard, and I followed him right into sin. We went out a dancin' and drinkin' beer. We done all the stuff wicked people do. That's why there was soon a little one on the way."

Momma would put her head in her hands and shake something awful when she got to that part. Then she would lift her head and keep on a testifyin'.

"Praise God, Brother Eddie did right by me. That's why we got married.

"It broke my daddy and momma's heart, but they fixed us a little house over here 'cause they wanted Brother Eddie to finish high school.

"Once my little Susie was born though, I got under

conviction real bad, thinkin' how she would grow up out in the world, all because of my sin.

"One night, I heard the saints in here a singin' and I couldn't take it no more. I went and scrubbed all that paint off my face, took my baby up in my arms, and set out a runnin' to the house o' God. I didn't stop runnin' 'til I had hit that altar up there. Praise Jesus. I don't know who took my baby that night. I just know somebody did. And I stayed up there at that altar 'til I broke through to victory.

"Praise Jesus, Brother Eddie come a lookin' for me and walked me home. He told me that if I wanted to come to church he would come with me. And that's what he's done all these years now.

"So, I want to praise Jesus for savin' me, sanctifyin' me, and fillin' me with the Holy Ghost. I got off the path for a while but then I done what the song said: 'I took the way with the Lord's despised few.' Halleluiah."

I heard that testimony plenty of times. Some of the details got changed with the tellin', but that's right close to what she said each time.

I was glad the devil didn't get my Momma, glad that the Lord had delivered her from the spirit of vanity and the vexation of beauty. As far as I could tell, she kept her promise to let the Lord beautify her with salvation 'cause she never painted her face again.

I know now that Momma started giving that testimony when my sister Susan started to change. She had Momma's eyes and hair and it was clear to me then that the devil would probably try to fool her, just like he had Momma.

I reminded Susan of that when she got in trouble for passing notes to Freddie McFarlin at school. She begged me not to tell Momma about it and I didn't. But it worried me just the same.

A fourteen-year-old girl in Mingo County ain't got no chance against the devil, that's for sure. If he fooled my Momma, he could fool anybody.

6

DADDY

MICHAEL COOPER

The power never came upon Daddy to handle serpents, but it weren't 'cause he was afraid. He killed a rattler once up on Pigeon Ridge while we were out lookin' for sassafras. Sliced off its head with a hoe! I remember it like it was yesterday, 'cause the snake kept twistin' around after it'd lost its head. That scared me more than the snake itself.

Despite not havin' the anointin', Daddy kept most of the church rules, at least as far as I could tell. But it was more like he didn't care about it one way or another. I always thought Daddy's attitude about church rules irritated Pappy. It was like something Pappy couldn't get his finger on. He couldn't claim that Daddy didn't keep the rules, but he didn't seem to find any pleasure in how Daddy went about it.

I can't explain it any better than that.

Granddaddy liked Daddy though. He said Daddy was one of them steady types, which meant that he was a good man who doesn't have the Spirit fall on him much.

Of course, some people said the same thing about Granddaddy Mullins.

People teased Daddy about his red hair, and though his name was Edward, people at the coal tipples usually called him Red.

No doubt about it, some of Daddy's ways were peculiar. Take like when he said grace. It was like he had learned all the words ahead of time.

"Lord, we thank Thee for this food, which Thou hast provided. May it be nourishing to our bodies, even as Thy word is nourishment to our hearts." I heard him pray those words many times; the very same words!

It was strange for a Holiness man to pray like that. Most Holiness folk prayed over the food the same way they prayed at church.

For instance, Pappy might say something like, "Thank you, Jesus, for this food, praise Jesus, which you've given t' us, and we ask you t' remember everyone that's hungry, especially them sweet little children cross the waters whose pitiful faces I seen yesterday in the magazine. Oh Jesus, them little children over there a starvin' while we have this wonderful food t' eat. Help us think about 'em as we enjoy what these sisters have prepared for us here today. Amen."

A prayer like that made Daddy's prayer sound kind of uppity. Course, I never said anything about it. I knew Daddy was doing the best he could.

All of us were proud Daddy had finished high school. Momma tried to fit it into every conversation she could.

"Eddie got his diploma from over there at the high school, you know," she'd say.

"He still can't figure out how to fix cars much, but they don't teach stuff like that in high school. Course, he can tell you all the names of foreign countries and who was the kings and queens of all them places. Stuff like that. Lordy, Lordy, what good's any that gonna do for anybody down in the mines?"

Everyone would laugh when she said things like that, even Daddy. Sometimes he looked a bit pained over it, but on the whole, he knew she was trying to brag on him the best she knew how.

Momma seemed plumb mystified by what my daddy found interestin'.

For instance, there weren't many books in my house a growin' up. I don't know where we would've put 'em if we had had any. All of us had a Bible of course, which we took with us to church—King James Bibles, which were the only Bibles we knew anything about back then. Then there were Daddy's books, up on the kitchen shelf.

Daddy kept maybe ten books from his high school up there. Momma got her way in almost everything except for those books. They were sacred territory. All of us knew that nobody was supposed to move them or get them down to look at without asking. Nobody ever said anything about it, but we all knew that's the way it was. I can still see those books in my mind's eye, back where they really belonged: up on that shelf. Later on, after all that happened, the books would always seem out of place.

The three I remember most were:

An Introduction to English Literature, an old beat-up

blue book called *The New Oxford Book of English Verse*, and *Think and Grow Rich*.

Momma would get nervous when she saw Daddy readin' those books. If he sat down and started openin' one up, she would always think of some chore that ought to get done. It's like the chore had come to her suddenly, just as Daddy was takin' his book off the shelf. I've wondered about that many times.

Sometimes it was funny, like the night Daddy was readin' *Think and Grow Rich*. He bought it that time he was tryin' to sell insurance on account of the long coal strike. It struck Momma funny, that book. One day she was lookin' at him a readin' it and commenced to laughin.' I can still see her there, standin' in the middle of our cracker-box house back in Mingo County.

"Well Eddie," she said, "if thinkin' made anybody rich, you shoulda already been richer than Cooter Brown!"

Daddy laughed and nodded.

"But there's a lot more in here than just making money, Irene," he replied, thumping the book.

"Like what?"

"Like learning to expect good things instead of bad. Like looking on the bright side of things. Like trying to make your life better."

"Make your life better? That's what heaven's for, Eddie," Momma said.

"I suspect you're right, Irene, but sometimes people can get a little of heaven here if they learn how to think right. That's what this book here is a sayin'," Daddy replied.

"Well, maybe I can help you get a little bit o' heaven later tonight, 'less you would rather keep on a readin'," Momma said.

Daddy laughed hard when she said that and then looked down like something needed hushed up, his face suddenly the color of his hair.

It would be years before I had any idea what their joke was about.

Sometimes though, Daddy's books caused a fight.

"Eddie, if I was gonna stick my head in a book, I would at least make it the Word O' God," Momma said.

"Now, Irene, let me be for a minute. I've been working all day and I need to collect my thoughts."

But Momma wasn't done.

"Pappy always says that readin' too much stuff other than the Bible ruins lots of people."

That particular remark ticked my daddy off something fierce, and it caused him to say something I knew he regretted as soon the words poured out of his mouth. He lifted his head, stared straight at Momma, his eyes just a blazin'.

He set his jaw and then spoke, real slow and clear. "I suspect Pappy did say that, Irene. It makes all the sense in the world that he would say something like that, seein's how he's barely literate."

Well, Momma looked like she had been shot. When she answered Daddy, her tone was full of something like fear mixed with anger and a tad of surprise.

Her voice shaking, she replied, "My Pappy's a Man O' God, maybe even a prophet. Course, how can I expect you and the Coopers to know anything about that? You didn't grow up knowin' nothin' bout holiness."

But Daddy wasn't finished either.

"My folks were Methodists, Irene. I heard plenty about holiness."

"You call what they do holiness? What with all their broaches and fancy clothes, not to mention their televisions?"

By that time, Daddy was getting that look he got when he started backin' up from an argument because he knew it wasn't getting him anywhere.

"Irene, what's any of this got to do with my folks? I was just wanting a few minutes to myself, that's all."

It was the saddest I ever saw my daddy. He stared at the window for a long while, even though it was dark and there was nothing out there to see. Then he suddenly slammed his book shut, set it up on the shelf, and left the house, slamming the door behind him. His truck threw gravel when he pulled onto the road, and he was gone a long time.

Daddy didn't do such things as that, which is why it scared me so much. That was just a little while after my eleventh birthday, but I don't know why I remember it that way.

I do know that a few nights later, everybody else was going over to Spice Creek Holler. I told 'em I needed to get some homework done and they let me stay.

When I saw they were gone, I got Daddy's book off the shelf to see for myself what had caused such a fuss. I opened it up to where I thought Daddy had been readin'.

I didn't know if I had found the right place, but I started readin' anyhow. Found out it was a poem.

I remember thinking, *All that fuss about a poem?* It made me wonder if there was something in poems that goes beyond the actual words.

I decided to figure one out.

There were some strange things in that poem, some dark and mysterious things. For instance, some of the words weren't spelled right. They spelled tiger "tyger" for one thing, though they put it the right way in parenthesis. I figured tyger must be some old timey way of spelling tiger. Either that or a tyger was a special kind of tiger, maybe bigger, or maybe with superpowers of some sort, which is where I finally landed. Since nobody was home but me, I said the words out loud, making them sound like some sort of spell.

> *Tyger! Tyger! Burning bright*
> *In the forest of the night,*
> *What immortal hand or eye*
> *Could frame thy fearful symmetry?*

Even though I didn't understand it exactly, I liked the poem right away. I could see a tyger in my head, runnin' through the forest. There's plenty of forest in Mingo County, so that didn't take much imagination.

And whatever "symmetry" was, it was fearful, which made me feel scared. Also, symmetry was something that could be framed, like when Granddaddy builds a house.

I had just learned in a comic book that "immortal"

meant not dying, so I understood that. However, the only hand or eye that couldn't die was the eye and hand O'God. But why did God use symmetry to make his frame for the tyger?

I thought I could ask my aunt Dorcas about these things next time I went over to Logan County. She was a schoolteacher and understood things like that.

Before my folks got home, I wrote the words I wanted to ask about on a piece of notebook paper and put it in my pocket where I could keep it to myself.

I just kept readin' that poem over and over until they got home because I had figured out why Daddy had been readin' this stuff' all those years. These books were full of important secrets about things, things most people never get around to learnin'. If my daddy knew what it all meant, he was important too, which made me proud. But I was a bit scared readin' it for myself, on account I was only eleven.

I figured there must be a good reason why nobody opened the books except Daddy. Not even Momma ever read Daddy's books. And now I knew that Pappy was leery of them because of what Momma had said, which meant they probably contained some sort of devilry. That too was fearsome.

Nonetheless, I knew I would find a way to open the books again. They had stuff in 'em people are supposed to know. It was like I had just found one of the most important things in the world and would need the rest of my life to figure it out.

I did worry about that the stuff in them books though. They were probably what kept my daddy from ever getting the anointin' at church. But it didn't make much sense why things would work that way.

When I heard the truck drivin' up the road and the hound dog makin' a racket to let me know about it, I put the book back on the shelf.

I fell asleep that night thinkin' about a great and spooky tyger a runnin' through the woods up Dry Creek Holler, everything dark but the stars overhead and that one fierce, beautiful beast, burnin' bright, lightin' up the forest through the night.

It was a fearful feeling thinkin' about that tyger.

If a kid didn't have a daddy like mine, who knew such stuff already, it would have been just too scary to contemplate.

7
DEVIL'S BAIT
MICHAEL COOPER

Sister Minnie Goins had a mustache. One of my earliest memories, in fact, is about askin' momma about it, 'cause she said that was a sorry thing to say about a lady.

Something happens to folk while they are a growin' up that changes their minds about what's important. Along the way they decide that since some questions have no answers they should stop askin'. Kids don't know that yet. They'll ask questions about whatever it is they want to learn.

For instance, for a kid, even if he's Holiness, askin' "Who created God?" is a perfectly good question. I asked Granddaddy that very question once. His silence and smile worked together to make me think I shouldn't ask the question again, which I didn't.

There would come a time when my old curiosity came back, but it would be a long time comin'.

Back then I just knew that sister Goins had a mustache, which was a fact I found impossible to ignore.

That mustache made me wonder about things. If the Bible said women "should not wear that which pertaineth to a man," why had God given sister Minnie Goins a mustache, which, as far as I could see, very clearly pertaineth to a man?

"Well, son, there are some things like that," Daddy said, tryin' not to laugh. "Some things just don't fit into any box of any kind. We figure out ways to explain things, we sort 'em out in our heads—but then along comes something that doesn't fit in those boxes. So, you just have to start over and re-sort everything. Other times, you just shrug your shoulders and move on."

She was a widow woman, sister Goins, whose husband had died in the late fifties down in the mines, on account of the ceiling a cavin' in. He and three other miners went down in the hole that morning and never came back up. It's an old story in Mingo County. Those who live there know what I'm talkin' about.

Her boys, Bip and Shank, didn't live around home when I was a kid. After they came back from Korea, they moved other places to get work. Bip lived over in Cincinnati. Shank lived up in Akron. I met Bip once, but he didn't come around much. But Shank came down right often.

Sometimes, he brought his Korean wife, Mi Rae, along.

I saw her and Shank once at the old Harding feed store, up on Mitchel Branch.

I got upset some at first because of it bein' a sin for Shank to marry a foreign woman. God told his people not to mix their seed with the heathen. But it was confusing. For one thing, Shank had never been noted for righteousness anywhere in Mingo County, so it was entirely possible that God didn't even care what Shank did.

Also, when I saw her up close I knew why he had done it, 'cause a spirit of lust fell upon me as soon as I saw her.

I had been noticin' that particular spirit creepin' up on me lately. But there was something in Mi Rae that was just too powerful to fight. It learned me how heathen women affect men o' God, just like Pappy had said in his sermon.

He was teachin' the saints why godly women need to dress holiness.

"A short skirt and a sleeveless blouse may be all it takes to flame the fires of hell in a man," Pappy said.

"You can read for yourself what the Word O' God says about it. Jezebel, Delilah, Herod's daughter—bless God—the devil used all them women to open up the gates of perdition. Even prophets and kings got fooled by the SPIRIT OF LUST in these WOMEN!"

(His face got beet red when he shouted the words 'spirit of lust' and 'women' because he had a powerful anointin'.)

"Bless God, ya add a little lipstick and smear on a dab of rouge, put ya on a pair of dangly earbobs, git yer hair all short and wild lookin' and you've mixed yourself up a witches' brew that will bring down even mighty men O' God. Yessir.

"Some poor soul can be peacefully makin' his way to heaven and suddenly forget God and his own name t' go off a whorin', chasin' the bait Satan smears all over some woman.

"Now you men o' God, you listen to MEEE! There's a HOOOOK behind that BAAAIT! The devil's gonna git that hook in ya, and then he'll drag ya DOWN! Oh, you'll fight and fuss, but ain't nothin' you can do 'bout it once the hook is in ya."

Everything Pappy had described was right there in front of me. Dangly earrings a hangin' from her ears, a skirt made of next-to-nothin', a tiny band of silver wrapped round her ankle—something I had never even seen before—hair all short and wild lookin'. All of it just like Pappy said. Besides all that there was a fragrance around her that plumb set me on fire.

For days after that, I pondered about how God beautifies the saints with salvation and how the heathen stir up the lust of the flesh. But Lord have mercy, even though all them things were a part of the world, which will soon melt away with a fervent heat, it was just hard to see things that-away sometimes.

It gave me a spirit of compassion for Shank. He had done a bad thing, marryin' that Korean woman like he did. But what I felt in that feed store helped me know that if any man got too close to the likes of Mi Rae, he would have no defense.

I couldn't imagine how a good Christian man could resist reachin' for that bait and gettin' caught on the devil's hook. Once that happened, he'd be like a trout, a floppin' around while he gets drug out of the river of life and pulled right into eternal damnation.

It was a fearsome thing to ponder, but I couldn't stop

thinkin' about it. That's why I think meetin' Shank's wife in that store had something to do with what happened betwixt me and Inida Goins.

———

I had known Inida Jean Goins all my life. We had played under the pews at church when we were little, long as we didn't get too loud. Course, usually the adults were yellin' so loud that we played however we wanted.

Inida was Minnie Goin's granddaughter, which is why she sometimes came to the Holiness Church of Jesus Christ with Signs Following. Everyone felt sorry for Inida on account that when her mother Lila got to be a teenager, the devil got a hold of her. It was an affliction for Sister Minnie, who always talked about it in her testimony and would ask for prayer that, "her wayward children would come home."

I found that confusing because Lila lived in the same house as Sister Minnie. When I asked Momma about that, she said it was on account that sometimes Lila went out "a prowlin'." I imagined Lila must go on huntin' trips of some kind, which I suppose she did.

Lately, Inida had been comin' to church, and I noticed she wasn't the same as before. She made me feel afflicted, which I think she knew and was glad about. Anyhow, she was a year older than me and wanted to remind me of it as often as she could.

One night we were at the back of the church, just talkin' and stuff. Suddenly, she leaned over and whispered in my ear. "Mickey! Wanna play a game?"

"What game?" I asked.

She opened up an old hymnbook somebody'd left on the pew and pointed to the title, *Blessed Assurance*.

"Under the Sheets," she said. "*Blessed Assurance Under the Sheets.*"

"What?" I felt stupid. I wasn't gettin' it.

"Just add 'under the sheets' to the songs."

So I flipped the book to page 134, "*Heaven is Calling– Under the Sheets.*"

Now it was her turn. "Page 47, *Just as I Am–Under the Sheets.*"

We went back and forth like that until we were laughin' so hard I thought someone would come and chew us out.

But I stopped laughin' when she leaned over, put her hand on my leg, and then in a voice like I had never heard before, low and gruff like she was out of breath, whispered, "*O Why Not Tonight–Under the Sheets.*"

Then, she bit me on the ear! It was almost enough to hurt but not quite. I don't know how to explain it any better than that.

It was like the time I stuck a knife in the electric socket, tryin' to pry loose the toaster plug. The shock flowed through my hand and up my arm. Now it was flowin' out from my ear and into my whole body. I had dropped that knife as soon as I got my wits about me because gettin' shocked doesn't feel good. But this kind of shock felt right nice, though it did strange, embarrassin' things to a person. It all left me not knowin' what to say 'cause I was ashamed, afraid, excited—all them things at once.

I got scared though cause I thought Pappy Mullins was lookin' back at us. So I told Inida we had better straighten up. I suddenly felt wicked, though I wasn't sure what I had done wrong.

I didn't get much sleep that night.

I kept thinkin' about what Inida had done and wonderin' why she had done it. It got me to thinkin' about something my Momma liked to tell when her family got together.

She said that one of the hardest lessons she had to teach me was not to bite people. She claims I bit everybody and everything, though of course I don't remember.

Anyway, when I was four, Sister Hatter was teachin' the children the story one morning about Daniel and the lions. I roared, evidently pretendin' I was a lion. Everybody laughed, so I fell down on the floor and bit my cousin, Beulah Mullins, on the leg.

Well, she commenced to cry and go on like she was a dyin', something she still does actually, and Sister Hatter told me that the devil would come and get me if I was bad, which made me cry too.

Momma came a runnin' with Beulah's mother, Aunt Tina, and found out what had happened from Sister Hatter.

Momma yelled out, "When you get home, your daddy's gonna set your little butt on fire!" Which of course, made me start cryin' again.

Momma told me to hug Beulah and tell her I was sorry, which I did. But when I hugged her she repeated what my Momma had said, "Your daddy's gonna set your little butt on fire," as she bit my shoulder so hard it left a mark.

That's when Aunt Tina jerked Beulah up by her arm and wore her out, right there in the back of the church in front of everybody. Course, Beulah let loose with a bloody shriek.

Momma said I never bit anyone again.

It had never occurred to me that anyone but a child would ever bite anyone else, but Inida Goins had proven that wrong. And something else; while I knew I never wanted Beulah Mullins to ever bite me again, I had to admit that if Inida Goins tried to bite me, I wouldn't have the good sense to stop her.

Now, what kind of madness is that?

It was a mystery why sometimes hurtin' just hurts and why other times hurtin' feels good. I just couldn't figure that out. Life is full of puzzles like that. It can drive you crazy tryin' to understand 'em.

———

Inida didn't come to church until the Labor Day picnic, about a month later.

When I saw her, I told Momma I was goin' to the Goins' table to get some chicken. I knew nobody at that table was walkin' with the Lord, except for Sister Minnie, of course, and I thought I need to explain myself.

Lila's boyfriend, Billy Joe Jarrell, had come back from fightin' communists on the other side of the world somewheres, and everybody said he took dope, on account of what he had seen over there.

I liked him though. He had a dragon on his arm, which made an impression. Daddy said that was a sign of low life. Momma said it was a sin to mark upon one's flesh like the heathen. I supposed both them things was true, even if what he was doin' over there was something good, like fightin' communists. But a dragon on somebody's arm was something anyone'd want to see.

Granddaddy Mullins had asked Billy Joe not to smoke at the picnic, out of respect for the saints. Billy Joe said he wouldn't. Even Daddy said that it was respectful and that he appreciated Billy Joe for it. Takin' these things into consideration, I figured nobody would care about me hangin' out with the Goinses.

Billy Joe had his nephew Robbie with him, who people said was slow. Robbie talked funny and always wanted to hug people. But he was nice and didn't hurt nobody.

When I got to the table, Robbie ran to hug me and hollered out "Mikeyyyyyy!" real loud, which I hated. I didn't say nothing to him about it though.

I was makin' my way to Billy Joe to look at that dragon up close, but I saw that Inida was standin' by a plate of chicken on the picnic table, which I needed to get on account of havin' told momma that was why I was comin' over there in the first place.

When I walked over to where Inida was, I took my time a lookin' at the plate.

"Breast or thigh?" asked Inida.

"Breast," I replied

"Is that so?" she said in that low voice, like she did at the church that night.

I swear it gave me the chills!

She grinned as she put the chicken breast on my plate and then said, "Wanna take a walk?"

"I dunno. Where to?"

"Somewheres," she said, raisin' her eyebrows as she started walkin'.

I quickly set down my plate on the table and followed her to over to where the trail begins and kept walkin' into the woods. We had just rounded the bend, at that place where you can no longer see the picnic area, when either my hand found hers or hers found mine. Whichever it was, I felt the same kind of shock as when she bit my ear, just not as powerful.

We kept on walkin' like that for a little ways when she suddenly said, "I'm tired. Let's sit a while under this oak."

"Already?" I asked.

But she had already sat down, so I sat down beside her.

I was tryin' to figure out what was going on when it was like we sort of leaned in toward one another. I either I kissed her, she kissed me, or we both kissed each other at the same time. To this day I have no idea which it was.

What I know is that the electricity got nearly unbearable because she slipped her tongue past my lips. Now, that was something else strange. It made me feel like I was losin' my breath, but I wasn't scared; it was like I was about to die but didn't care; it was like it didn't matter what was going on anywhere else or to anybody else. If Gabriel had blown his trumpet I might not have noticed. It was a puzzlement and a wonder. There just wasn't any words to explain it.

We would have stayed that way for a long time, a kissin' and carryin' on, except I suddenly heard a fearful, piercin' sound a cuttin' through the spell I had fallen under.

"Michael Cooper! Michael Journeyman Cooper!"

"Ain't that your Momma a callin'?" Inida asked

"Yeah." I said it like some one who has just been called to the Day of Doom.

"Shouldn't we go back?" Inida asked.

"Yeah, in a minute," I said.

The problem was, there was no way I was going back; not yet anyway. I had suddenly realized I was in no shape to walk among righteous people, so I needed time to get myself decent and presentable. Wickedness is a bewitching thing. It does things to a person that you can't do anything about. So here I was, reapin' the wages of sin. I could almost feel the hook that had laid a hold on my soul.

By and by though, I got the courage to stand up and start walkin' toward the clearing.

When I got there, momma was standin' with her hands on her hips lookin' for all the world like the wrath of God on judgment day. Behind her were all the saints, tryin' not to appear as though they were lookin,' though I knew full well they were.

Lila and Billy Joe were over at their table a laughin', though I could tell they meant no harm in it.

"Come over here, honey," Lila said to Inida, which she did.

Me? Well, I had lowered my head and was lookin' intently at a line of ants a walkin' from somewhere far away, headed to a bush just a stone's throw from where I was a standin'. It brought to mind the Word O' God,

"Go to the ant, thou sluggard; consider her ways, and be wise: which having no guide, overseer, or ruler, provideth her meat in the summer, and gathereth her food in the harvest."

I had memorized that verse for Sunday School class a few weeks before. Now it was shoutin' at me from somewhere deep in my bosom. Even ants knew better than to do what I had been up to back there with Inida Goins.

"I know what you were a doin', young man," Momma said.

"We weren't doing nothin'," I replied. "Just takin' a walk."

"Right. And I'm Howdy Doody. You think I was born yesterday? You think I'm stupid?"

"No ma'am."

"Well, we're going to have a talk when we get home. That's for sure."

"Yes ma'am." I walked over to my Grandma Mullins' table.

I picked at the chicken and ate some potato salad but I was too miserable to eat or to talk to anyone.

Then Granddaddy said everybody needed to go early on account of the storm. The clouds had been gettin' dark and the wind had started to grow chilly.

It felt outside like the state of my soul, all stormy and dark.

Pappy talked about how the apostle Paul said we all

do the things we don't want to do and don't do the things we want to do. It was kind of hard to understand, but Pappy explained it this a way:

"There's two people inside you a fightin.' One of 'em is your old man and one of 'em is your new man. The new man wants to folla the Lord, and the old man wants to folla the devil. The good man wants to be righteous. The old man just wants the things of the flesh. And that old man, he'll jump right up if you don't watch out and take you over. Next thing you know, you're out there a committin' the sins of the flesh. Yessir. Praise Jesus. That's just the way it is. Oh saints, ya better find a way to put that old man t' death or he'll git ya fir sure."

Now what Pappy was warnin' us about had happened to me. My old man had jumped up and taken me over. I had been completely defenseless. My old man wasn't anywhere near dyin'. But what made me ashamed the most was that I didn't want nobody to put my old man to death.

Not yet, anyway.

————

On the way home in the back seat, my sister Susan kept grinnin' at me and shakin' her head. She would punch me to get my attention and then rub her fingers together in the way that means "shame on you."

Like I needed any more shame on me! Shame was already on me, hangin' on me like the dark Mingo County clouds that were scrapin' the tops of the mountains that very moment.

When we got home, we ran into the house on account of the rain. We had hardly got through the door until Momma began, raisin' her voice above the thunder.

"You leave that Goins girl alone, Michael Cooper. Do you hear me?"

"Yes ma'am."

"She ain't no little girl no more. She's been around the block more than once already, if I don't miss my guess. If God don't git a hold o' that girl, she'll turn out to be a floozy, just like her mother. There's things 'bout the world you don't know, Michael Journeyman Cooper!Are you listenin'?"

"Yes, ma'am."

Momma only evoked my entire name in times of great seriousness, and the effect on me was right strong.

"It's time your Daddy talked to you, like fathers are supposed to talk to their boys. Sure ain't a woman's place.

"Lordy, Lordy, child. Not yet fourteen years old and already took off into the woods with a Goins girl.

"Jesus, Jesus!"

I finally raised my head to glance at Daddy, who looked like someone on his way to a hangin'.

I knew then that Daddy hadn't killed off his old man neither.

———

The next morning, Daddy was runnin' coal over on Buffalo Creek. He said I could go over with him and that when we were done we would go see Grandpop. I was always up for seein' Grandpop, but we both knew we were going to have that talk because there was nothing neither of us could do to keep from it.

Daddy did his best talkin' about difficult things when he was drivin' the coal truck. It made it easier for him somehow, and I didn't mind it as much either. It happened that way a bunch of times.

"We're getting some good rain this year, son," he said.

"Yeah, I guess we are Daddy."

"People's crops already looking healthy. That's a good sign."

"Yes, sir."

"Grandpop's a good farmer. I never was much count at it."

"You're a good farmer, Daddy," I replied.

"Well, I can do it if I have to, and it helps with the grocery bills. But your Grandpop, now he's got a green thumb. He's just plain good, your Grandpop. Yes, sir. He is a right good man."

We kept drivin' in silence for a while, but after a few more miles, Daddy started talkin' again. "Son, I need to talk to you about the Goins girl."

"Yes, sir, I know."

"I suspect you didn't do anything wrong out there in the woods, son. You're just growing up, that all. And, your momma don't mean you no harm. She's just afraid."

"Afraid of what, Daddy?"

"Well, son, there's powerful force that can rise up in boys and girls your age. Them forces change a boy into a man and a girl into a woman and that's the way the good

Lord meant it to be. But you gotta learn how t' control them forces. If you don't, they can mess up your life something awful. And it's worse for girls.

"You think you won't do anything wrong, but them forces will just take over and you can't help yourself. If they hit both the boy and the girl at the same time, nothing can stop them. They will just carry that boy and girl away, like a mountain river in the springtime carries big trees and such. You'll be thinking you're just enjoying the girl's company, kissin' and carryin' on—touching each other's bodies and what have you—then, before you know even what has hit you, bam! Those forces will take hold and carry you on into fornication.

"Do you know what fornication is, son?"

"Yes, sir."

I had listened to the boys at school talk, and even though they didn't use the word fornication exactly, I had figured out it was the same thing Pappy and Grand-daddy Mullins usually preached about. I had put that all together a couple of years back. I turned out to be wrong about some of the details, but I had gotten most of it right.

"Me and Inida Goins weren't fornicatin' Daddy," I said as confidently as I could.

"Didn't think you were, son. Inida's a pretty girl and there ain't nothing wrong with her. Ain't nothing wrong with you either. I'm just saying you're curious and can wind up getting each other all worked up. Things might happen before you get a chance to stop. Sin slips up on people. When it does, you spend your life a payin' for it.

"They'll come a time to make love to a woman. You

want that woman to be your wife. That's the way the Good Lord wants it to happen. There ain't no shame in it when it happens that way. No shame a'tal, though some people act like there is."

He was quiet for a while so I didn't say nothing either. But I knew he wasn't finished.

"Son, they call it makin' love 'cause that's what it's supposed to be about. It's a beautiful thing when that's what it is. Men who talk nasty about women aren't after love. They're just after a woman's dew lily. And when they get a hold of that, they're done with 'er. A man who acts that way ain't no count.

"After a man treats a woman like that, a lot of them women start sinkin' real low. They never get their pride back. Oh, the men go on and live however they want to. Even get to be deacons and such. But the women can't get no forgiveness anywhere.

"That ain't right. But that's the way it is."

"Is that what happened to Lila Goins, Daddy?" I asked.

It took forever for Daddy to say anything, but after a while he replied, "Yeah, son. That's what happen to Lila."

"Is she really a floozy, Daddy?"

"No, son, she ain't. Lila's just a woman who wanted someone to love and for someone to love her back. She ain't no different than any of the rest of us that-away.

"Son?"

"Yes, sir?"

"Treat a woman the way you want other boys to treat your sister. They ain't just body parts. They're people. Don't forget that, hear me?"

"Yes, sir," I said, delighted the ponderous talk was over.

But he wasn't quite done.

"One more thing, son."

"Yes, sir?"

"Them body parts ain't that bad though, are they?"

"No sir, they ain't," I said with a grin.

Then we laughed. We laughed real hard.

There in that bend on Buffalo Creek Road, just outside Robinette, I understood my daddy thought I was gonna become a good man someday, and I decided I would do everything I knew to do to make that happen.

But Lord Almighty, how was I gonna stay away from Inida Goins?

8

KILLING OFF MY OLD MAN
MICHAEL COOPER

Growin' up any kind of Holiness was an affliction for a kid in Mingo County. But the kids from signs-followin' churches had it particularly rough.

I tried to make the kids at school think I was at least part of the regular holy rollers, like the ones from organized churches. People in those churches shook and fell out in the Spirit, just like us, so kids made fun of them too. But if even those kids from organized churches knew you took up serpents, you were plain doomed.

When kids at school got to makin' fun of Holiness kids—course, they called us Holy Roller kids—the ones from the organized churches would shoot back, "Well, at least we don't handle no snakes, like the people over at Pappy Mullins' church."

I always dreaded that because I knew what came next.

"Ain't you a Mullins?" somebody would ask. "Don't all the Mullinses handle snakes?"

My face would turn hot as a coal stove when they said that kind of stuff. Course, that made things worse. I wanted to be in Outer Mongolia.

Girls wanted nothing to do with me.

The boys, on the other hand, loved to have me around because I was always good for a laugh, especially in the locker room. If things got quiet, someone might say something like, "Hey Cooper, how often do you handle your snake?"

To which somebody might add, "Well, who else is going to handle his snake if he don't?"

Or, if they were unusually bored, the inevitable mockery of tongues-speakin.

"SHANDA KANA TA SKUTU! Interpret that, Cooper," Jasper Holcomb said that one time he got used by the Devil to rob me of my salvation.

"Sure, you jackass," I replied. "It means, don't answer a fool in his folly."

Jasper, who went to Blizzard Ridge Baptist Church and was always talking about the Bible, responded, "I guess snake handlers get to call people fools, even though Jesus said that callin' folk fools sends you straight t' Hell."

My skin turned cold when he said that. A spirit of anger had made me deny the Lord and give a bad witness before the world. It made it worse that Jasper was right. Jesus did say not to call people fools. Now I had done something worse than lust, something that if I didn't make right somehow would cut my soul off from God.

Granddaddy, who had been doin' most of the preachin' over at the church, had preached on the very passage Jasper had just quoted a few weeks before: "If ye call your brother a fool, you will be in danger of hellfire."

Well, that's what I just done. I shouldn't have called Jasper a jackass either, 'cause Holiness people don't talk that way. But at least sayin' "jackass" wouldn't send a soul t' Hell.

A spirit of dread came upon me. For days I couldn't think about nothin' else.

What I said back to Jasper Holcomb was a mumbled "No, we ain't supposed to say that."

But there was a storm in my soul. Here I was, not yet fourteen years old and already fallin' into the sins of the flesh and failin' the Lord, like Peter did when they led Jesus away. I was weighed in the balances and found wanting, fallin' into the pit where my sins dragged me down 'neath Jehovah's dread frown.

I could hardly repent there at school, on account the Holy Ghost might come upon me. People sure wouldn't understand that! That's why I just prayed a quick promise to make things right as soon as I got to church.

I worried the whole week Pappy would find out. He knew things people did in secret, which was something that had me tore up in knots.

I found out later that Sister Bertha Solomon was a dreadin' the same thing. She had played cards over in Charleston while visitin' with her sisters. Sure enough, Pappy revealed in church what she had done. He didn't say it out exactly, but he kept talkin' about things saints do when they're away visitin' their relatives and they think no one sees him.

Course, she knew then that Pappy had the spirit of

discernment on 'em and was givin' her a chance to come clean. So, she stood up and commenced a cryin' about what she had done. She confessed that her sisters, who went to an organized church over in Charleston, had told her there weren't anything wrong with playin' cards, even though people had said such stuff back in the old days. Pappy just shook his head when he heard that and everyone started cryin'. They weren't mad at sister Bertha; they were just sad about how low Holiness people in organized churches can sink, especially over in the city.

Pappy told Bertha that Jesus always goes after the lost sheep. She just needed to make things right. So she ran right down to the front where Pappy was a standin'. When he laid his hands on her head, the power came upon him and then flowed into her. They both looked electrocuted, and she started shoutin' out, "SHANNNANANANANANA!" as she fell out and jerked on the floor for a good while.

Pappy saw that Bobby Lynn Collins and some other folks had come with guitars, drums, tambourines, cymbals, and what have you. So he told them to start singin' and playin', which they commenced to do.

> *"He's God when the lightning flashes; he's*
> *   God when the thunder rolls;*
> *He's God in the Amen corner; He's God down*
> *   in my soul."*
> *God is God and God don't ever change*
> *God is God and Jesus is His name."*

As the saints kept singin' 'round sister Bertha, helpin' her press on to victory, I stayed in the back, scared of what I had done at school and for the powerful spirit of lust I had for Inida Goins. I was afflicted with an awful dread. What had been done in secret was about to be shouted from the housetops, and so the spirit of conviction just got stronger and stronger until I thought I would explode.

I was still tryin' to figure out what to do when Granddaddy walked up to the serpent box. I had already been lookin' at the message carved in that box: *Holiness Unto the Lord*. The phrase had been rippin' my soul to pieces. So by the time Granddaddy opened the lock, I knew I had to do something.

Now, a serpent usually won't strike anybody if he's under the annointin', and even if it does, it won't kill nobody. But if someone in the church has a spot, wrinkle, blemish, or any such thing, bad things can happen to folk. I'd seen that for myself and was under the fear of God.

Finally, I just couldn't stand it no more.

I ran to the front and blurted out, "Saints, I got terrible sin in my heart. I called Jasper Holcomb a fool for pretendin' to speak in tongues, and now I'm in danger of fallin' into hellfire!"

Pappy stared and then shouted back, "Son, it takes a man to confess when he's done wrong! Sometimes when we git persecuted for his name sake, we git weary with it. But you ain't goin' to hell. You are saved and redeemed. All that's under the blood. You let that go now!"

When he said that, I knew I didn't have to say nothin'

'bout Inida Goins and all the lust she had stirred up in my soul. Pappy had said everything was good betwixt God and me. I got so happy about it, I just shouted out something, I don't remember what exactly, and then the power hit me at the top of my head and went all through my body.

I didn't intend to take up serpents. Young people aren't allowed in churches with signs-followin' to take up serpents anyhow 'til they're grown. But before anyone knew what was happenin', I broke through the veil and picked up a copperhead Leroy Mullins had hung about his neck and had commenced to put back in the box. I danced all over the place with it before I came to myself and knew what I had done.

When it was all over, no one said much. Course, everyone hugged me and told me to keep a walkin' with the Lord. Most everybody seemed happy for me except Daddy. He didn't say a word about it. To tell you the truth, he looked plumb grieved.

But Granddaddy talked to me later that week about getting baptized, which I had never done. He said we would do it down at the river the following Sunday.

When Sunday came, all the saints were gathered at the river bank singin' the song they usually sang for baptism.

> *I'm a child of the king, yes I am, yes I am.*
> *I'm a child of the king, yes I am, yes I am.*
> *I belong to the Lord, yes I do, yes I do.*
> *I'm a child of the king, yes I am.*

Well if I hold, hold it, hold it, til I reach that
    other shore
I'm gonna praise his name forever; won't
    have to suffer anymore.
They'll be no one there to mock me; no one to
    laugh in my face.
But my journey won't be over til I reach that
    heavenly place.

I'm a child of the king, yes I am, yes I am.
I'm a child of the king, yes I am, yes I am.
I belong to the Lord, yes I do, yes I do.
I'm a child of the king, yes I am.

Granddaddy asked Pappy if he wanted to say a few words, and so Pappy talked a while about Noah, whom he always called Noey, and about how the whole world got covered up with water because of the peoples' wickedness.

"Sin was a risin' to heaven and sickened the nostrils of God. That's right, saints, sin stinks! Yessir. Praise Jesus. God told Noey that a flood was a comin' t' wash everything away. Everybody died because they'd gotten so wicked they refused to get in the ark of safety. But bless Jesus, my great-grandson is gonna drown his old man in this water, just like the people back there in Noey's day. He's goin' down in this water here, his soul all full of pus and corruption, and he's gonna come back up—PRAISE JESUS! SHATA HA!—he's gonna come up a brand new man. His old man's gonna be dead."

When Pappy finished, Granddaddy said a prayer and

plunged me in the cold waters of Laurel Branch, washin' away all my sins and killin' off my old man.

———

Granddaddy talked to me after the baptism about how I shouldn't handle any more serpents until I got older. He allowed how the Spirit had come upon me in that service but that had been a special moment, he thought. People were always watchin' churches like ours, and if they knew that people as young as me were handlin' serpents, it would cause a lot of trouble.

I told him I understood.

Granddaddy was saying what he did because he really thought that a way, but I also knew my Daddy had probably talked with him about it. That made more and more sense as the weeks went by because I started noticing that my Daddy had a lukewarm spirit when it came to the signs.

I didn't know why it troubled Daddy like it did, but though he didn't say anything about it, I knew he was a ponderin' something.

What really surprised me was that Momma seemed to be troubled too.

A few weeks after that, I turned fourteen.

Things were changin' somehow, though I couldn't quite put my finger on what they were. Momma and Daddy would be talking and then get quiet if my sister and I came into the room.

As for me, I had been sanctified, delivered from lust, and forgiven for denyin' the Lord like the apostle Peter. I started readin' the Bible every chance I got. If the saints went forward, I didn't stay in the back, where the spirit of lukewarmness and fleshly desires grabs a person.

I didn't handle any serpents either, on account of Granddaddy asking me not to, and also because I didn't want the unbelievers to criticize the saints. But every time they brought out that box, I got grieved. Something was missing from my life, and I just couldn't tolerate it. It was like a hunger deep inside, and it wouldn't go away.

That's why, about the time school was lettin' out for the summer, I got carried away in the Spirit one Sunday night and forgot myself. When the saints were takin' up serpents, I stayed on the other side of the room, but then I started shoutin' and so before I knew it, I got up there with everybody else. By that time, I was so caught up in the Spirit I didn't noticed how I was bumpin' up against aunt Bess, who had been holdin' that big brown copperhead, the one with all the spots. It must have been about three feet long.

When it struck, I just kept on a shoutin' at first. It really didn't hurt like you think. My thoughts were way off, like someone else was a thinkin' 'em. But I do remember thinkin' that a safety pin had come undone and stuck me in the arm. What I did notice clearly was that the music had stopped and that I was feelin' right strange. It was like I had been watchin' a movie that had suddenly stopped, and I couldn't yet figure out yet where I was or what I was a doin'. Momma and Granddaddy Mullins had rushed over to me and were tellin' me to lay down on the front pew. Everybody else were a prayin'.

I don't know how long it was before Daddy got there.

It couldn't have been long. He told everybody to get away from me, and then he picked me up and carried me to the car. Someone said something about "trustin' the Lord and pressin' on to victory," but Daddy yelled back, "My boy's going to the hospital!"

Momma was cryin' like she didn't know what to do, but Granddaddy said, "Eddie's right, Irene. He gonna do what he needs to do. He's gonna get that boy some help."

My world was just breakin' in two. I knew I was probably dyin' but I wasn't afraid. What worried me the most was that my Daddy and Granddaddy might be fallin' away from the truth, or at least gettin' a lukewarm spirit. But I was gettin' too sleepy to think much more about it.

I remember how Daddy pulled up to Mrs. Sadie Workman's house over by the church 'cause she worked for a doctor and that she gave us some cloths because I was throwing up. She told Daddy to take me on to the hospital over in Logan because although copperhead bites are not usually fatal, this bite was dangerous 'cause I was on the small side.

Daddy got back in the car, slammed his door, and headed for Logan like he had gone crazy. It's a wonder we didn't get killed.

He didn't say anything once we got on the road, but as he was backin' up into the road, Daddy said, "Son, Mrs. Workman says you're gonna be all right. You're gonna live, boy. You hear me? You're gonna live."

As sleepy as I was, I knew Daddy was tryin' not to cry.

I puked all the way to Logan. By the time we got to the hospital, my arm had swollen up and was hurtin' really fierce, especially where the serpent had struck me. I don't remember much else until I woke up in a hospital bed, the next morning, I think. I saw that I was in a gown, and there were tubes of something hooked up to my left arm, the one that wasn't bit.

I remember the lady standin' over me sayin, "He's back with us! He's going to be fine."

I must have gone right back to sleep after that. When I woke up, the sun was already shinnin' and my first thought was that I obviously wasn't dead. The second thought was about how bad my arm was hurtin'. The doctors had cut out a big piece of flesh around where the serpent had bite me and there was a bandage on it.

I saw Daddy talkin' to a doctor in a long white coat.

"We've saved that boy's arm," the doctor was saying. "But if he was my boy, he sure wouldn't be going back into that mess."

"He ain't goin' back," Daddy said, looking down at the floor. "We're moving somewheres else."

I never told anybody that I heard what Daddy said to that doctor. I just thought about how everything would have been fine if a spirit of disobedience hadn't taken me over. I wondered how it was that I had been so sure that it was the Holy Ghost that had come upon me, only to go on to disobey my Granddaddy and open my soul up to be fooled by the devil. Now, the saints were goin' to be persecuted for righteousness's sake, all because of me.

Them's the things I keep thinkin' about layin' there in the Logan Hospital, recoverin' from the sting of the serpent.

9

LOGAN

MICHAEL COOPER

When I started gettin' better, Daddy told me we were movin' to Amherstdale, up Buffalo Creek. That's just a little ways from where Grandpop and Granny Cooper lived, over in Man.

Daddy said we was a movin' on account of his work. Course, I knew it was really on account of me. Daddy, and I think Granddaddy Mullins too, had decided. I knew that 'cause I heard him say to the doctors about "not lettin' me go back into that mess."

I never told Momma about what he said, knowin' it would cause a powerful feud. I knew it all the same though, and it bore down on me.

I couldn't decide if Daddy was right or not. 'Cause if it had really been the Holy Ghost that told me to pick up the serpent, I wouldn't have needed any doctor to save my life. On the other hand, maybe we hadn't given Jesus a chance to save me. Maybe just rushed off to the doctors instead of trustin' in the Lord. That line of thinkin' appealed to me at first, but it didn't go anywhere since Granddaddy seemed to be agreein' with Daddy.

As I saw it, Daddy and Granddaddy were on one side, Pappy Mullins was on the other, and Momma was caught somewhere in-between.

When Grandpop and Granny Cooper came to see me, Daddy said I would be stayin' with them for a while, since the doctor I would be seein' later lived closer to them. Momma didn't say anything about it. She was mostly quiet durin' that time.

I also found out I would be goin' to school in Man after I got out of the hospital.

It was all so confounding and confusing.

Anyhow, I stayed at the hospital for a few days while the doctors made sure my arm was goin' to be all right. I heard a nurse tellin' somebody in the hall how they thought at first I might lose a part of my arm. I wondered then if I might get a hook for a hand, like a pirate. I didn't want to lose any of my arm, but on the other hand, there weren't a kid anywhere around with a hook for a hand, so I wondered what that would be like.

Those were the kinds of things I thought about mostly. It was scary to think about Jesus because I didn't know if I had made him sad by disobeyin' Granddaddy over the serpent, or if I was only pretendin' to be in the Spirit, or if I had been given a test for trustin' in God but had run to the doctors instead—I just couldn't figure none of that out.

I just knew something big had happened and that nothin' would be the same again.

Course, it turned out I was right about that.

———

The morning I got out of the hospital, Daddy drove us to Kistler, and we ate at Dolly's Shake and Burger. It was the first time we had ever gone to a restaurant. I'd heard Pappy say once that restaurants cook old food and then charge you an arm and a leg for "that little bit of nothin' they put on your plate. I wouldn't waste my time or money on food like that."

That's why I had put restaurants in the same category as picture shows and ball games, places Holiness people don't go 'less they have to. But the undeniable fact was that it was the best hamburger I had ever had. And the shake? I got a chocolate one. It made me nearly forget about the serpent and everything else. I think if Pappy had ever had a milkshake like that he might have come to a different conclusion about restaurants! Course, I kept that to myself.

We went on up to Amherstdale, then to see the house we was goin' to be livin' in. Course, I would be livin' in Man for a while. But after that, I would get my own room in our new house. That's the kind of things Daddy was talkin' about when we drove up.

It was a bigger house than anybody had up in Verner, at least anybody I knew. It looked even bigger from the road, on account of it being up on the hill across the railroad tracks. We didn't go in that day because the people who had been livin' there hadn't got out yet.

It belonged to Mr. Petry, who owned the coal truck Daddy was gonna drive. Daddy explained how he was gonna make more money here and that Mr. Petry was helpin' him do that somehow. Anyway, I could see that people in Buffalo Creek had nicer cars and houses than we did over in Mingo County. Anyone could see that.

It crossed my mind that we might be goin' down to Egypt, sellin' our souls to Pharaoh, givin' up the Kingdom of God for the wealth of this world and the praises of men. Pappy warned people about it all the time and told stories about them who had done it.

Junior Dolittle was one who had done it. He got a job over in Charleston sellin' cars and started makin' money. Pappy talked about it at church one Sunday.

"Next thing you know, Junior bought himself a big RCA color television set," Pappy said.

"Put it right there in his living room where everybody'd see it. Yessir. Sister Workman saw it herself when she was over there seein' her sister. She decided to visit with Junior and Betty before comin' home, and that's when she knowed how the Dolittles had gotten themselves a television. It grieved her the whole time they were a sittin' there. It wasn't on, but the thing was a burden to her spirit just a sittin' there. Might as well have a pipe connectin' your house to Hell as to have one of those things . . . invitin' all the corruption of the Devil hisself to pour into your house."

All television was bad but a color television was worse. And if it was a big color television? Well, that made a bad thing sheer evil. I wondered if we'd be gettin' us a television, maybe even a big color television, seeings how we had moved over here to Egypt. I worried about it, but I also hoped it would happen.

I think that's what afflicts a soul: you want something and don't want it; you believe something and don't believe it. Like there's two people inside you a fightin' and neither one can win and bring an end to it.

Anyway, movin' away and makin' money seemed to be what made folk fall away from the truth. Before you know it, they'd get ashamed of the signs and start acting like treacherous Lot, who moved away from Abraham and settled over next to Sodom.

"He didn't want to become a heathern, exactly," Pappy said. "Lot just wanted to eat all that good food, carry on with the rich people, and forget he was kin to Abraham up there in the mountains. Happens all the time. You know what I'm a talkin' about—somebody shout 'AMEN!' Folk move over to Logan or Huntington— they get to makin' a little bit of money— pretty soon we don't see them but every few weeks or every few months. Finally, they won't stay for church even when they come home 'cause they ain't got time! Yes sir! They got to rush back to their new lives over there next to Sodom."

After showin' us the house in Amherstdale, Daddy drove me over to Grandpop and Granny Cooper's. Momma never got out of the car, but she waved at us and smiled. I figured she was scared about me livin' out of the ark of safety over here in Logan County. Granny Cooper told me to go back and hug my Momma.

I thought that would make things worse, but I went back to the car anyway and said, "I'm just stayin' for a little while, right?"

"Yeah," Momma said. "Be sure to brush your teeth and don't perplex Mr. and Mrs. Cooper."

"I won't Momma."

"Michael?" her voice trembled. "Don't forget that you're a Holiness child."

"OK, Momma. I won't," I promised.

Grandpop and Granny had fixed me up the room that had once been my Daddy's. They said if I wanted, I could fix it up different, so it would feel like mine. But having a room to yourself is already pretty important and so I didn't have a mind to change it none. But when I looked around and saw the little shelf next to the bed with two books on it, I knew right away Daddy had put them there. One was *An Introduction to English Literature.* The other was the old, worn-out blue one: *The New Oxford Book of English Verse.* I picked it up and turned to page 483.

"Tyger! Tyger! Burning Bright, in the Forest of the Night," I read in the spookiest voice I could muster up.

I read that poem every night before goin' to bed while I was at Grandpop and Granny Cooper's house. One night, I also read the poem beside it.

"Love seeketh not itself to please," I read out loud.

It went on about something connected to Heaven and Hell and how a piece of dirt tries to decide which one he wants to be in. I didn't make much sense of it and decided I would have to read it lots of times before understanding it.

The next Monday, I went to school at Man High school, over on East McDonald Avenue. I had decided to tell people my arm was bandaged because I had been bit by a snake—only Holiness people say "serpent"—but not to say that it had happened at church. I had thought about the story and how I would tell it.

I would say, "I was at my Pappy's place, just goofin' off with my relatives, when a copperhead came out of nowheres and bit me."

I remembered how Granddaddy had told me that it would bring trouble upon the saints if the unbelievers knew I had handled a serpent on purpose. I didn't want to lie about what I had done, but I also needed to tell the story in a way that wouldn't 'cause nobody no trouble.

Anyway, it turned out that some folks get excited to meet a person who's been bit by a serpent. Most of the time, they just wanted to know if it hurt or why I wasn't dead. I told 'em it wasn't that a big a deal.

"It's kind of like gettin' dog bit," I said.

Course, gettin' dog bit hurts more at first but then goes away. A serpent's sting can hurt your whole life. I didn't say none of that though.

People over at the school in Man are called hillbillies, which is stupid. Everybody in the mountains is hillbillies. Also, they take a goat to the games. I've heard tell that folk in other places eat goats, like in the Bible. They don't do that in either Logan or Mingo County. In West Virginia, goats don't do much of anything 'cept climb up hills and eat clothes off people's clothes line. I went up and touched the goat. He didn't mind. I just couldn't figure out what a goat was doing at a ballgame. Kind of like me that a way.

I went to the Methodist Church with Grandpop and Granny.

They did everything out of a book. They even sang all their songs out of a book—which weren't like ordinary songs no how, more like poems put to music but with words that nobody knows what they mean. They had the numbers of the songs up on a board in the front of the church, which meant that everybody knew what they were goin' to sing aforhand! That was about the strangest thing I had ever seen.

The preacher preached short, which was good, otherwise we would've all been asleep before he got done. He never got the anointin' and neither did we. He just talked. Not that he said anything bad or anything. What he said was all right. It just never got quickened.

On the way home, Grandpop said to Granny, "Preacher Grundy did a right good job this morning. I don't get as much out of it as when Preacher Grover was here, but I'm getting tolerable of it."

Granny said she agreed.

I thought about how I would be goin' to that church for weeks and weeks—the whole time I would be with Grandpop and Granny— and wondered how I could make that church tolerable enough to go for that long.

While I was stayin in Man in that room of my own, I thought every day about Mullinses and the Coopers, how they're part of me and I'm part of them. It came to me in those days I would have to figure out if I was gonna be more like a Mullins or more like a Cooper. It was gonna be hard to be both, that was for sure. The Coopers always figure out why they're gonna do before they do it; the Mullinses don't know what they're gonna do this afternoon. For instance, Granny Cooper sometimes told me what she was gonna fix for dinner while we were eatin' our breakfast! The Mullinses, on the other hand, wouldn't decide what to eat right until it's time to cook.

Then there's the matter of how you put stuff in your house. If the Mullinses like a picture out of a magazine, they'll just cut the picture out and nail to the wall. It might stay up there for years if nobody needs the space for something else. The Coopers have to talk about what to put on the wall before anybody puts it up. They talk about where it will look the best and then they measure the picture and the wall with a ruler. The picture, which they buy in a store somewhere, has to be so far from the floor, so far from the ceiling—just so-so. After Grandpop fixes that picture or whatever it is he's decided to put up on the wall, he calls Granny in to see what she thinks. Sometimes he moves it just a tad this way, and then she makes him move it back just a tad the other way. It's right funny how complicated they make something like that.

If anybody at the Mullins' would ever ask where they should put something up on the wall, the one they'd asked would just say, "Suit y' self. It ain't my picture."

I figured out that the Coopers think things probably will turn out tomorrow pretty much how they turned out today. The Mullinses don't know if there will even be a tomorrow. The Russians might drop a bomb. Gabriel might blow his trumpet. Uncle Hershel might get the itch. Nobody but the Lord Almighty Hisself knows what's gonna happen tomorrow, and even if anybody did know there'd be nothing he could do 'bout it! There's a day you're gonna get married. There's a day you're gonna die. You're gonna have so many kids. You're gonna make so much money. You're gonna get the croup on an appointed day in an appointed year. All that's been decided already, and its gonna happen just the way it's been set out by the Lord Hisself.

No man knows the day or the hour. That's God's business, knowin' all that stuff, though sometimes you can see a little bit of it in a dream or maybe in the Farmer's Almanac.

The Coopers, on the other hand, act like people's got somethin' to say about how things turn out. One week when I was there, they drove to the elementary school to vote in the election. I had never met anybody that did that. I was plumb mystified.

Pappy said, "The Good Lord puts up kings and takes down kings, bless God. The folk up in Washington or over there in Charleston pay people money or liquor them up for their votes. The election is already fixed over there in the country club before the votes are even counted. Saints O' God don't have no business with such stuff as that! The Good Lord let's things go on for a while, then he writes up on the wall, like he did that day in Babylon: YOUR TIMES UP, NEBUCHADNEZZAR! Yessir. We ain't home yet, but where we're a goin' there ain't no elections."

Course, like I said, the Coopers weren't Holiness.

I asked Grandpop once about voting in the election. He explained how in our country we decide together how we want the future to turn out. I liked the idea, but what is strange about it is that if everybody else decides something you didn't like? I mean how are you gonna make yourself go along with stuff you don't care for?

When I asked Grandpop, he said that although he didn't like President Nixon much, we still call him out in our prayers. We don't talk bad about 'im or nothin'. Once everybody decides, we all have to make do. That's what Democracy means, he said. I suppose he was right, but I didn't see how anybody in the mountains could find a way to go along with it.

Because of things like that, it was strange at first, living with Grandpop and Granny. But after a while, the quiet didn't feel like a tomb, which is what Momma had said about things "over there at the Coopers." It was more like sittin' under a tree in the summertime when there ain't nothing much to do. You just watch the clouds go by, eat you an apple under the tree, and listen to the birds a chirpin'. You don't want to do that forever, but while you're doin' it, it feels like the best thing you've ever done.

Granddaddy Mullins preached once about Jesus being in a storm and tellin' the wind to be still. I thought it was probably more exciting bein' in the boat when the waters had been stirred up. After a while though, the disciples had more excitement than they could stand. When a person gets to that point, he's right glad for somebody to come and calm things down.

That led me to the conclusion that I could be a Mullins when I needed something exciting to happen, and I could be a Cooper if I needed things to settle down. I figured that's why Daddy wanted me to spend time with Grandpop and Granny after bein' stung by the serpent. I didn't need the waters to get troubled for a while.

I don't think Momma ever figured any of that out.

After five weeks stayin' with Grandpop and Granny

Cooper, Daddy took me Amherstdale. They had already moved our things over there but it felt funny, livin' in a different house. It made the family seem different somehow, like we didn't have all our parts.

People in other places have a mom and dad, sisters and brothers. Mountain people have aunts and uncles, cousins and old people related to you in all kinds of ways. We don't live with all of them in the same house exactly, but they are never far away. We walk down the road to an uncle's house and get in the fridge to see what's to eat over there. If the uncle ain't there, he might be over at our house, talkin' to our mom. The dogs all know us and wander from place to place. Our own house is like "homeroom" at school. We start the day and usually end the day there, but we are also at home lots of other places. The family is the whole thing, not just homeroom.

Most Sundays, we went back to Mingo County. After a while, we would go to church and hear Pappy or Granddaddy preach. But it wasn't the same. We weren't strangers or nothin', but we weren't exactly part of things either. Not seein' your kin every day, or at least knowin' that you can see them if you want to, is an affliction.

Momma cried sometimes.

That winter, Pappy had got over bein' bit by a serpent. He always did. The serpents had bitten him many times and had turned his fingers all gnarly. He would sometimes show his hands to folk. Using a finger on one hand to point to the fingers on the other he would say, "This one was a mean o' rattlesnake. He was full of the devil! This one here was when I got ahead of the Lord and didn't wait on the anointin'.'"

Then he might say, "This one here is when my old woman got mad at me and threw a knife."

Ma Mullins would laugh or frown, dependin' on her attitude (or his) at the time he was tellin' the story.

One time she said, "Mister, if I had thrown a knife at you, you wouldn't have no finger to show off to nobody!"

He died that winter though.

Granddaddy said Pappy just plumb wore out.

After that, Granddaddy Mullins kept holdin' services. He just didn't have the serpents. Granddaddy said that takin' up serpents was a revelation for Pappy's times. A lot of people back home didn't like that. Some of 'em claimed Granddaddy was gonna join up with the organized folk, which was a lie straight out of Hell! Momma told me Pappy would roll over in his grave if Granddaddy was to do such a thing.

The next couple of years, I took the bus each morning to the school over in Man. The days, weeks, and months run altogether in my head. So, I don't remember much from those days.

Course, I remember now how Daddy talked about the state of the dams up the head of the holler. Some big shot over at the coal company told a friend of Daddy's that those dams weren't worth owl bait; that the people who built them "didn't have enough sense enough to pour P-I-S-S out of a boot, even if the boot had directions on the heel. One dam has already broke up already a couple of years ago, and the ones left aren't any better," the man said.

I heard lot of talk like that but it didn't bother me much.

When it kept on a rainin' like it did that February though, and Daddy said the dams were a fillin' up, people started talkin' more about it. Most times, someone would say, "Y'all stop that talk now. You're scarin' the kids."

That was true. But we didn't let on.

10

SLEEPWALKING THROUGH THE FLOOD

SAMUEL CANTERBURY

This is one of the places where I, the editor and commentator of Brother Michael's story, must gently intrude.

Michael simply didn't write enough about this period to offer details in his own voice. We must reconstruct the events surrounding the flood from public records, personal interviews, and, when available, from Michael's brief notes.

It may seem strange that Michael did not write much about the single most important, formative event of his life. It would be several years before he was able to face how the ravage and ruin caused by Southern West Virginia's negligent guardians had impacted him personally. By that time, he had, in a sense, become a different person, and so his reflections, while important and moving, often come across more like the words of a spectator than as a participant.

Tucked away in one of his poetry books, I found a single sentence that he wrote within weeks of the flood:

"I saw the Albright baby today. His momma threw him up to higher ground before she went under."

Both the brevity and pathos of this sentence are striking.

What we know is that on Saturday morning, February 26, 1972, a sixty-foot-high, five-hundred-and-fifty-foot-wide dam made of coal gob, rotting timbers, standing trees covered up with debris by bulldozers, and whatever other kinds of material had been available at the time of its poorly engineered, amateurish construction, suddenly gave way.

One hundred and twenty million gallons of water and sludge, together with the toxic material of a now-liquefied dam, rushed through the sixteen towns and villages of Buffalo Creek, exploding power stations, tearing apart schools and churches, and erasing most signs of civilized life as it gushed through the narrow valley. Rising at times as high as forty feet, the watery hell writhed for over two hours through 17 miles of horror. When it had finally exhausted itself, 125 people were dead, 1,100 were permanently injured, and 4,000 were homeless.

President Nixon was in China, making peace with his old enemies. Meanwhile, the owners of Pittston Coal were quietly planning how to keep the eyes of everyone who mattered away from the dead, the wounded, and the homeless people of Buffalo Creek.

By the next day, Pittston had prepared two separate statements. One, prepared for reporters, declared that the disaster had been "an act of God." The second one, tailored for the Securities and Exchange Commission, read: "the disaster will not have any material effect on our consolidated financial position."

In the following months and years, as the nation remained riveted by the Watergate hearings; as a major war erupted in the Middle East; and as a new geopolitical order began to emerge; lawyers, social workers, coal company operatives, and government investigators slowly gathered their evidence, wrote their reports, and shuffled their papers among themselves. Meanwhile, the survivors of a disaster caused by the incompetence, indifference, and greed of the community's major employer, struggled to maintain their sanity and discover some reason for staying alive.

It may seem callous to move on with our story after this short and perhaps dismissive account of the Buffalo Creek disaster. However, this is precisely what Michael Cooper, the subject of this book, did. If we want to experience his story as he himself experienced it, we must do the same. At any rate, his reaction to natural disaster was not that unusual.

We usually study history by focusing on the names, events, and dates our teachers tell us will be on the test. Those who live through history's great events and find ways to survive the antics of our so-called great men, rarely experience life the way the future enshrines them.

For moms and pops, grandparents, and kids, the world's great events are like the flashes of a constantly changing, distant kaleidoscope. Real life plods on. Neither the rise and fall of great men and women nor the events that occupy them creates much of a ripple in the everyday world of working men and women.

Working people are born, get married, have careers, get sick, and die without getting so much as a day off. Working people care when a president or a king dies. However, when they lose a husband, wife, father, mother, sister, or brother, they become inconsolable. If, God forbid, they lose all of these at once, along with neighbors, churches, and schools, they often forget why life matters, or even why it ever mattered.

We see ourselves as individuals only when times are good. When the ceiling of civilization threatens to crash in on us, crushing the communities that allow us to experience individuality, we discover the awful truth: we are mostly family fragments, cells of larger organisms that birth us, sustain us, and form the meaning that makes life worthwhile.

That's why, as the president of the United States fought off his looming impeachment, the vice president resigned, China ceased being America's enemy, and the head of the Soviet Union addressed the American people on national television, the people of Buffalo Creek sat outside the cheap trailers they had been assigned, smoked their cigarettes, and stared out into space.

In the waning days of February 1972, Michael Cooper was too young, too inexperienced, to articulate such things. There would come a time, a terrible time, when he would put into words the horror and loss he lived through on that February day. In the meantime, it was as though he was sleepwalking through a nightmare.

Michael shuffled from funeral to funeral, ate enough not to starve, said inappropriate things to people who didn't care, dropped out of school, stopped attending church, and, from time to time, read poems out of an old blue book in the bedroom that had once belonged to his father.

In a notebook dated five years to the day after the Buffalo Creek Flood, Michael began writing about what life was like for him in the aftermath of the disaster.

We can therefore, return to his own voice to learn about what happened from late July, 1972, until he left West Virginia for college.

———

M.J. COOPER

It had been five months since the flood and I hadn't slept through a single night. I wasn't sure I wanted to live, much less work or study. So, I just walked through each day in a daze. I couldn't tell you on Saturday what I had done the previous Monday.

It was worse when it rained. The slightest patter of rain on the roof and I was awake, eyes opened, heart just a poundin'.

I hated how I saw and heard things through some kind of fog. I got afraid I would become like Milton Workman, an old drunk that hung out over at Punky Hatfield's store. Milt was one of the nicest men you would ever meet but he was fit for nothing. He ate. He breathed. He slept. He drank. He would talk with you for a while if you wanted. Sometimes he whittled while he listened. He had no apparent purpose for livin' but to find another drink.

Is that what would happen to me?

I didn't want that. But one of the football players at the school showed me how a few shots of shine could settle the noise in my head.

Conversations I didn't start and couldn't end kept rushin' through my brain. They had no theme or order. It was just random bits of voices and phrases. Sometimes there were images, sometimes not. The words just came and went, without makin' any real connection with each other.

I would hear Daddy's voice sayin', "Skip, the slag is messin' up the crawdads. Bait won't be worth a dime this year."

Pappy might answer, "Well, it rains on the just and the unjust."

"Wanna take a walk?" I heard that in Inida's voice.

"Lordy, Lordy, Son," Momma's voice said.

"Act of God," said a man in a suit.

"Son, hurry up; the water's a comin'!" That was Daddy's voice, and it scared me each time as much as it did when he first said it.

I heard shrieks and cries in those days, people calling for help and nobody coming to help them.

The worst were the sirens, the high pitched shrieks that sounded like they were announcing the break of doom.

One day at Hatfield's store, all that was goin' on in my head when I heard someone a singin' outside myself, "I hear her voice in the morning hours she calls me, radio reminds me of my home far away."

"SHUT THE HELL UP!" I shouted.

Everyone stopped to stare at me 'cause they hadn't been sayin' anything. It was just a song on the radio. I was sorry, but that song was just unbearable to hear, and I had to get somebody to shut it off.

Somedays I figured that us leavin' Pappy Mullins to start a new life in Buffalo Creek had brought the wrath of God down upon everybody. Maybe we had been like Jonah, runnin' from the presence of God. If that was the way it was, then our family had doomed everybody around us.

Course, that didn't make sense. I was the one more like Jonah than anybody else around me, and I was still alive. Besides that, what kind of God kills people like that, just to make a point? Those people up the holler hadn't hurt nobody.

Mostly, I couldn't figure out why I was still alive. Must be some reason. But how was I supposed to know?

Sometimes, my arm that got bit by the serpent would throb, and I imagined it might be rotting off from the inside out.

That's the way it was for the year and a half after the flood. The waters had washed away part of my mind, and I couldn't seem to get it back.

I would walk from Grandpop's house to Hatfield's, then wander over to the school yard to hang around other people who had lived through the flood. I didn't want to talk much to them and they didn't want to talk to me, but we seemed to cling to one another like drowning people often do, not because they have much hope of getting back to land but simply because they don't want to sink alone.

11

THE SOUL'S HARBOR
MICHAEL COOPER

I started walkin' out of the fog the afternoon a sentence dropped into my head out of nowhere: "GO TO MINGO COUNTY TO SEE GRANDDADDY MULLINS."

It was the first week of August, best I recall. I knew Grandpop had put some gas in the '62 Corvair he had bought for me. So, the next Sunday evenin', I threw some clothes and toiletries in the back seat and headed out Route 8 to the last place I had called home.

I knew Granddaddy and Granny Mullins wouldn't like the way I was a livin' nor the way I looked. I also knew they wouldn't say anything about it. They would give me a hug and tease me about my hair, which I hadn't cut since the week before the flood. I hadn't shaved either. I looked like the Old Man of the Mountain. I didn't care.

It was still light out when I got to Mingo County. I had got as far as Medford's, that old general store that used to be on the right just before you get to Verner. I decided to pull in and get a root beer before going on to Spice Creek. Medford's had one of those old pop coolers. Big pieces of ice floated on the water all around bottles which hung by their tops from a bar. You would slide the bottle down to the end of the row and then lift it out, nearly freezing your hand off in the process. On a hot day, there wasn't anything like a bag of pork rinds and a root beer from one of those old coolers.

Our old country stores had a distinctive smell. If I were to offer a formula for the fragrance, it would be to take a bag of sawdust covered with mildew, some old tobacco, a bit of peppermint, a bunch of cedar shavings, and pieces of other stuff collected several decades old. Even though the odor is not that pleasant, it kind of smells like home and so is, in its own strange way, comforting.

I was noticing that smell as I got my pork rinds and then walked over to the cooler. I pulled out the drink and then realized it was Johnny Shelton standing behind the counter. I knew he didn't recognize me 'cause he was lookin' me over suspiciously, like I wasn't from there. I didn't let on that I knew who he was. He wasn't old enough to run a store anyhow, I figured. What did I care what he thought? So, I decided to pay and drive on to Spice Creek.

Anyhow, as I was walking to the counter, I heard the screen door open behind me. I didn't turn around to look to see who it was until I heard Jonny say, "Hey, Inida."

She answered him and started walkin' up to the counter as I turned to look.

Now, there are just some sights that get frozen in your mind and then go on to haunt you forever. Most of 'em are bad. Perhaps this was one of them. It sure didn't seem like it at the time though.

Her reddish-brown hair was hangin' down her back, not in the Holiness way but well-trimmed and brushed. She was wearin' a long blue skirt, with embroidered flowers that seemed to pop out from it and a pair of Roman sandals—the kind that lace up half way to the knee. Peering out from the sandals were sculpted feet with long slender toes, the nails painted bright red. She had on a white peasant blouse gathered at the neck with a blue cord tied in a bow under her throat. She smelled of rosewater and musk.

When she saw me looking at her she smiled a sort of polite "I don't know you" smile and said hello. Then she really saw me.

"Michael!" she shouted. "Oh my God!"

She was crying hard when she grabbed me.

"Oh Michael," she kept saying. "Oh Michael."

I didn't feel much of nothin' but I was moved that she did. I think she could see that I was doin' the best I could.

"Where are you going?" she asked.

"To Granddaddy and Grandmomma Mullins' house," I replied.

"Will they be worried if you take time to talk to me?"

"No, they don't know exactly when I'm coming."

"Then drive with me over to the park where we used to have those church picnics. It's only about a mile from here. We can sit and talk for a while."

She held on to my hand like I might run, which I had no intention of doing, until we got in my Corsair and drove to the park.

I noticed that the park hadn't changed much, which I was glad about.

We got out, walked over to a picnic bench, and sat down.

I hadn't talked to anyone much about what had happened. I didn't say that much about it to Inida either, at least at first. I just said that Daddy had died in his truck, my sister hadn't made it across the road, and that I wasn't sure how the flood got to Momma.

I said that I was livin' with my Grandpop and Granny Cooper over in Man, that life wasn't going anywhere, and that I hadn't amounted to much.

At some point, I started trembling. At first I thought it was because I was cold, but then I realized it was still plenty hot outside. Something else was causing me to shake, which didn't feel good. It didn't feel good at all.

Inida didn't say anything much after I started shakin'. She just stood up and put her arms around me, holding me while I cried for what seemed like an hour.

It felt stupid, cryin' like that, but I couldn't stop. There wasn't anything to do but go with it.

When I had stopped cryin', I just stayed there with my head pressed into her shoulder. It felt like I was frozen. I didn't say anything or move. After a while, Inida stepped back and looked right into my face.

"Michael," she said, "would you like to make love to me?"

I thought I hadn't heard right.

"What?" I replied.

She put my face between her hands and looked into my eyes.

"Make love to me, Michael," she said. "I've wanted to make love to you for as long as I can remember."

I couldn't think of a thing to say to something like that. Finally, I just blurted out, "Inida, I would like that, but I'm 'shamed to say I just don't know much about it."

She laughed. "Well darling, I think you'll figure that out as we go along."

At that, she walked back to the car, got a blanket she had seen draped across the backseat and then walked over to the edge of the clearing. She said we would be able to see anyone coming from there.

She told me to untie the blue cord of her blouse and then she pulled it over her head. After that, I discovered she had been right about me bein' able to figure things out. Things seemed to move along right naturally after that.

Making love to Inida was probably not that memorable for her but it certainly was for me. That was not merely on account that it was my first time. It was because it hushed all the noises in my head. I poured my grief, confusion, longing, and fear into waves of sensual tenderness which, at least for the moment, left me feelin' grateful for being alive.

When we had put on our clothes, Inida said, "Michael, let's lie here for a minute and watch the sun go down." Then she lay her head on my chest. We laid there like that on the blanket until I fell asleep.

I woke up after a while and saw she was sittin' beside

me, legs tucked beneath her, runnin' her hands through my hair.

"We need to get back, Michael," she said softly. "I have to pick up milk for mom and the store closes at nine."

I nodded, stood up, took her hand and started walking toward the car.

After we got to the market, she bought milk, I kissed her goodnight, and told her I would be by to see her the next day.

———

Granddaddy Mullins was sitting on the porch playing his mandolin when I drove up, but when he saw me drivin' up he nearly broke into a run to meet me. I had seen him only briefly a couple of times in the year and a half since the funeral and so he was surprised. He must have hollered for Grandmomma as he left the porch because she was soon moving as fast behind him as her stocky self could move.

After hugs and tears, we went on inside, where I ate the soup, cornbread, and fried apples Grandmomma had fixed. As I ate like I had not eaten for months, Grand-momma just watched me and chuckled, sometimes wiping tears from her eyes, though she claimed they were "still a hurtin' from the onions."

When I finished, she looked me over real good and said, "Good Lord, child, you look like you've been a rollin' around in the grass. And you haven't shaved for months! When did you start havin' to shave anyhow?"

I laughed the way one does when he's holdin' back tears, but I couldn't think of anything to say. So I just started walkin' outside.

Granddaddy had gone back out on the porch and was playin' on his mandolin, singin' about a ship that has made it to harbor after bein' out in a storm.

"I've anchored my soul in the haven of rest," he croaked, in his old, out-of-tune voice. *"The tempest may sweep, o'er the wide stormy deep, but in Jesus I'm safe ever more."*

I suppose when sailors are working to stay afloat during a hurricane, they don't have much time for thinkin' about home. It's when they sail safely into port that they notice the sea is calm and the sky above them is full of stars.

I wasn't ready for Jesus. Had I thought about it, I would have known Jesus wasn't ready for me either, on account of me just havin' committed fornication and all. But despite that, I had made it to harbor. I was safe. Which is something I hadn't felt for a long time.

After just listenin' to Granddaddy sing a while, I went back inside, showered, and went on to bed. I didn't think another thought until I heard the rooster wakin' up the sun. That's when I smelled the bacon, biscuits, and apples.

It was a new day in Mingo County. I sure was glad to see it.

Those weeks in Mingo County with Granddaddy and Grandmomma felt like I was living in a magical kingdom. Some days I made love to Inida. I listened to Granddaddy play his mandolin. I ate good food. A few times during those weeks I thought I had finally found something that would go on forever.

It didn't, of course.

12

APPALACHIAN APOCALYPSE
MICHAEL COOPER

The Goins' place was about three miles south of Verner going toward Tamcliff. Even though it was on the other side of the railroad, you could see it from Route 8. You just had to know where to get on the old dirt road, cross the tracks, and then backtrack to the Goins' property. Driving up to the house, I could see that Minnie's tomatoes, beans, and squash were doing well, and the corn behind the house was already high.

Minnie's husband, Charlie, inherited the house from his father—old man Goins was the only name I ever heard him called—just a couple of years before Charlie died in that mine accident. Everything went to Minnie when Charlie died, which is why she had lived there since.

It was a two-story house, partly made of logs from over a hundred years ago, but someone had added on to it a few decades back. Granddaddy Mullins told me once that when he was little, old folk used to say that the Goins had run a boarding house before he was born.

It was startin' to fall apart. Billy Joe had tried to keep things repaired, but things had gotten away from 'im. The paint was a peelin' and the upstairs porch looked plumb unsafe. Two hounds came from under the house, barking at me as I pulled up. I laughed a little because there's nothing like the sound of a coondog. It's just they made me think of Daddy, and so the laugh kind of died in my throat.

Lila and Billy Joe were gettin' ready to take Minnie to Logan, to some big store over there where old women like to shop.

"I'd as soon a savage cut me with razor blades and drop my hind end into a sea of alcohol than to go to that store," Billy Joe said to me on the porch. "But I reckon there's no gettin' around it."

Even though he was complainin', I knew he was fond of Minnie, and that since he'd been puttin' off taking her to that store for a while, today had to be the day. Some things are like that; they just have to get done and so you might as well just get them over with.

After talkin' with me a bit, the three of them left. Inida put her arm around my waist as we watched them go.

We set down on the porch and made out for a few minutes. I was ready to go inside and finish what we had started, but Inida wanted to talk.

"A few weeks ago," she said, "I took acid."

I just stared at her. I had heard about LSD. People in places like California had been takin' dope for years, but I didn't know anybody in Mingo County who did it.

She didn't like my silence much, but what was I

supposed to say? It's like when somebody blurts out, "My uncle has three testicles." You understand what they've said, you're just not sure why they said it or what you're supposed to say back.

Inida crossed her arms over her chest. "Hey, look! It didn't harm me any," she said. "I think I'm a better person than before I took it."

"Really?" I responded. "I heard it destroys your brain."

"Do I look like my brain is destroyed?" she asked. "Acid showed me how wonderful life is. Since takin' it, I've noticed how the trees and flowers are alive—really alive. I can almost hear them talk. The world has become so intense.

"Really, Michael, what are we supposed to do with a life that goes on, day after boring day . . . older people tell you to grow up and accept life as it is . . . but is growing up supposed to just be about learning how to survive meaningless life and then die anyway at the end of it?

"I took acid! Now, I experience real life all around me. I'm swimming in life—every cell in my body feels alive."

"You gonna do it again?" I asked.

"Yes sir; I will, Michael Cooper. Yes, I will! The question is, will you?"

"I don't even know where I would get LSD," I said.

"Now, that's not an answer!" she said loudly. "I *do* know where to get it." Pointing toward a trailer about fifty feet behind the house, she continued. "We get it right over there."

I hadn't remembered ever seeing that trailer in the times I had visited the Goins' place before.

Somebody, Billy Joe, I guess, had stretched an electric wire from the house over to it, and had propped the wire up with a couple of long boards planted in the ground. The weeds between the house and trailer had been cut back some, but the lot still looked a bit wild, like people who used it cared about it some, but not that much.

"Don't be a party pooper, Michael! I swear you act like you're fifty years old," Inida said.

"Listen, I met the coolest guy a couple of months ago. His name is Elijah, and he's been living in the trailer for a while. He hitchhiked all the way from Oklahoma to North Carolina! He wanted to see the reservation over there and walk through what he calls 'old Cherokee country.' He's an Indian. A real one! Anyhow, after being over in North Carolina for a few months, he met a truck driver in Qualla who was driving to Logan and decided to go with him. Then he hitchhiked over to Williamson. That's where he met Billy Joe, probably doing some drug deal if the truth were told. Anyway, Billy Joe offered Elijah the old trailer to live in for a few weeks.

"Elijah's the one who let me try acid and I know he still has some. I've already told him all about you, and he said you could come over and try some if you want. Hey, after all you been through, what can it hurt?"

Tugging on my hand, she had already started walking. "What do you say?" she whined. "Come on! Let's go on another little adventure!"

"Who knows?" she added. "Maybe I'm your heart doctor! The one person in your life who keeps your heart from stayin' sad!"

Sometimes, a person will be out taking a walk and

will suddenly feel as though he has entered some sort of shadowy place. He looks up to see what has dimmed the light, but since he doesn't see anything, he just keeps on a walkin'. That's what happened as I walked from the house to the trailer. Something somewhere dimmed my light. I didn't know who had done it, why they had done it, or what I could do to stop them. That's why I just followed my feet as my feet followed Inida, not thinking about much of anything.

As we approached the trailer, I saw that somebody had stepped out of it and was standin' in the doorway.

"Must be Elijah," I said to Inida.

"Yes sir. That's him," Inida said, laughing.

Elijah Quantisis's hair was black, except for a half an inch wide of white runnin' through it. He had it pulled back in a ponytail and it was hangin' to his waist. A necklace of what looked like tiny bones was wrapped around his neck. His jeans were worn. He had a white shirt with blousy lookin' sleeves with these large cuffs covered with probably a dozen buttons.

Elijah wasn't big. Still, there was just something about him that made you want to stare. You wanted to figure him out if you could. You knew right away he was physically fit, like someone who has worked hard or played a lot of sports.

He was smiling as we walked onto the small wooden porch.

"Come into my parlor," he said, moving his hand in a big sweep like rich people used to do long time ago at dances.

The windows and the door were open, though there

were screens over both, to keep out the bugs. Sweat was pouring down my face and back, and the air felt like we was swimming through it. August is like that in Mingo County. Course, ain't hardly nobody that's got air conditioning, especially them livin' in trailers. It can feel like you're livin' in the center of Hades.

I was looking Elijah over as I walked in, listening to the big electric fan inside that was keeping the trailer from baking people alive.

Elijah stared at me too.

"You were in the flood," he said.

Now, that's the first thing he said to me, which I didn't like much. The flood wasn't none of his business. Not at all!

"Yeah. Don't want to talk about it though," I responded.

"Sure, man. Makes sense. Hanging out here in Mingo country for a while?"

"Maybe."

He extended a hand. "I'm Elijah. I enjoy meeting people."

I took it but let it go really quick.

"All right," I said. "I'm not much good at it. Meeting new people, I mean."

"No problem, man," Elijah shot back. "People are what they are. You know what I mean? We should just let everybody be. I mean, if everybody respected everybody and wouldn't spend their lives trying to impress anybody else . . . the people we are supposed to meet come right into our lives just when they're supposed to. You can't force things. Stuff needs to unfold, like a rose."

"I suppose so," I replied.

Inida stepped between us and said, "Michael wants to go on a little trip, like the one I took."

"Is that right, Michael?" Elijah asked.

"I don't know," I said. "Inida was telling me about it. Sounds kind of interesting."

"Oh, it is that," Elijah said with a chuckle. "It is that. Acid helps people see the way things really are. The System—government, industry, religion—all the power players of the world—they are not too keen on us ordinary people discovering how things really work. But when you take acid, the whole world gets naked. You can see right into everything. Nobody can pull the wool over your eyes after that."

I wasn't convinced. After an hour or so of talkin', and Inida urgin' me to go on an adventure, I decided to give it a try.

———

Nearly an hour had passed from the time I had eaten the sugar cubes and nothing much had happened. I kept strumming the guitar Elijah had laying around, singin' old songs—I don't remember what exactly—except the one about John Henry, the Black mountain man who worked himself to death laying railroad track.

Layin' rail wasn't easy. As a crew heaved a new rail into place, two men with sledge hammers were waiting on each side to drive a stake in it, joining it to the rail already nailed down. As soon as the first hammer struck, the other one was starting down to strike the rail again.

What keep the two hammers in rhythm was the crew, singing a workingman's chant.

The old men told us when we were kids that this was how the railroad made its way through West Virginia. It's why we have so many songs about railroads, even in church. But the one about John Henry was probably the first.

The song tells the story about how John Henry was a drivin' those spikes into rails when his boss started teasing him about how he was gonna get replaced by a steam-run rail-drivin' machine. The machine, the boss said, would do everything John Henry could do but twice as fast. John Henry laughed. He said he could win any old race against a machine. The boss decided to humiliate John Henry. The boss, who must keep his workers in their place, arranged a contest between John Henry and that rail-driving machine. John Henry won the race as it turned out, but then died when his heart gave out on him.

A man just can't just keep a working without any rest, on account of men not being machines. That's the real story the song tries to tell us, but of course nobody pays much attention to what a song says, even those who like the song.

Well, I sang every verse of it waiting for something to happen from them sugar cubes. When nothing did, I started singing a few lines of another mountain song.

> *Take this hammer to the captain*
> *Take this hammer to the captain*
> *Take this hammer to the captain*

Tell him I'm gone, Tell him I'm gone.

So that was the song I was a singing when I saw notes pouring out of my guitar. They were all different colors, vibrating all together in strange patterns, flowin' from the guitar out into the room and into my friends' ears.

The notes then flowed from their ears into their bodies, filling up their veins and arteries as it moved through their hearts, pumping in rhythm to the strums of my guitar. The colors of the music ran deep down into their cells and even further down, into the molecules and chemicals from which the cells are made. The notes flowed into every level of their bodies until their skin were radiating the colors and pulsating with the music. It was a sweet symphony of feathered angels, singing and dancing round reason's fine-wrought throne.

I laughed. Here I was, deep in the mountains of Mingo County, seeing the secret of everything, observing the world not as it appears but as it really is.

The colors slowly became fragrant, smelling first like evergreen and sandalwood then like honeysuckle and sassafras. Taste and touch, sight and smell—the universe was alive. It was watching me as I watched it, seeing me not only from outside myself but from my insides as well. I was barely separate from everything that was, that had ever been, and which will ever be. I was in the room but not in it—leaping out from myself without leaving myself—out, out to someplace beyond space and time.

I put the guitar down to hear the men out on the railroad who were singing and laying track. The grass and trees swayed to the rhythm of their hammers and set the time for the music flowing through them into the world. The melody became mixed with something bent and pungent so that my mood shifted from joy to growing apprehension. I no longer wanted to see anything more beneath the surface of reality but I knew I had no choice. I had forced my way into seeing and so my wish would be granted, whether I liked it or not.

Looking past the singers, I saw blood oozing from where the spikes had pierced the rails. It flowed in the space between the tracks, forming streams of blood as far as I could see. One by one, the great trees began to fall, announcing their death with loud blasts and then pouring their vegetative essence into the sanguine sea.

Ancient drummers beat upon animal skins stretched across hollowed-out trees. Painted dancers moved around fires to their rhythm, emitting fierce and terrible cries. The pain of their cries gushed through the sounds of the music, forming streaks of wounded purple and stained yellow in the blood that oozed from the drummers. The dancers were consumed by the dance and joined their life force to the bloody current gushing down the railroad tracks.

I tried to return my awareness to the trailer. I was ready to leave the terrible world I had entered. Unfortunately, I had lost my way.

I saw then that John Henry and his fellow workers had formed the banks of a great crimson river. It ran into the hollers and poured down the holes leading to tunnels, through which their blood then descended into the honeycombed caverns of carbon that consume the Appalachians from within.

As I beheld the blood pouring into holes, clouds of soot began bellowing up from where the blood had poured in. Wherever it drifted, it banished beauty, until the hollers grew grey with death. It choked all the animals, plants, and people of the mountains so that the smell of the burning offal overcame the sweet fragrances that had breathed glory and life into the hills on the first morning of Creation.

My emotions now raced past my reason, alerting me to a greater terror than I had yet seen. For behind the Soot came the Great Serpent, hissing in rhythm to the hammers and the drums, coiling itself around the villages of Logan and Mingo; Boone and Raleigh, Kanawha and Wyoming Counties. Writhing and hissing, it gyrated through the mountains, pulsating with all dark energy it sucked from the veins of the people. The muck and mire suffocated the mountains as the Living Soot railed in high-handed defiance of the light of creation. The Soot extinguished the breath of men and beasts however it pleased.

My friends constrained me because they claim I had begun to howl, though I do not recall it. I remember only that I had lost my speech and found it hard to breathe. I had suddenly understood the great secret of the Appalachians: that the great serpent had been sucking my life, killing my family and friends, destroying through fear, poverty and despair all related to me by blood and soil, consuming even those we thought were bosses and owners but who were only the puppets and pawns of a darkness they could not see. The darkness had deceived us into killing one another through feuding, murder, and fraud, and, when all else had failed, through due process of law.

But then I saw something more heinous than these other ills, for the Great Serpent was controlled by something yet worse, yet more powerful, yet darker than itself.

Rising high above the Appalachians was a monstrous beast, as black as the inside of an unlit cave. All light fled before it and the hills shook as it strutted through its domain. It was haughty and aloof, taking no thought of life, death, joy, or pain. Its odor was foul, and I retched as it stood above me glaring and then commanding me to hear the words belching through its sneering lips.

"Son of the hills!" it shouted.

"I AM KING COAL, CREATOR AND DESTROYER OF MOUNTAINS AND MEN. I WAS BORN BEFORE ALL TIME IN THE FURNACE OF THE STARS, FORMED BY AN IMMORTAL HAND THAT WAS GUIDED BY AN ETERNAL EYE. I AM THE CENTER OF THE HILLS. I AM THE MASTER OF THE HOLLERS.

"I AM THE GENIE OF THE LAMP. I OFFER WEALTH AND POWER. I GIVE MY GIFTS AND I EXTRACT MY TOLL. THOSE WHO OPEN MY LAMP, AND ALL THEIR CHILDREN, AND ALL THEIR SERVANTS, BELONG TO ME—FOR ALL GENERATIONS UNTIL TIME BE NO MORE!"

The monster seemed to quote some eternal degree that rested on an authority far above mere human government so that all argument was futile. I knew then that I, and all the people of Appalachia, would surely perish. For whether we stayed on the land or left it, whether we drugged ourselves with moonshine or wealth, we had all been cursed. Some unknown offense committed by our ancestors long, long ago had sold us into slavery. There was no escape. We were without hope. We could find small measure of relief in our songs, dance, and drunkenness. But we would never be fully human or whole until death delivered us from our eternal servanthood to ignorance, poverty, and despair.

Oh God, I thought. *The rose is sick. The invisible worm flies in the night, through the howling storm.*

One again, I strained with all my might to return to my physical body and to the material world but felt myself trapped in this part of the universe where living persons are uninvited. Perhaps, I had committed the unpardonable sin by forcing my way into this dark corner of reality.

Meanwhile, King Coal glared. Forcing me to acknowledge that his curse extended to me personally, he peered into my eyes and continued the tirade.

"PISS ANT! DO YOU HOPE TO DO ME HARM? IN THE END, YOU TOO WILL FEEL MY BITE. YOU HAVE SEEN WHAT OTHERS DO NOT, BUT IN THE END, YOU WILL LEARN YOUR PLACE!"

Distraught by those sights and sounds, I could no longer bear to live, not even another minute. Had my friends not restrained me, I would have done away with myself.

Restrained now in both body and mind, all I could do was mourn. Our poverty was far greater than the loss of mere home and goods. We had been robbed even of our spirit because King Coal had demanded it as collateral before I had ever been conceived.

Entranced by despair and resignation, I had not noticed how King Coal had begun to shake and shrink. When I did, I prepared myself to see a yet more terrible sight than what I had yet seen. But I wondered: if the terrible serpent had turned out to be the servant of King Coal, what sort of being would have the power to conquer him?

Shaking as though every fiber of my soul would unravel, leaving me without form or substance, I looked for the source of King Coal's distress. I saw to my astonishment that it was a tiny lamb, standing peacefully in a field.

A fragrance from before time pushed away the stench.

I wept.

Around the lamb were colors of music that had fled before the great clouds of soot. Amazed at its beauty, I looked for that power which had forced the monster's retreat.

I could not see it, but it made itself felt. Then I heard it, a sound more terrible than the hissing of the serpent or the roar of King Coal, but also more wondrous than I can relate. The power thundered its defiance of all that is ugly and oppressive and promised to reveal the secret of all time, so the lowly and the fearful might be delivered and made alive.

"Hear the voice of the Bard, who Present, Past, and Future sees!" the power said in a language I had always known but had never heard. "The Lamb is the secret of time; the reason for all things. The Lamb is true, good and beautiful. The Lamb heals and revives. And this day, the Lamb makes his claim for the lawful repossession of these lands and all they contain."

My body was now dissolving into dust. Somehow, I knew that this had been happening since I had been a child and that nothing on earth had the power to regather and reorder the particles of my being. I would be deconstructed. Unless something arrested the dissolution, I would be utterly undone.

It came to me then that the colors of music coming from the lamb might extend to where I was. If only those colors could reach my ears and eyes, I would be reassembled.

Somewhere from the deepest levels of existence, under all thought, emotion, and awareness of self, came a nearly inaudible and anguished sound. My soul uttered its hope that the lamb might come to my aid and to the aid of all those now perishing under the oppression of the serpent and its perverse king.

"I a child and thou a lamb!" was the cry. But the colors grew dimmer and the lamb began to fade.

I slowly began to feel the rough texture of an old carpet on my back and the weight of human hands on my arms and legs.

The vision retreated. I was back in my own world, unsure of whether what I had seen was from an intoxicated brain or a glimpse of reality beyond time and space. I had dreamed a dream; what could it mean?

I'm not sure. Perhaps, the tension between what is

and what we imagine to be is nothing more than the fearful symmetry of existence, our awareness that the entire world lies in a grain of sand.

It is, at any rate, something none of us will ever fully comprehend.

13

CHOOSING EXILE

MICHAEL COOPER

It had been a week since I had tried acid and was still tryin' to make sense of it. I didn't want to do it again. I just wanted to talk to someone about it. That's why I decided that Wednesday afternoon to drive over to the Goins' place and find Inida.

No one was home at the Goins', but I saw that the trailer door was open. I figured I would see if Elijah knew where everyone had gone. I didn't think to call out his name first. I just walked up to the screen door. Not seeing anyone, I opened it a bit before calling out his name. You know that feeling when you realize someone has heard you but they're not saying anything back? That's what I felt.

He might be in the back, I thought.

Stepping just inside the door, meaning to call out his name again, I looked down. There on the floor, right at my feet, were two naked people staring up at me. One was Elijah. The other was Inida.

I had got halfway to my car before I heard her

shouting my name. She had pulled a dress over her head and was running behind me, crying and begging me to stop.

"I'm sorry, Michael," she said. "I'm so sorry." And I figured she was, but I was in no mood to stop and talk.

It might sound crazy but I didn't feel much anger. I had dropped into some sort of deep, dark hole, like when one of those stars collapses on itself and starts pulling in everything around it.

When I got in my car and drove away, I knew only a few things for certain. One of them was that I was going to climb out of this hole—not just the hole of despair caused by being betrayed, but the hole I had been born in. I was going to climb out of poverty, ignorance, and powerlessness. I was going back to high school. I was going to graduate. I was going to college.

The second thing was that I intended to leave coal country forever.

What I had seen on LSD may not have been real but I couldn't shake it. Appalachia was cursed, by who or by what I wasn't sure, but I did know I wanted no part of it.

———

The Wednesday morning after going back to Man, I saw Diana Blessing over at Hatfield's store. I usually avoided her because she was always bugging me about going back to high school.

Diana was one of the social workers who came over from Charleston to help us get our lives back. Most of the time, they didn't make much sense. Diana was nice enough. I just didn't want to hear it anymore.

That morning, she cornered me and I couldn't get away. She wanted me to know about a scholarship fund that Pittston Coal Company had set up for children of flood victims.

"You are eligible for some of that money, Michael," she said. "You can get yourself a first-class education."

"I'm not interested in anything from Pittston," I replied.

"Understandable," she said. "But another way to look at it is that if you don't use that money, it will go right back into their corporate pockets. So why don't you use their money to start a new life? Wouldn't your parents and sister want you to do that?"

That made sense, and so I told her I would think about it. A new life somewhere else was exactly what I wanted.

I would have to finish high school, of course. But if I worked hard, she said I was likely to get a scholarship from Carnegie Mellon, up in Pittsburgh. That wasn't very far; I could even come home on holidays if I wanted.

First though, I had to get back in school, and I was already a year behind. Course, lots of kids from Buffalo Creek were in my same situation, which is why I didn't mind it that much.

Grandpop and Granny Cooper were excited about the idea of me going back to school and perhaps on to college. They said they had some money to help me with my clothes and stuff. Course, I now owned the old property up in Verner. It was just too sad to go back there right now. Anyway, Granddaddy Mullins was taking care of it for me. He even had somebody living in it, though he said it wasn't in such good shape.

The following Monday, I went over to Man High to talk to Mr. Barns, the guidance counselor. I told him I wanted to start back at school. He helped me fill out the papers and gave me a test to figure out what I should study. One of the things on the test showed that I should study literature, which is how I ended up in Mrs. McDaniel's class.

That sure turned out to be a good thing! Without Mrs. McDaniels and Diana Blessing, I wouldn't have gotten to Carnegie Mellon and would have had to work for the mines.

One thing I didn't know was how Diana Blessing was always checking up on me, which would've made me mad. When she found out I had signed up for school, she went and talked with all my teachers. She did that the entire time I was in high school. Every year, she and Mrs. McDaniels were plotting about how to get me to college. Diana even wrote the coal company and several colleges, wearing them all out about helping me get an education.

I found all that out later.

Back then, I just knew I had to finish high school. That's why I kept at it, day after day for the next three years. Mrs. McDaniels helped a lot. Other people did too. Sometimes I didn't feel like going but went anyway because the only ticket out of West Virginia was a high school diploma. Also, I figured if my Daddy could do it, so could I.

After graduating, I had to wait another year because

of some papers that got mixed up. That was okay. I worked at Hatfield's place that year, stocking groceries and listening to people talk about how they were getting their lives back together. That's what I was doing too, and their stories weren't different than mine, in that way.

I went to the Methodist Church sometimes, but it only made me angry. The people were nice, especially Pastor Grundy. But it was God I didn't know what to do with, and that is a bigger subject than I can address here.

I went out with some girls, which was fun. I just knew where all that ends up. So, I made out with them and all of that; I just had no interest in things going much further.

I smoked marijuana twice. It tasted like old rubber and made my head feel swimmy. Mostly, I felt old and worn out, even though I wasn't through high school yet. I didn't want to die but didn't yet know how to live. I mostly read Blake and Wordsworth, wrote down stuff in my journal, and worked over at Hatfield's.

———

SAMUEL CANTERBURY

That is the extent of Michael's written reflections about life after the flood. The only other piece of writing I have found is a large post card he sent to the Coopers, dated August 28th, 1976. On the front is a picture from above of Fort Duquesne. On the back, in nearly illegible small script, Michael wrote:

After I rode the Greyhound Bus to Logan, we went on to Huntington and Charleston. In Charleston, I ate apple pie at the Post House beside the terminal. On the way to Pittsburgh, I saw lots of towns, including Wheeling and the Ohio river! I crossed into Pennsylvania. It sure is strange, being outside West Virginia. The picture on the front shows the rivers around Pittsburgh. That's a little bit scary, but I won't be living too close to water!

14

PITTSBURGH

SAMUEL CANTERBURY

During his years in Pittsburgh and Ukraine, Michael didn't write much about his personal life. His journal entries are sporadic and usually express his developing ideas about life and faith. For this reason, there are significant gaps, sometimes representing several months, in his personal story. I have tried to fill in these gaps with material gleaned from interviews with those who knew him during those years.

I also have read correspondence from him, to him, and, in a few cases, about him. His academic papers, written for courses at the university and the seminary, are much as one would expect: mostly about demonstrating his competency in his chosen areas of study. They were, for this reason, not often helpful for this book. Nonetheless, taken together, these sources, including the academic papers, offer important glimpses into Michael's intellectual, spiritual, and emotional development and add depth to what otherwise would be a colorless account of those years.

Professor Sofiya Stefanyik, who knew Michael perhaps better than any other living person during his time in Pittsburgh, made several helpful suggestions for improving the early draft of this book. That was altogether appropriate, seeing that during Michael's college years, when they had been students together, Sofiya was easily the most important person in his life. Indeed, over half of his journal entries from that period involve her in some way.

The first one reveals not only how much she impressed him initially, but also hints at how deep her influence would go in time.

———

M.J. COOPER

There was a slight hint of Asia in Sofiya's eyes and she had nearly platinum hair. She was tall and had a well-formed body, not the kind that advertisers use to sell stuff, but womanly and real, like the kind normal people like. She wore regular clothes but knew how to arrange them in ways that made her look dignified without appearing haughty.

When I first met her, she had a way of wrapping a single braid of hair around her head, leaving the rest of her hair to fall around her shoulders. I'd never seen a woman wear their hair thataway, and it rather afflicted me.

I'm embarrassed to admit that this what I first noticed. But I learned in the twelve-step groups to tell the truth the best I can. In my defense, I wasn't yet twenty! Also, a pretty body and face will turn your head for a moment or two—there's no denying that—but then you go about your business. What kept my attention on Sofiya were the comments she made in class.

She knew how things fit together. That's the best way I can explain it. I had always thought knowledge was like bits and pieces of unrelated facts, which meant that things like engineering and literature had nothing in common with religion or marketing.

Knowledge, in other words, was a collection of facts in a given field. That made me see the relationship between different fields like colors of thread—a bit of red here, some yellow and orange over there, and a spool of purple in-between. Some people like one color; some like another. Throw all the thread together though, and it just makes a mess.

When I was little, I once crawled under a quilting frame the church women back home use to make a quilt. I stayed there looking up at the underside of the quilt until Grandmomma said, "Hey! You need to move your little butt out from under our feet!"

By that time, I had seen that the underneath of a quilt is nothing but fluffs of thread running this way and thataway. Course, I knew it looked different from above, up where the women were a working. From their point of view, the threads I was looking at from beneath were busy forming flowers, squares, and circles . . . stuff like that.

I knew after meeting Sofiya that I had been looking at knowledge from underneath. She looked at knowledge from above, in a way that formed a picture of the world. She talked about scientific theories in literature class. She quoted novels in philosophy class. That was an amazing thing to me—realizing that knowledge about stuff fits inside a bigger picture and that the picture is why knowledge about anything even matters. That's why I progressed from starin' at her bountiful endowments to wanting to learn how she put things together.

She was both smart and beautiful, which was a rather nice combination. It made me decide that I wanted to be a part of her life forever.

Over the weeks, I made up my mind to talk with her. I just didn't know how to go about it. Every time I got close, it felt like I was gonna break out in the itch.

Then came that day she was walking past the pumpkins in front of the student center. We had both just left the philosophy of science class and were headed in the same direction—to a lecture across campus. A plastic skeleton was hanging from a light pole and somebody had put an old pair of tennis shoes on its feet. She stopped for a minute and laughed.

When I saw her laughing at that skeleton, I remembered something Pappy used to say.

"Things that are supposed to happen are like persimmons," he would say. "If you eat one too soon—Lord have mercy! Some of you out there know what I'm a talkin' about. If you wait too long, you'll be consuming corruption; it'll make you sick as a dog. But if you pick that persimmon at just the right time—well, glory, there just ain't nothing like it. A just right persimmon goes down sweet and easy 'cause the appointed time has come to eat it."

As I figured it, the weeks before now had been too early and tomorrow might be too late. Now being the appointed time, I needed to make my move. Sofiya wasn't a persimmon, but Pappy's thought about there being a right time for things seemed to fit anyway.

"You Russian or something?" I asked. Now I swear I couldn't think of anything else to say. My words had disappeared like a mountain mist after the sun comes up.

She stared at me, pointed her eyes toward the top of her head, and then pulled her mouth back. I knew what that look meant: "Oh Merciful God, deliver me from this fool!"

Slowly and deliberately, she formed her response. "I'm something."

She started walking away, but I kept pace with her. Problem was, my mouth was still open but I wasn't saying anything. And, as she said later, she thought I would probably trip over something because I kept looking at her instead of where I was walking. Amused, she decided to see how deep my stupidity went.

"Did you want to practice Russian?" she asked. The syrupy attitude she had put on took away my thoughts.

"I don't know no Russian," I finally blurted out, losing in an instant the months of hard work I had spent trying to lose my mountain dialect.

"Well, there are several Russian classes here. Russian clubs too! If you want to learn Russian, I'm sure the Russians will help you," she continued.

"Won't help me none," I replied. "I'm from Mingo

County, West Virginia. We hardly speak English down there. Tryin' to learn Russian wouldn't be a good idea. I might hurt myself." I managed to laugh and so did she.

Perhaps, I thought, this really could be the appointed time.

"So, now I know you are a mountain man from southern West Virginia," she said, "and that is why you have that accent. You also want to know if I am Russian. You told me all of that but still failed to tell me your name."

"Didn't know I still had an accent," I replied. "My name is Michael Cooper. Michael Journeyman Cooper. And I didn't mean any harm. I was just curious because you look different than anyone I've met before. In a good way! I mean . . . what I'm tryin' to say is . . . you are pretty and I am amazed by the things you say in class and I am not . . . I don't know how . . . Heck, if you don't mind me asking, where *are* you from?"

"Well, I'm from Pittsburgh," she answered. "I grew up just a few miles from here. That's why it's so interesting that you thought I was Russian. But I'll tell you what. I'll let you off the hook. I'm Ukrainian. My grandparents moved to America when my father was little. So, you were close. We don't like it much when people call us Russians though."

"Then I swear to God, I will never even say the word Russian around you again," I replied.

She laughed. I thought it was because I had said something clever. Later, she told me she laughed because my face had turned purple.

She stopped walking then and held out her hand.

"I'm not offended, Mr. Michael Journeyman Cooper from Mingo County," she said. "It's a common mistake. So, loosen up. But if you want to talk to me, why didn't you just say so instead of going through all of that?"

Lord have mercy! I had never wanted anything so bad in my life.

By the time we had gotten to the lecture, I had found out her full name was Anichka Sofiya Stefanyik. I had to ask her to spell it and wrote it down. She made doubly-sure I hadn't written Sofiya the wrong way. The rest of the day, I repeated her name over and over in my head so I wouldn't forget how to say it or write it down.

During the lecture—I have no idea what the man said about paradigmatic saturation or whatever the heck he was talking about—the thought crossed my mind it might be possible for a goddess like Sofiya to fall in love with a snake-handling Holiness kid from Mingo County. Even if that couldn't happen though, I was right certain she might make a good friend. And, as it turned out, I was right, at least about the last part. In fact, outside of my family, I never had a better friend anywhere.

———

Sofiya remembered her early days with Michael differently.

"Michael was always intriguing, no doubt about that. Sometimes though, he was just plain weird," Sofiya said. "I kept meeting him at first simply because I wanted to figure him out. Maybe that was the emerging anthropologist in me!"

"I often said to my brother, Victor, that Michael was either brilliant or crazy—or perhaps both," she said with a laugh. "Victor always voted for brilliant. He admired Michael from the first day he met him. I went back and forth on what I thought about his mental stability.

"One thing for sure though; Michael was different.

"Because of his woefully inadequate preparation for college, he struggled, and had to find creative ways to grasp the material he encountered in the books and lectures. I mean, we studied some heady stuff, at least for undergraduate students—writers like Kuhn, Merleau-Ponty, Polanyi and the like—which means we were not only trying to make sense of their complex ideas but learning the jargon they used to express those ideas. Michael constantly complained about it—the jargon, I mean.

"It was the subject of many an argument—the role of jargon, the kinds of specialized vocabulary every discipline develops. I believed back then, and believe still, that specialized vocabulary is not only convenient but essential. I mean, who wants to hear a neurologist saying to his colleague, 'The brain camera shows that the patient's squiggly kind of brain waves have taken over, and he doesn't have any of the smoother ones that flatten out, even when he sleeps. I'm afraid he might be in deep doo-doo.'

You want to hear a neurologist saying something like, 'The patient's EEG shows a brain nearly always in Alpha state; it rarely records Theta or even Beta patterns, even in sleep. This implying that the patient's sleep patterns are disturbed, indicating either a neurological or psychological issue.'

"Michael wouldn't hear it. To him, jargon exists to keep people from entering the conversation. For him, language was always a class issue."

"Writers could use every-day words to say the exact same things," Michael said to Sofiya more times than she could count.

Once, while struggling to make sense of Michael Polanyi's concept of "tacit knowledge," Michael created a fantastic metaphor that involved envisioning a person's interior life as something like a little village.

"Polanyi is sayin' that we're are not just one person but several persons all wrapped up together," Michael explained.

"One of our parts is like a scout: it runs ahead of us into the future to see where things are going. The scout doesn't make complete sense out of the future, but he understands enough to form an opinion about what's comin'. The scout then runs back to the present and reports what he saw to the other parts of the self. The opinion that results from the scout's intuition is always a bit unclear and may even be wrong. In the end though, the scout's opinion about the future is the reason a person does what he does and thinks what he thinks. That's what tacit knowledge is.

"It's kind of like prophesy," Michael continued. "Prophesy is someone talkin' about stuff he doesn't know much about. People who remember what a prophet said may understand what he was trying to say better than he did himself. I've seen stuff like that—

prophesy, I mean. In a way, Polanyi must be talkin' about the same thing. He just didn't use that word because it was religious and spooky sounding. That's why Polanyi made up a brand-new term nobody understands. It's really quite unnecessary."

"It was always strange to hear Michael use religion, especially the sort of religion he had experienced, to express philosophical and scientific ideas," Sofiya said. "He was always doing that—drawing examples from his own life to explain complicated concepts. Later, in seminary, Michael would do the same thing with theology. I have several letters where he explains the ideas of some obscure Patristic thinker using pop music lyrics, odd mountain expressions, and sermons he heard as a child. Michael didn't acknowledge any barrier between the world of abstract thought and the common sense of everyday life.

"Michael was also fascinated with how knowledge from different fields, from different eras of life, and different eras of human history fit together to create our picture of reality. He said once that knowledge develops like extending a telescope. In other words, as we learn something new, we don't discard things we knew before but rather absorb and reinterpret that old knowledge in the light of the new."

"Take Einstein for example," he had said to Sofiya.

"Einstein reinterpreted Newton. So! Most of us, most of the time, get along fine seeing the world like Newton saw it. That means Newton's understanding of the world fits somehow inside Einstein's theory of relativity. The same goes for quantum mechanics. We know, somewhere in the back of our heads, that the universe is not exactly as we once thought. For nearly every purpose in everyday life though, Newton does just fine. The layers of everything we knew yesterday are there behind the stuff we just learned today.

That's the way knowledge works in the real world."

"I think Michael's view of intellectual life is why he never ridiculed the mountain religion he had known as a child," Sofiya said.

"He seemed fond of mountain religion, even the parts of it I thought abusive and barbaric. So, although Michael didn't want to go back to his past, he was always clear about how he believed his past had made him who he was, and that he couldn't dismiss it without losing his entire self.

"I was just explaining this to Rwanna not long ago because she seems to process life similarly. She was raised on a reservation, you know.

"Anyway, I had no intention of forming a long-term relationship with Michael. I was just intrigued by his weirdness and wanted to figure him out. But then the days and months went by, I took him home for the holidays, he became friends with my brother . . . after a while I just couldn't imagine life without him and sometimes I still can't.

"My relationship with Michael scared my father to death.

One night, after Michael had just left the house, my father's anxiety exploded. 'Surely, you're not thinking of making a life with that hillbilly!' he shouted.

"Oh yes," I said, putting on an air of sophistication.

"We plan to live in a cabin near a coal mining community. We're going to study Appalachian folklore and kinship structures.

"My father started playing with his pipe and looked as worried as I had ever seen him. That pleased me, I'm sorry to say.

"In our second year at Carnegie Mellon," Sofiya continued, "I took Michael to see St. John the Baptist Cathedral. We didn't go for a worship service, just to see the building. Michael, who seemed fascinated by everything in the church, couldn't stop talking.

'Why are there so many pictures?' (He had never seen an icon before and seemed to have no concept of what it meant.)

'Why is the table so big?'

'How old is this church, anyway?'

"At one point, standing in the center, looking at the altar and icons, he suddenly whispered, in a kind of awestruck voice, 'Sofiya, what IS that smell?'

"At first, I thought he meant my perfume, which struck me as strange. It seemed an inappropriate thing to say while walking through a church. So, I turned and glared at him but realized immediately that I had misjudged the situation. Michael was indeed intense and I might even say aroused. But it wasn't about me. Something else had provoked his passion.

"I don't know," I said. "Incense?"

'It smells like God,' he whimpered.

"That's when I knew Michael would never be mine," Sofiya said. "Not in that way.

"I had already thought that he might be falling in

love with me and so had wondered what I would do were he to express his feelings. We came from such different worlds, you see . . . there were other problems though . . .

"Anyway, as we were standing before the altar that day, I knew I had a rival for Michael's affections, saw that he was one of those God-intoxicated people who either go crazy or become a saint . . . it didn't matter which. The effect is the same for those who love people like that . . . disruption, unpredictability, and heartache.

"At the time you see, I was a philosophy major and had been gradually drifting away from my faith, except in the sense that my faith was a vital part of my family and community life. Michael, on the other hand, was about to go deeper into faith. Far more serious, as far as I was concerned, Michael was about to plunge into the parts of my faith I considered the most embarrassing. Soon, he would start showing an interest in visions, weeping icons, and all the other kinds of medieval hocus-pocus I hoped my religion would outgrow.

"Neither he nor I knew, as we stood in front of the iconostasis—that's a decorated screen that separates the altar from the congregation in Eastern churches—all of that was about to happen. I did get a glimpse of it though and it soured me.

"I would soon discover my life's path too—when I changed my major to anthropology. But I already knew Michael was going in another direction. I just wasn't ready to acknowledge it yet. I didn't know what I wanted, to tell you the truth. I had all kinds of stuff churning around in my insides—but that day in the church revealed something I could not easily dismiss.

"Sam, you asked me if I loved Michael," Sofiya said.

"The answer is 'yes,' I did love him. The curious thing though was this; except for a couple of near misses after too much wine, our relationship never took an erotic or even a romantic turn. That may have been because of our many differences. It was also because marriage and family did not seem to be the way forward for me.

"You must understand, I was born to be a scholar. Although I dated a few men when I was younger, and even a few times later in life, things like romance, eroticism, domestic life . . . these were simply not priorities for me. Other young women focused on who slept with whom, who was good-looking, and who was not—I just wasn't wired that way.

"Nonetheless, I liked being with Michael. He saw the world through such different eyes and helped me catch glimpses of the world as he saw it. He was as exotic as any Taoist or Hebrew prophet and infinitely curious about the way other people saw things. He even was fascinated by the secular, feminist viewpoint I was beginning to adopt. It never seemed to offend him. He just experienced it as strange, as something he needed to investigate. If I was in one of my moods, he would listen to my rant while he made coffee. He would only interrupt to ask a question.

"Michael was just a good person, Sam! He was naïve, sometimes silly, and a bit neurotic. But I'll tell you this . . . Hell! Pass me that box of tissues over on the lamp table, if you don't mind!

"If Michael and I . . . well, if we would have become romantically involved . . . I think we might have killed one another! As it was, we reached something in one another no one else seemed capable of doing, for either of us.

"I know Michael was physically attracted to me; I wasn't stupid. But he also seemed a bit fearful of women in that way, which was something I found refreshing. On one hand, he was one of the few men in my life back then who seemed to care about me as a person. Other men ran their eyes over my body—said stupid things . . . I did catch Michael looking at me like that too, several times. The difference with him though was that he seemed to be fighting with himself, forcing himself somehow to experience me as a person.

"I respected him for that.

"So, that pretty well sums up what I thought about our relationship. But that day at the church? It showed me something about Michael that he didn't know about himself, something I did not at all like.

"Michael was in love with God."

————

Michael's short reflection about the visit to St. John's offers an interesting contrast to Sofiya's story.

"There are Bible characters hanging around the walls in Sofiya's church," he writes. "She calls them icons. I figured out what some of them were about. They are beautiful. I don't think I've ever seen more beautiful art.

"The one on the back wall, just inside the front door on the right, nearly scared me out of my wits though! It shows King David holding a harp. While Sofiya was in the restroom, I was pondering what the symbols in it might mean when suddenly the figure in the icon began to move. Well, I shouldn't say it *did* move but that it *seemed* to move. That sounds crazy but it didn't bother me much until I heard the voices coming out of the icon.

"The first thing I heard was Bobby Lynn Collins. He was singing.

> *'Little David was a shepherd boy,*
> *He killed Goliath and shouted for joy.*
> *Little David play on your harp,*
> *Hallelu, Hallelu,*
> *Little David play on your harp*
> *Hallelu.'*

"After a while, I heard everybody back in Verner joining in—Momma and Granddaddy, even Pappy—as clear as if they were in the church beside me.

> *'Joshua was the son of Nun.*
> *He wouldn't stop until his work was done.*
> *Little David play on your harp.'*

"I knew they were singing to me, and the part that shook me the most was when they sang that part that says, 'Don't want to stumble; don't want to fall. I wanna be ready if the Lord should call.'

"Lord! Here I am, trying my best to start a new life, but my old life has no intention of letting me go.

"Anyway, I didn't talk much on the way home. I was thinking about whether everybody is given a harp of some kind they are supposed to play and the world can't be whole unless they play it. But what is my harp? How am I supposed to play it?

"Stuff like what happened tonight in that church don't just happen for no reason. It's maddening though to figure out what they mean, but it's like reading road signs. You gotta figure out what the signs mean. Otherwise, you end up in the wrong place!

"On the way home, I stayed wrapped up in my thoughts.

"Sofiya was quiet too."

15

THE REVENGE OF A
NEGLECTED PAST

SAMUEL CANTERBURY

T hree weeks after Michael Cooper was granted a Bachelor of Arts (with a major in English Literature and minor in Philosophy) his past unexpectedly and inconveniently demanded his full attention.

He had found an inexpensive apartment four blocks from St. John the Baptist Cathedral and had been offered a job in the fall teaching English literature at Central Catholic High School. This job was usually available only to Catholics but had been offered to him because of the recommendations from clergy at St. John's and because the faculty had been unimpressed with the other applicants.

The promise of work gave Michael a few weeks to rest and allowed him to shift gears before beginning his working life. He had several friends and seemed reasonably happy. Unlike many of his peers, he had nearly no debt because of the generous Pittston scholarship. His past life had grown distant. Except for an occasional letter or phone call to his grandparents, his conscious attention was fully on his present and future.

What Michael was about to discover however is that the past rarely demands one's conscious attention. We are aware of its continued influence from time to time, but for the most part, our past functions like a subterranean stream, gurgling quietly beneath our day-to-day affairs. Sooner or later though, the past demands a moment in the sun. When it does, even the person from whom that stream erupts may find its force mysterious and uncontrollable.

We often work to prevent such an eruption by suppressing the past, denying its existence, doing whatever is necessary to keep it underground. The past always wins this struggle. It will eventually resurface despite our opposition. Michael found this out in the early days of July 1979.

After not hearing from him for several days, Sofiya and her brother Victor went to Michael's apartment. When he did not respond, they opened the unlocked door, walked in, and found him lying on the couch. He was fully clothed and conscious but barely coherent. The apartment smelled of vomit because he had thrown up several times in the trash beside his couch. He had not washed or shaved. His hair, normally kept so carefully combed, was disheveled.

When Sofia and Victor finally got Michael to sit up and talk, they cleaned up the room and made a pot of coffee. Although still groggy and confused, Michael became coherent but had no opinion about what had happened or why, or about what should happen next.

Michael insisted he had been drinking for days, though Victor and Sofiya found only a handful of empty beer bottles in his apartment. He continued to express profound shame for his actions but could not say why he had decided to drink—something he had rarely done— or why drinking so little had affected him so much.

They decided Victor would stay at Michael's apartment until they could develop a plan for Michael's care.

It was Michael's good fortune that Victor and Sofiya had an uncle by marriage who happened to be a major donor of St. Luke's Clinic, a mental health center launched by the Episcopal Church decades before. Though now under the direction of a not-for-profit medical business and thus not officially affiliated with any religious body, the clinic was often host to several resident patients who were either clergymen or other kinds of church-related personnel.

This uncle, William Gladstone Rochester, was a convert to his wife's Ukrainian Church and had endeared himself to his new religious community by opening to them his long family connections. This made him a friend of the bishop, a frequent visitor to the seminary, and a reliable support in times of family distress.

That's who Sofiya called. After listening to her tearful entreaties, Mr. Rochester called the clinic. The clinic assured Mr. Rochester they would be all too happy to find a bed for this worthy young educator.

Michael would end up staying at St. Luke's for a month.

It may seem difficult to believe now, but in this not so distant past, medical practitioners were free to create a treatment plan based on the needs of their patients rather than on a business plan created by the medical corporation that employed them. Although a strange concept for us now, this was the norm for most of recorded history and was still the norm as late as 1979.

At any rate, we can only surmise what occurred at the clinic from the records released after Michael's death. Other than a single lengthy session I believe indispensable to our story, I have chosen simply to include a few of the notes made by various doctors and therapists about him. Even a reader unacquainted with therapeutic jargon will note the challenge these mental health workers faced in trying to understand Michael's inner life.

Note #1:

> I have ruled out schizotypal personality disorder for the following reasons. First, what one might judge as idiosyncratic locution is more likely a dialectical characteristic of the geographical location and religious sect in which he was raised. For example, the patient's use of the word "family" is nearly always a reference to an extensive clan rather than to an immediate family. He also uses other terms slightly or, in some cases, notably differently than the ways those same terms are used by the broader English-speaking community. However, this does not seem to be due to any pathological issue but is rather a feature of his early social environment.
>
> Religious terminology is another important feature of his everyday speech. An example is the frequent use

of "backslid," by which he means existential alienation from his religious community of origin.

Therapists: please take note. The patient uses several terms in unique ways. Always ask him to define the meaning of those words that seem out of context to you.

Note #2:

The patient's stories about his life (and the lives of family and friends) blend without apparent boundaries into biblical stories. He experiences biblical characters as close and present realities rather than as literary inventions, or even as remote historical persons. He references biblical characters much as one who recalls stories heard from grandparents about more distant ancestors. Thus, persons separated from him in time are nonetheless a personal part of his sense of ongoing family life. This includes biblical persons. The patient does not struggle with schizophrenia, however. He can distinguish entities in the external world from mentally constructed ones. Nonetheless, figures of the past, even of the distant past, seem extraordinarily present to him and exert a real and present influence on his thoughts and actions.

Note #3:

The patient experiences strong and constant dissociative ideation. In his own words, "I often see my life as though I were watching a movie. As he recounts events from his past, one notices the dissociated stare of his eyes and becomes aware that the patient is removed from his present time and place.

Note #4:

The patient does not exhibit true clinical signs of alcoholism. The recent binge activity seems more related to anxiety over long suppressed trauma than what we would more frequently label as addictive behavior. Furthermore, the patient greatly exaggerates his behavior, seemingly from a need to identify an external, present cause for his distress than to acknowledge any interior cause related to his traumatic past.

Note #5:

The patient has an intense longing for home, which feels to him as utterly and irretrievably lost.

Note #6:

The patient feels he has become disloyal to "his kin" due to his decision to create a life removed from his ancestral home. This is deeply connected to a feeling of ambivalence about his recent educational accomplishment. In his mind, his recent academic degree has decreased his connection to his past and perhaps endangered his membership in his community of origin. He experiences his loss of an immediate family as having severed the way he connected to his broader clan and region. Without a clear sense of personal boundaries, this loss of immediate family has left him believing he has no real connection to the world at large.

A quote from the patient is worth recording here.

"When Pappy died, our family just fell apart."

Objectively, it appears that the various family members of the patient's extended clan were becoming less dependent upon one another and were moving steadily toward healthy individuation when the flood occurred. The patient however, experiences this differently.

Note #7:

The patient exhibits signs of extreme stress that mimic pathological issues but are instead normal human reactions to the trauma he has faced. Thus, there is real potential for full recovery, given the right tools for rebuilding his life. We thus see no reason to distrust his ability to carry out the responsibility of his pending employment as a teacher. At the same time, we highly recommend ongoing treatment and participation in competent small group work.

Note #8:

The patient is reluctant to talk about the trauma of his religious past, which included practices such as carrying poisonous reptiles, drinking toxic substances, and adhering to a strict code regarding sexuality, dress, and speech. These elements have led to a persistent, non-relenting sense of guilt about trivial issues encountered in everyday life. It is likely the patient would be helped by some form of religious ritual or authority in processing the shame imposed by religion as he understood it as a child.

Note #9:

The patient most definitely suffers from a life-altering trauma of which he is only marginally aware. Intervention must therefore include a therapeutic modality that uncovers the largely unconscious networks of memory and reflection that lead to the dissociative state in which he tends to experience much of life.

16

GOING UNDER
SAMUEL CANTERBURY

By the time she worked with Michael Cooper, Dr. Frederica Nesis had been practicing for several decades in the Pittsburgh area. In the recording of one of her most significant sessions with him, one hears the voice of a confident and seasoned practitioner.

Those who worked with Dr. Nesis before her retirement speak glowingly of her ability to treat patients who had stumped others. At the time she worked with Michael, she was not on staff at St. Luke's. She rarely worked there in fact, and so we can assume that someone either called in a favor or funded the extra expense to involve Dr. Nesis in Michael's care.

I spent an entire day listening to the cassette tape and reading the clinical transcripts of what was probably the turning point of Michael's treatment under Dr. Nesis care. That evening, I went to Cabin Creek for some target practice. I felt as though I had been personally present. The following week, I reconstructed Michael's journals, his reaction to Dr. Nesis, which pulled me further into the sessions. This was especially true of his emotional account of the flood.

The session begins professionally one might even say abruptly.

"Mr. Cooper," Dr. Nesis said, "the doctors and therapists at St. Luke's believe you are dealing with issues related to the disaster you experienced several years ago. Does that make sense to you?"

"Yes," Michael replied. "I don't know what I can do about it though."

"I understand," Dr. Nesis said.

"The daily level of stress you seem to experience is like that of a soldier returning from combat. We are still learning how to work with this sort of trauma. One thing we have learned is that most mental health professionals would not recommend the use of hypnosis for treating trauma. However, your case worker believes you may be an exception. You have a unique background that suggests you may profit from trance work."

"Hypnosis?" Michael laughed. "Will I cluck like a chicken?"

"Hopefully not," Nesis responded. "I need a fully engaged human being to work with me. Circus tricks wouldn't do either of us any good!

"Let me explain what trance work is like.

"Imagine the contents of your mind as arranged something like the contents of this room. Right now, you are seeing things I cannot. For example, you can see that painting of grazing sheep. From where I am sitting, I cannot see it. Like me, you are aware of items in this room that you cannot see at the moment. You know they are there because you saw them as you walked in. If you turn your head—yes, like that—you can see those items. When you do, you no longer see the painting. Directing our inner attention works similarly to the way pointing our heads works in the outer world. Deciding what we want to observe changes what we see, in both our inner, mental environment and in our shared, physical world.

"So, the contents of your conscious mind are like items in this room that you are seeing now, without turning your head. Everything else in the room is like the contents of your *un*conscious mind which you are not presently seeing. Interestingly, there are things in your unconscious mind you have not looked at for a long time. A trained coach like me can help you turn the 'eyes of your mind' toward those things.

"That is what clinical hypnotherapists do. We use different modes of speech, stories, and other tools to coach individuals who want to look at the contents of their unconscious.

"It is important to know that you always remain in control. You will not do anything or say anything against your will. You most certainly will not be clucking like a chicken unless, of course you decide that you want to do that for some reason!

"Does this sound safe to you?"

"Yes," Michael said. "It's interesting. Besides, I am ready to get to the bottom of this stuff."

"Ok then," Dr. Nesis said. "Let's get started."

"Are you comfortable?" Dr. Nesis asked. "If not, you can sit in another chair. You can or even lie down on the couch over there. It's entirely up to you."

"What works best?" Michael asked.

"The chair works just fine. Last week a patient sat in that very chair and immediately went into trance.

"We will start with a few relaxation exercises.

"In a session like this, I gradually shift from my normal, day-to-day speech and into a different way of communicating. We have learned that patients already know the way into therapeutic trance because everybody everywhere trances out naturally several times a day. A therapist's job is simply to support the patient's *natural* way of shifting from the conscious to the unconscious.

"You said you wanted to get to the bottom of things. That's an interesting thing to say—the *bottom* of things. We spend so much of our time on the *surface* of things, not often aware of the many, many things—many, many emotions—we might examine at a safe time and a safe place like this. We all want *under*-standing; want to know what stands under. But how seldom we really look under, look *under*neath, the apparent, the surface, the publicly visible.

"I think you will find it interesting . . . informative . . . enlightening . . . to *under*-stand some things, though they may be things you have already known . . . but at a *deep*er level . . . Things you have known and know even now, but will *now* know in a *deep*er way . . . for one can know and yet not know, all at the same time . . . This is something you are now finding *in* yourself *entrancing* . . . At the same time, your body has already been and is now noticing things you don't always consciously notice."

Dr. Nesis goes on like this, using phrases with two or

three different meanings, constantly changing the tone and rhythms of her speech as she continues.

"You may now wish to close your eyes . . . not needing to be concerned with what I am saying . . . just relaxed . . . that's right," she said softly.

Her voice had taken on a velvet-like quality, similar to the way a mother soothes a child.

"I will ask you questions from time to time about how you are doing. You can respond with a simple yes or no. Is that all right?"

Michael softly expresses his agreement.

"We can even play with this, this *under*-standing a little," Dr. Nesis continued.

"You may notice *now* sensations on the bottoms of your feet, which are, as you *now* realize, touching the floor. It may seem interesting to *under*-stand, to look at the world from this interesting place of standing- *under*, how the unconscious mind constantly feels such sensations and has been feeling them your entire life.

"But now, in this safe place and safe time, the unconscious mind is revealing to you the sort of work it constantly carries out *underneath* your day-to-day life.

"Notice now the sensations in your back. Since you first sat down in that chair, the chair where so many of our patients have gone deeply into trance, your unconscious began examining the back of that chair. Now, you are sensing what the unconscious has sensed all along. And so, it seems that you are now entering *deeply, deeply* into the chair . . . almost as if your body has found it safe to become a part of the chair . . . almost as if there is no difference between the chair and yourself."

In her journal, Michael says by this point he found himself drifting as in a pleasant sort of fog, without real direction or concern. He knew what was occurring around him but had stopped thinking much about it.

"The unconscious part of yourself is responsible for so many things," Dr. Nesis continued. "And it is amazing to become acquainted with it and to recognize the parts of ourself we have not acknowledged for a while.

"Just as the unconscious explored the chair without your conscious mind thinking about it, the unconscious is constantly directing our breath. Moment by moment, hour by hour, day after day, we take a breath in . . . a breath out . . . a breath in . . . a breath out . . . and we now slow our breathing down to the rhythms the self adopts when it is *utterly* and *totally* relaxed."

Michael did indeed find that his breathing had become deeper and that he felt something akin to floating.

"We are fully in the present," the psychologist continued. "We are not in the past. That is why we may, in this *present* state, explore things from the past, things that were perhaps too frightening to acknowledge as they happened or even immediately after they happened. Your unconscious self, which you are now experiencing in this moment, knows how to keep your conscious self safe; keeping to itself things that were once too difficult to experience as fully as you may now do in this present, safe place."

Michael heard her words as though from a distance, her voice now nearly a part of his own thoughts.

After a long pause, Dr. Nesis continued.

"You can choose now to see the parts of your past that you wish to observe, see them as though in a movie, *your* movie, and see them at a pace that is right for *you*. As you see this personal movie, you can, if you wish, share what you see and feel with me.

Michael was aware now of the tears on his cheeks, flowing in a way that was neither pleasant nor unpleasant.

"I hear Daddy's voice," Michael said quietly. "He's talkin' to Momma and my sister, Susan."

"What does he say?" Dr. Nesis' voice said far away.

"He says, 'Lila, I was up at the head of the holler yesterday looking at the dam. If this rain keeps up I don't know where all the water's gonna go. I mentioned it to Rich Workman yesterday, up at the left fork tipple. He said he heard Jack Kent worrying that the water behind the dam up there above Three Forks was raising up way too fast to drain off'—

"Daddy's talking about that old dam; the one that broke up first. It was about to break up and destroy everything," Michael said with noticeable anxiety.

"Michael," Dr. Nesis said gently, "this is a movie of things that happened a long time ago. Keep watching it but pull away if it gets too difficult. Be kind to yourself.

"Now, as you remain in full control, tell me what happens next?"

"I smell bacon and coffee," Michael said. "I'm hungry. I ain't payin' much attention to Daddy. I just want to eat."

Michael felt that he was examining the house in Amherstdale as it had been in those moments just before they left it. He wanted to be there. Wanted to stop time. Wanted to remember the last few moments he had been with his family.

"Mr. Farley drives up in his '68 Chevy pickup," Michael said. "He's yellin' but we can't hear what he is a sayin' . . .

"I think he's cussin' about something 'cause I make out that one word—Dam! Dam! I wonder what he's so mad about, 'cause I'd never heard him cuss before. He was a church goin' man and didn't cuss.

"I hear Susan a laughin' because Mr. Farley has got hisself so worked up.

"But Daddy gets up and stands in the doorway. He tells us to be quiet so he can hear.

"Dam's broke loose!" Mr. Farley shouts. "You've got to run!"

"We look and see the water a risin'. The creek is already over its banks. It's startin' to run between the house and Daddy's truck.

"Daddy tells us to run to the truck but Momma says it ain't that bad. She says she can at least finish her coffee. Daddy shouts that there ain't no time to drink no coffee. He says the water from the dam's gonna fill up the whole holler.

"Susan tries to grab something but Daddy pushes her out the door and she starts cryin'.

"Momma tells Daddy he's actin' crazy, scarin' everybody. She tells him to calm down.

"I'm laughin' at Daddy and Momma fussin' like that. I'm also aggravated at Daddy for pushin' Susan and scarin' her.

"Then I go out on the porch to see for myself. The water's a risin' so fast. I see it comin' up. I know then Daddy's right. I start yellin', 'Daddy's right, Momma! Oh my God! We've gotta get up to higher ground.'

"Susan is crying real hard. She says she's scared.

"Daddy picks Momma up. He shouts at her, 'Irene, get your butt in the truck! I'm amazed to hear my Daddy talk to my Momma thataway. I'm really scared.

"We are runnin' to the truck.

"Daddy gets there first. He gets Momma in the car.

"I am runnin' with Susan 'cause she is having a hard time.

"Daddy comes back to help us. He tells me to run on while he helps Susan.

"We are just a few feet from the truck. Daddy sees we can't make it. The low spot between the truck and us is now filled with water.

"Daddy yells at Momma to start the truck. He tells her to drive fast out of the holler. I know he thinks we can make it to the road if we run fast enough. I remember the place he's thinking about, further up, past that low spot.

"Daddy has Susan in his arms. He is running through water just above his ankles. The sound of the creek is really loud now. I turn to see what's causing the noise. It looks like a wall of ink running past the house. I stop to watch for a moment and see the house tearing loose from the ground. I start running again.

"Oh God! Oh God!" Michael sobs.

From somewhere far away, Michael hears a tender voice. "Michael. You are not there. You are watching something that happened long ago. Breathe slower, now, slower.

"Gently now . . . what do you see?"

"I see Daddy slip. He and Susan goes down in the water. He reaches for her and pulls her up. He puts her on the branch of a tree and shouts my name. I can hardly hear him. The water is now around my knees and the current is really strong. I know I can't reach him now. I see the swing from our porch comin' at me. I think I can float on it toward Daddy. So I grab it and throw myself on it. It holds me up but is movin' toward the creek, away from the road.

"Daddy plunges in the water toward me. He reaches the swing. He uses his feet to push against something—I don't know what—and gets the swing lodged between a fence and a rock.

'This won't hold son. You got to let go!' he shouts.

"I'm afraid. I call out for God for help but a burst of water washes over me. I let go of the swing. I go under. I get pushed by something and can't get my head back above water. My hand finds some sort of board that doesn't move. The water is rushing all around me but I keep hold of the board. The water finds another path and so it gets lower for a moment where I am. I stand up and I'm at the edge of the water.

"I see that the board I'm holding to is a part of a house and that I can climb out on to it and get to land. I make it to land and then I start running toward the road. I get to the road and start running up and down by the water. I'm lookin' for Daddy and Susan. I'm yellin', commandin' the water to go down in the name of Jesus.

Then I fall. People I don't know come out of nowheres and pull me away from the water. It's still risin' up and the house I had been hangin' to has given way now and is lurching into the current.

"Everything turns black. I wake up in the back of somebody's truck. The truck is movin' up the side of the mountain, on some old dirt road. The truck stops. Someone drags me out of the truck bed and lays me on a blanket. They cover me up because I don't have on any clothes. People are cryin' and groanin' all around me.

"I try to get up to find Daddy and Susan but the people won't let me. They keep pushin' me back down.

"Some big man says, 'Son, you ain't goin' nowhere. I'll tie you up if I have to. It's too dangerous to go down there until the water passes. That's what your Daddy would want.' I know the man is right. That is what Daddy would want.

"So all I can do is cry; cry and pray."

Michael was weeping and rocking now, trying to remember that he is in Dr. Nesis's office, hundreds of miles and many years removed from Buffalo Creek.

Even listening to the session many years later, one is aware of a weighty, pregnant silence that seems to go on forever.

"Michael?" Dr. Nesis finally said. "Please take as long as you need to reenter this present time and place. You know the best way and the best pace to do that. When you are ready, you can open your eyes.

"That's right. You've done some really difficult work today, Michael, recalling those terrifying events."

Michael opens his eyes and finds the room sucked

dry of energy and life. He stares into space for a while before turning to Dr Nesis. When he does, he sees that her eyes are teary.

"You don't have to talk anymore today, Michael," she said quietly.

But he spoke anyway.

"They never found Susan. They found Daddy's body two days later, not far from Man. They found Daddy's truck too. People say Momma left it beside the road so she could jump in the water to find Susan. No one ever saw her after that. By the end of the day, they were all gone."

Speaking slowly, somberly, Michael said, "I am the boy in the swing! I always thought I watched that boy from the bank. I don't know what to do with that."

"Most of us remember what is safe for us to remember, Michael," Dr. Nesis replied. "We remember the past in a way, and at the time, that feels safe to us.

"Those who find the courage to face the truth about their past suffer working their way through illusions they once adopted to protect and comfort themselves. But those once comforting illusions keep us stuck in trauma. Letting them go is the only way to freedom."

17

ENTERING THE COCOON
SAMUEL CANTERBURY

In the spring of 1980, after several months of catechism, Michael Cooper was converted to Byzantine Catholicism. He briefly mentions this in his journal but doesn't go into much detail. It appears that he experienced this conversion as being mostly about joining the congregation at St. John the Baptist. The greater implications of what he had done seem to have only gradually become apparent. He took his decision seriously enough, however. In fact, some of his friends found the way he embraced his new spiritual path disturbing.

Sofiya, for one, had strong opinions about Michael's Catholic practice.

"Michael was attracted to the very elements of my religion that most troubled me," she said.

"If he heard about a weeping icon or a reported apparition somewhere," she added, "he went to check it out. He said that he understood that such things are often the result of an overworked imagination and that they are even fraudulent! None of that bothered him. Michael had a nearly medieval view of the universe, you see. He saw humanity as living in some sort of middle territory between light and darkness. He took all of that quite seriously. It wasn't just metaphor to him.

'This overwrought spirituality wore me out. When I talked to him about how I felt, he just laughed. He never seemed to get mad about it. Nonetheless, he persisted. It was like he wasn't all that comfortable with the modern world.

"So, no, to answer your question, I don't think Michael ever really converted to Catholicism. He just pulled his own weirdness into our church.

"You know who liked Michael? Old women! They were always giving him rosaries, religious pictures, and the like. He would go on about it like they had just given him the winning ticket of the lottery! If a group of them gathered to pray on some obscure feast day, Michael was right there with them.

"Something else that bothered me was how Michael often wept in church. Not out loud or anything, just quietly. Still, I didn't like going to church with him. I avoided it when I could. It was like he was on another planet. I loved him, but on the matter of religion we just couldn't see eye to eye.

"On the other hand, when I was in despair about a private matter a few years ago, something that had serious implications for my religious beliefs, he dropped everything and drove up to Pittsburgh. What he did for me that week proved I never had a better friend than him. That was when he understood why it wouldn't have worked for us to get married. That was also the day he gave me his father's poetry book, the one he rarely let out of his sight all those years. It's right over there, in that glass case.

"But that's a conversation for another day!"

From the fall of 1981 to the spring of 1984, Michael attended Saints Cyril and Methodius Byzantine Catholic Seminary, located just outside Pittsburgh.

These were years of significant development for him as he came to grips with his past, was forced to notice the gap between contemporary American culture and his own Appalachian religious upbringing, and, as we have noted, came face-to-face with the trauma he had experienced in the flood. During this same period, a Redemptorist monk named Father Maximus joined Sofiya in exerting influence on Michael Cooper's continuing journey.

His academic papers from this period are technical, interesting perhaps, for theology students, but not offering significant insight into his personal life. An exception to this is a short reflection on the Gospel of Luke, written in 1983 for a class on the only non-Jewish writer of the New Testament. Michael's paper on Luke expresses a view of spiritual life considerably different from both theologically liberal and conservative writers. Although his view of reality and spiritual life seem at first far removed from the likes of Pappy Mullins, a closer examination reveals other-worldly assumptions held by Appalachian Christians in most denominations.

(For those interested, this paper was published in 1998 by Fuller Theological Seminary in a collection enti-

tled *Voices From The Diaspora: Theologies of the Disin-
herited.*)

I trust the reader will excuse this brief detour into
Michael's academic life. The reader surely wishes to
proceed with our fascinating story, which, I assure you,
is my desire as well.

However, I thought it would be helpful to point out
that despite Brother Michael's common touch, he sometimes wrestled with profound questions. Nor is this
unusual for those with Appalachian roots. Sheer survival
in mainstream American culture requires mountain
people to constantly examine the ideas and practices of
their pre-Enlightenment, shamanistic background. For
good and ill, a Celtic soul lies at the deepest strata of the
Appalachian diaspora no less than in the present inhabitants of the mountains. Whether the members of this
diaspora live in a trailer park, run a billion-dollar
company, or teach in an Ivy League school, a similar
understanding of life is either directly motivating their
thoughts and behaviors or exerting enormous influence
on them.

Another way of saying this is that Appalachia is not
mostly a geographical location; it is a state of mind.

Michael was studying the great ideas of Western civilization as a foreigner or a tourist, not as a native-born
son of Western culture. Furthermore, his past was
increasingly conversing with his present. Indeed, in
retrospect, we see his dimly perceived future pulling
both his past and present toward itself. The diverse
forces we have mentioned—academic life, therapeutic
care, personal friendships, and religious influences had

begun working together to form the unique person who would, in little over a decade, unsettle the controlling powers and console the suffering powerless throughout southern West Virginia.

For the moment though, Michael Cooper was simply a theology student, working through the demanding course work of a seminary dedicated to preparing deacons and priests for service in Eastern-Rite Catholic churches.

This would prove to be neither accident nor detour.

Eastern-Rite Catholicism emerged in the fifteenth century as the result of a brief union between the long estranged Orthodox East and Catholic West. That union rapidly unraveled in other places. The Ukrainian Church however, maintained the connection that fell apart elsewhere. Because of this, Ukrainian Catholic priests, unlike their Roman counterparts, maintain much of their Eastern Orthodox heritage, including the right to marry.

Michael had joined a group that the centuries have constantly forced to define and defend itself. In this sense, he was fully at home.

We know that Michael loved the seminary chapel. This sacred space had been remodeled in the early 1970s, a few years before Michael attended there. At the time of the remodel, it had been graced by the iconography of Christina Dochvat, a Ukrainian immigrant from Philadelphia. Years later, Michael sometimes remarked how often he had found retreat in this beautiful setting. It is not too much of a stretch to see the influence of this chapel on the healing houses Michael would go on to found years later.

It was in this seminary chapel where Michael first met Father Maximus. Fortunately for us, he wrote several pages about that meeting soon after it occurred.

———

M.J. COOPER

I went to the chapel yesterday to meet Father Maximus, who heard my confession.

Victor had been encouraging me to meet with him because he thought Father Maximus to be a discerning man who helps people discover their calling. I finally gave in and made an appointment. I had seen him around campus and had even heard him lecture a couple of times, but had never talked with him personally.

Father Maximus is in his early seventies, with a beard as white as coconut that goes halfway down his chest. His shoulder length hair matches his beard. The sleeves of his simple black cassock end just above his wrists, in large openings without cuffs. He wears a large medallion just below his heart that hangs from a gold-plated chain and depicts a colorful Madonna and Christ. His sky-blue eyes dance, which complement a perpetual smile.

The chapel was quiet when I entered, like a rose petal falling to the snow. My heart was pounding as I walked toward him. I thought he might hear it! Father Maximus was standing in front of a couple of chairs that he has positioned a few feet from the iconostasis. As he sat in one of them, he motioned for me to sit down in the other. He then made the sign of the cross, prayed quietly for a moment, and offered me the book he had been holding.

Pointing to a page he had marked, he said in a quiet but deep voice, "Please read this as slowly and deliberately as you can, doing your best to pull your mind into your heart."

"Have mercy upon me, O God, according to thy lovingkindness," I began.

"According to the multitude of your tender mercies, blot out my transgressions. Wash me from my iniquity, and cleanse me from my sin. I acknowledge my transgressions. My sin is ever before me. Hide your face from my sins and blot out my iniquities. Create in me a clean heart, O God. Renew a right spirit within me."

Swallowing hard, I continued. "O Lord, open my lips; and my mouth shall show forth your praise. For the sacrifices of God are a broken spirit: a broken and a contrite heart, O God, you will not despise."

Father Maximus waited a moment, retrieved his book, and then continued. "O Lord, receive your servant Michael who now repents of his sins. Overlook all he has done, forgive his faults, and pass over his transgressions. For if you should mark iniquities, O Lord, who could stand?"

He then indicated for me to begin my confession.

"Forgive me Father, for I have sinned," I said.

I talked about my spiritual journey and about the impure thoughts I often have about Sofiya. I told him I have misused alcohol and that before I came to the seminary, I had gotten drunk and had to be admitted to a clinic. I also confessed that the worst sin I have committed was blaming God for the death of my family.

"Tell me a bit more about that," Father Maximus said.

Over the next half an hour, I told him the story of the flood, how I had fornicated with Inida Goins, taken LSD, and stopped going to church.

When I finished, we sat together in silence.

Then, he abruptly blurted out,

"By the grace and mercy of God, and through the power granted to me, I, an unworthy priest, forgive you, my brother Michael, and absolve you from all your sins, in the Name of the Father, and of the Son, and of the Holy Ghost."

He made the sign of the cross and I thought the confession had ended. Turns out, he was just getting started.

"Michael," he said, "St Augustine said that God made us without asking us but that God won't save us without our consent. Does God have your consent to take over your life?"

I nodded.

I told him that Pappy, my grandparents, and all the rest of my family had all read the Bible and tried to live right but added that I couldn't seem to make much sense of religion.

We talked for nearly two hours. I don't remember everything we said, but I wanted to write down a few things, so I wouldn't forget them.

There was one thing he said I found perplexing. When I had been talking to him about getting drunk,

Father Maximus said, "A caterpillar suffers more in the cocoon than when crawling on the ground."

He could tell from my face that I didn't see what caterpillars had to do with anything. He kept on talking though.

"If a caterpillar changing into a butterfly could numb itself, it probably would. That must hurt—legs falling off, wings bursting through its back—all that change can't feel good. Unlike butterflies, human beings going through change often do something to make the pain go away, at least for a while. Unfortunately, sometimes the way people numb themselves just leads to more pain.

Father Maximus smiled and then looked up at the iconostasis, as though asking for help. Then he looked at me and asked, "Michael, do you know the story about the prophet and the ass?"

He meant Balaam. Of course I knew that story! I had always thought Pappy told it so he could say the word 'ass,' which would have been a sin otherwise. Same thing with the word 'whore', in the Book of Revelation. Pappy liked talking about that passage too. "The Great WHOOORE of BABYLIN," Pappy would say, mostly meaning Methodists. I didn't laugh at the Revelation passage. That was too scary. But Balaam and the ass, well that was just too funny. I would stare up at the painting of Jesus behind the pulpit to keep from laughing.

"Yes," I said to Father Maximus with a smile. "I know that story."

The old priest laughed.

"Besides teaching us that a great prophet is sometimes dumber than an ass, the story tells us that God lets us hit a wall sometimes so we will stop going in the wrong direction.

"You are ashamed because you hit a wall, Michael. But look—you came here because you found out that the road beyond the wall—the place where God stopped you —is somewhere you don't want to go.

I teared up. He was right. I was afraid of what was beyond that wall.

"What do I do now?" I asked.

"Let's begin by making the sign of the cross," he said. As you do that, say the words: 'Lord Jesus Christ, have mercy on me, a sinner.' Do that as often as you think about it, until your heart is pierced by sorrow for your sins and you begin to sense your own longing for God.

"Here," he said. "I have something to help you."

He handed me a small yellow book. On the cover was a drawing of a man holding a stick, walking down a winding road. The title of the book was *The Way of a Pilgrim*. I thanked him for it and took it from his hand.

"Let's meet from time to time to talk about how you're doing," Father Maximus said. "For now, go in peace. And may the blessings of Almighty God, Father, Son, and Holy Spirit, go with you."

He stood, signed the cross over me, faced the iconostasis, bowed, and then slowly turned and walked out of the chapel. I waited a moment or two and then followed him.

Walking away from the altar, I heard lines from William Blake running through my head:

God Appears & God is Light
To those poor Souls who dwell in Night
But does a Human Form Display
To those who Dwell in Realms of day.

I remembered how I had promised Daddy I would become a good man and so before exiting the chapel, I faced the altar, bowed, and made the sign of the cross. When I got to my room, I knelt by my bed and opened the book Father Maximus had given me and began to read.

By the grace of God, I am a Christian man, by my actions, a great sinner, and by calling a homeless wanderer of the humblest birth who roams from place to place. My worldly goods are a knapsack with some dried bread in it on my back, and in my breast-pocket a Bible. And that is all.

18

IN THE BORDERLANDS
SAMUEL CANTERBURY

Father Maximus was the one who introduced Michael to the Redemptorists, a monastic society that places qualified clerics in local churches.

Two years after Michael graduated from seminary, several spiritual and personal factors led him to make a three-year commitment to this missionary society. His work would involve ministry in Ukraine and the United Kingdom. The provisional vows he took would give him time to discern whether he should take lifelong vows or, as he expected, return for parish work as a married priest.

First though, he needed to know where he stood with Sofiya.

Sofiya vividly recalls the night Michael talked to her about marriage.

"He proposed," she said. "Went down on one knee with a ring, read a poem—well, the whole ball of wax!

"And I loved him, Sam! I really did. I know I've told you that already but it's true. It was just that I was not ready to be married and, as it turned out, never would have been.

"And there's something else.

"In Eastern-Rite Catholic churches, a married man can be ordained as a priest. After ordination though, marriage is no longer an option. So, I understood his sense of urgency, but found it off-putting.

"My uncle was a priest, you see. I learned from watching his family that the wife of a priest is a constant object of criticism and gossip. God forbid she might express an opinion of her own!

"The truth is, married priests are married to the Church, just as in the Western-Rite churches. The only difference with us is that our priests can have a life-long female companion—although she will have little life of her own or have much of a relationship with her husband either, for that matter.

"Actually, I was already uncertain about whether I wanted to be married at all and the idea of being married to a priest made me even more reluctant. Don't get me wrong! I am Catholic and I respect the priesthood. Furthermore, I think priests should marry if they want. I just wasn't the sort of woman who could tolerate all that came along with that.

"So, I tried to explain all of this to Michael that night the best I could, but my hesitancy hurt him. He thought I was trying to force him to choose between what he thought was a calling from God and his love for me. That wasn't it at all but I understand why he believed that.

"Naturally, I was a bit concerned about his mental stability, but not too much. He seemed to have made a good recovery and was clear minded. I do think a part of me wanted to see that he remained in good emotional health.

"Anyway, about a month later, he told me he was definitely going to Ukraine. He reminded me that his commitment would be for three years and that he hoped things would change for us during that time.

"All in all, it was a sad time—for me and for him. We told each other things might be different when he returned, but I think we both knew it probably would not work out for us, at least as a married couple. I wasn't yet able to put into words all the reasons why, though I did later. Fortunately, we would retain our friendship through all of that, though neither of us knew that then.

"We just couldn't figure out how we were going to love one another without getting married! At the same time, we didn't want to lose each other. Our relationship was confusing! It would remain confusing like that for many years. In some way, even with him gone, it's still confusing."

By the time Michael finished his seminary training, Redemptorists in Canada and the United States were being given permission by the Soviet State to work directly with churches and monastic communities in Ukraine. For a few years, they would even be permitted to maintain foreign church workers in the county for extended amounts of time. Michael and two other students from his seminary, for example, would live there for nearly two years.

Mikhail Gorbachev's administration was making several initiatives at the time toward the West, as well as toward communities within the Soviet Union that had been previously marginalized. These initiatives deeply affected Ukrainian Catholics, a group accustomed to being caught between Eastern and Western forms of Christianity. It remained to be seen whether the emerging geopolitical situation would allow Ukrainian believers to serve as a bridge between Rome and Constantinople, to put the matter in historic terms, or whether they would once again, as had often been the case, be rejected by both.

Nor was this merely a religious question. The very word "Ukraine" means "borderlands," which the Russians had often interpreted to mean the place where their own country meets the West. Using the article made that implication clear—*The* Ukraine—something quite different than simply *Ukraine*. The Ukrainians and the Russians; as well as the Orthodox and Roman Catholics, had strong opinions about the meaning of this word "Ukraine" and were at odds with one another about whether the word should or should not be preceded by the article.

Were Ukrainian believers esoteric Catholics, people who in time should embrace Roman standards? This had been the unstated opinion of most Roman Catholic leaders in the past. Or, were Ukrainian Catholics unfaithful Orthodox Christians who, in a moment of political stress, had capitulated to the insatiable Western desire for religious control and hegemony? This was the opinion of many Eastern Orthodox leaders, especially Russian ones. The decision to use or disuse the article before the word "Ukraine" thus depended on whether this "borderland" belonged to either the East or the West as each faced the other, or whether it was an entity in its own right, a community able to play a mediating role between behemoths on either side.

In those days of cautious hope, Ukrainians dared believe they might escape being devoured by either the East or the West and might instead be invited to take their place as a people among the peoples of the world. Many Ukrainian Catholics spiritualized this role, hoping to escape both Romanization and Russification and embrace, as they had always wished to do, those elements of both West and East that would make sense for a national church like theirs, birthed as it had been, in the borderlands.

Michael knew this, not only because he had studied these specific issues but because he too was a borderland person, the member of a community that had been a part of the American social reality from the beginning but which had never been fully accepted by the other subcultures of the nation as an equal, or even as an honored participant.

Like Ukraine, Appalachia is neither North nor South, neither this nor that. It is a place set apart, an in-between, suspicious, and, to outsiders, a strange place—a place not easy to place within the great categories of the world. Like Ukrainians, mountain people are not merely an extension of other communities but rather a distinct people with a distinct heritage. During the War Between the States, to the great surprise of the North, the people of Appalachia refused to be automatically lumped together with the South. Unlike Ukraine,

Appalachia had neither the desire nor the potential to be a nation of its own. That is why most of it unenthusiastically sided with the North, even though its contemporary inhabitants often fly rebel flags. These characteristics, as mystifying as they can be to outsiders, signals its inhabitants to maintain a culture of its own—including its unique spiritual heritage.

Michael was already making these comparisons between Appalachian and Ukrainian history. In the next four years, he would work to grasp the implications, a struggle that would influence him to make the spiritual and social choices he would soon be making.

As was often the case during this period, our understanding about what was occurring with Michael comes from his interactions with Sofiya. A good example of this is a letter he wrote to her after a few weeks in Ukraine.

Dear Sofiya,

I have been in Ukraine now for a month. A German deacon visiting Ternopil offered to mail my letters from Stuttgart when he returns. Otherwise, I'm not sure when, or even if, a letter would get to you.

Since arriving, I have been living in Ternopil. However, most weekends I travel to rural areas throughout the Carpathian Mountain region. The area and its people remind me so much of home. Except for the language, I don't feel nearly out of place as I had imagined.

After Alexis and I landed in Kiev, we were detained in the airport for several hours. The customs officers yelled about everything—our crosses, bibles, prayer

books, cassocks, you name it. Some of the young officers wanted to talk though, at least when the older
ones stepped out of the room. These young officers
were particularly interested in Alexis and me, amazed
that Americans would be coming to live for a while in
their country. Some of the young people here have a
look in their eyes like thirsty horses who have just
caught the first scent of water.

Anyway, we stayed in Kiev that night. We headed
for Ternopil the next morning, traveling in a couple of
old cars I doubted could make a trip across the city!
One of them stopped three times on the way for
various kinds of repairs—I had no idea what was
happening. My Ukrainian is so bad. (Not any worse
than yours, I hasten to add.)

I have been given the task of accompanying a
young priest to Kiev twice a month. We are to meet
with Catholic students from the Western side of the
country. We will dress in street clothes and take the
train, so we won't draw attention to ourselves. My first
trip there was last week, in fact.

While in Kiev, I met a Greek woman named Zoe.
She is originally from Corfu and her father is a priest!
She received a scholarship from St. Hilda's in Oxford
but after studying there in England for a couple of
years entered an exchange program. It involved a year
of studies at the University of Kiev. When she told me
her major was economics, I said, "I have a friend back
home who reads Ayn Rand. She has strong opinions
about economics."

Now, I don't mean to rub it in, but Zoe has never

heard of Ayn Rand! Alas, that must be an American thing. (You have no idea how much I miss arguing with you about that!) She has challenged me to read *Das Kapital* and discuss it with her. I thought, 'why not?' That's the kind of things we do at the university anyway—we make connections with students.

As you might imagine, English-language books are not easy to get. Strangest thing though, I quickly discovered that Marx is readily available in English. It was cheap too! I have read most of it now. I must admit that it surprised to me to learn that Marx was not nearly as boring as I had feared. At any rate, it will give you and me some more things to argue about after I get home!

Seriously, I think Marx's description of the effects of the industrial revolution are not all that different than Blake's. I mean, think about Blake's rage against "these dark satanic mills!"

(Don't tell your father I said anything good about Karl Marx; he already thinks everyone from coal mining country is a communist!)

I do think Christians often forget that Christ (and the Jewish prophets before him) addressed similar issues as Marx and Engles. Zoe passionately points this out and seems hellbent on creating some sort of synthesis between Christianity and Marxism, which I don't think possible. (Of course, in terms of how Marx and Christ each address human suffering, I get her point.)

Well, this letter will get much too long if I keep trying to pick a fight, so I'll wrap this up.

I wanted to tell you that I met a molfar! I'm sure your family knows about these shamanistic characters. They play music on what West Virginians unfortunately call a Jew's Harp. After they zone out with their music, molfars tell a person's fortune and what have you. The one I met had a large mustache dropping over his chin. His shirt was dirty and worn but covered with colorful patterns. Father Yaroslav said that most people in the area wore clothing like this in the past. (We were near Mizhhir'ya.) The molfar mumbled something about me being a "man of woe, appointed to fight giants and demons, destined to defeat the darkness, but through much suffering and so forth." A deacon with us said afterward, "A healthy offering in that madman's palm would likely change your fortune really fast!"

That was crazy, but to tell you the truth it kind of made me feel at home. Evidently, mountain air affects people's minds the world over!

Tell your mother I'm eating tons of holubtsi, nachynka, and, most definitely, borscht. But for goodness sake, tell her none of it is as good as hers!

I think of you every day. Of course, I'm still hoping things will turn out well for us.

With Much Love,
    Michael

Father Alexis, the other student from Michael's seminary on this Redemptorist mission, says that most of his and Michael's work during this period was routine and uneventful. The leaders of their Order were cautious in how, where, and to whom these young Americans were exposed. The Cold War seemed to be winding down but we know this only in retrospect. At the time, no one could be certain about how deep the changes in the Soviet System would go, or how permanent they would be.

The young would-be Redemptorists spent most of their time in the Carpathians among rural people. The exception was Michael's twice a month visit to the capital, as seen in his letter to Sofiya. It was there in Kiev that his routine took a dramatic turn.

Michael spent two years in Ukraine traveling from city to city and through rural areas in the Carpathians. He would however usually return within a week or less to monastic centers in either Ternopil or L'viv. He studied the language, helped local priests petition Ukrainian communities in North America and Europe for financial assistance, and met with students in Kiev. Zoe Iordanou was one of them.

Zoe was twenty-four years old. She had an olive complexion, long black hair, a spirited disposition, and was inclined to reveal much more of her body and mind than most Soviet-era young women. She argued passionately with Michael from a Marxist interpretation of Christian practice which, in her mind, should be applied globally as well as individually.

One might say Zoe was one of those young idealists

at the end of a turbulent century about to be awoken from their beautiful dream of global brotherhood and economic quality among the world's nations. In retrospect, she may look naïve. At the time however, she was charismatic, beautiful, and invigorating.

Michael arranged to meet with her regularly. This was, the reader will recall, entirely consistent with the mission he had been assigned. His meeting with Zoe began shortly after Michael had arrived in Ukraine and took place during his twice a month excursions to the capital.

He was at the university for one of these meetings on April 30th, 1986, when he learned that the public transportation system had been shut down. He assumed this was due to the preparations underway for the May 1 parade—Workers' Day for most of the world. It was therefore impossible to get to the train station by bus. Rumors had it that the subway station was also closed. Michael, worried about being a foreigner in those circumstances, was hesitant to travel alone, especially toward the Western regions where nationalistic aspirations irritated the Russian leaders. The Redemptorists, connected as they were to an ecclesial expression of this nationalism, constantly warned their American guests to remain aware of this political reality.

When Michael discussed his worries about travel with Zoe, she remembered that there was an empty room with a cot just across the hall from her in the international dorm. One of the English students had temporarily returned home for a family situation. Zoe assured him that no one would be checking to see if anyone was in it.

Seeing no other option, he decided to stay there. Zoe told a couple of her English friends about the situation and together they formed a plan that would allow Michael to safely move in and out of the building, use the rest room and shower, and so forth. This arrangement would end up lasting a week.

During the day, Michael walked to cafes and parks frequented by believers, trying to learn what was happening and how he might get to Ternopil.

He wrote his thoughts about this in his journal that week.

Kiev, May 7, 1986.

I first knew something strange was happening on the day after May Day. The public buses all disappeared! I heard people talking about it but of course unexplained stuff liked this happens from time to time in the good old USSR. It gives everyone an opportunity to tell more jokes about Soviet efficiency. This was something different though—the buses didn't return the next day, nor did they return the day after that.

The next evening, at the end of the 10:00 news, there was a short announcement about an accident at Chernobyl. The announcer assured us, however, that everything was under control.

Then, last night, Secretary Gorbachev ranted on national television about some sort of foreign mischief —"a mountain of lies" to use his precise words, that was stirring up irrational fears about radiation poisoning. This morning, the Ukrainian minister of health said we should not eat green vegetables or drink milk.

What the heck is going on?

I met two people today who claimed that something terrible has happened somewhere near the border with Belarus. Ilia, a believer from Prypyat, claims his entire city was evacuated and that as he was leaving the city—in one of the public buses from Kiev, by the way—he talked with a group of coal miners from the East. They had been taken to Pripyat to dig a deep tunnel near the city for some reason. Ilia said you can see a huge fire out on the outskirts of his town but that no one knows what is burning.

The other person I met was a nun, newly arrived from Sweden. She says the Swedish government has publicly claimed that a radioactive cloud has been drifting across Europe and that its origin is from somewhere inside the Soviet Union.

Whatever is happening, it isn't good; and it isn't small.

Michael would soon learn, along with the other peoples of the Soviet Union, that a nuclear power station, located a hundred and thirty kilometers from Kiev, had experienced a major meltdown. The entire area around the plant had been exposed to massive amounts of radioactivity. Plant workers had died. Those trying to contain the damage were also dying. The medical community knew that thousands more would soon die from various kind of cancer and radiation poisoning.

The centrally controlled bureaucracy of the Soviet

State, already under massive strain, was unprepared to deal with this catastrophic mishap. As a result, its leaders lurched from one desperate reaction to another. Meanwhile, the people of Ukraine were frightened, disillusioned, and angry. A growing feeling of desperation was building that would soon lead to the disillusion of the Soviet state itself. At the time though, this was nearly unthinkable. Most people were simply thinking about how to survive.

It has been said that what we call courage in the face of great odds is simply the realization that one has nothing left to lose. However, courage is only one of the ways people cope with disaster. Another way is to momentarily lose connection to what has been one's deepest values.

That is what happened to Michael.

Michael was alone, in the middle of one of the twentieth century's most frightening moments. It didn't help that he was a veteran of disaster. Since every catastrophe creates its own climate, experiencing one sort of disaster doesn't necessarily teach a person how to face another. Indeed, survivors of a disaster know that if the event itself does not kill them, the residual effects may inflict pain for decades to come. That kind of anticipated sorrow can be devastating.

Two days after writing the entry above, Michael made a pot of tea in his borrowed room and was trying to express how man-made disasters affect those who experience them. Zoe listened. Usually, she was the one spitting out passionate platitudes about injustice. That night however, it was Michael's turn.

He turned his face to the window, looked out over a partially darkened Kiev, and felt as if his own light was going out.

"Governments deny responsibility for disasters to protect the dignity of their country, or, more likely, their own dignity. Good God! What is a government if not the embodied spirit of a people? But it's always the people who suffer. They die as their trusted representatives cover their own sorry asses. Governments suppress the truth. They oppose the people who try to help the victims. They even bully the victims.

"Tell me this Zoe, what kind of evil grips a man when he gets into office? I mean, those government officials over there in Moscow were once little boys, playing with toy cars in the very same villages as the people they now ignore. How do they even sleep at night?

"This new guy—Gorbachev—the West praises him as such a reformer. Crap! Him and all his cronies in Moscow and Kiev; ain't a one of them any more enlightened than Arch Moore, the governor of my home state. West Virginia is one of our country's poorest states by the way! Governor Moore was so angry after that flood killed over a hundred people. But who was our governor mad at? Was he mad at the coal companies? Lord, No! He wasn't mad at them. He was angry at the victims who he said were bringing shame on the state of West Virginia. As though the Blessed State of West Virginia was some paragon of virtue and enlightenment!

"Crap! Crap!

"Government, church, corporations—they're all nests of narcissistic, ethically tone-death, legalized thieves. All of 'em, like Blake, talk about it in that poem about soldier's blood running down church house walls."

Michael wrote later about that night.

My rant complete, I turned my face toward the wall, spent by my own unbridled rage and shamed by the awareness that my words were incoherent and point-less. I had nothing else to hurl at the darkness.

I stood there for a while, like a boy told to sit in the corner. I stared at nothing, not because I didn't want to see anything but because I didn't want to be seen.

"Michael?"

It was Zoe's voice, softer than I had heard it before.

"Michael," she repeated. "Will you just turn around?"

More because I realized how stupid I must look facing that wall than for any other reason, I turned to face her.

I liked Zoe.

For nearly two years, we enjoyed lively debates about politics, economics, and religion and I had not overlooked the fact that she was stunningly gorgeous. I dismissed that thought every time it came to me though. I was an aspirant for monastic life, for God's sake! What I saw between her open arms that night should have made me avert my eyes.

Unfortunately, I didn't. The two top buttons of her blouse had come undone, revealing more of her than I had seen before. I did muster enough self-discipline to lift my eyes to her face. But that didn't help. Her lips were as inviting as her breasts.

It was like a volcano went off inside me. I had to have her, and I wanted her right then. I just didn't care about the consequences.

I might have found a way to move past all these feelings, but she spoke, which kept me from fleeing into my thoughts.

What she said was, "Michael, forget about all of that for now. We can't fix the government and we sure can't fix the church. We can't even figure out what all is going on out there. But we have right now and we have one another."

When she said that, I rushed toward her and kissed her.

I forgot all about Chernobyl, Gorbachev, and everything else. I didn't pause long to say anything affectionate. I didn't even make sure that she wanted me in the way I wanted her. I was just aware of my own emptiness and what I thought was her availability. At least that's what I told myself that night: that she was as worked up as I was.

God forgive me. I'm not sure any of that was true. I just know I threw away any hope of a monastic vocation and probably the ability to become a priest—just like that!

Michael wrote little (and talked even less) about Zoe. By now, perhaps, it has likely become obvious that Michael found romantic, sexual, and erotic situations challenging. That is likely the reason this journal entry you have just read is the only reference in his papers that I found about his relationship to Zoe. Had Dr. Iordanou not helped me fill in the missing pieces of the story, we would have little explanation for the decisions Michael would make over the next few months.

After discovering that Zoe Iordanou and Father Alexis Romanyuk, who had known Michael during the Ukraine years, both lived in New York, I arranged to interview them.

At the time, Ms. Iordanou was representing the Greek government at the United Nations. When I called, and explained I was doing research on the life of Michael Cooper, she responded with restrained enthusiasm. Encouraged, I told her that I needed more understanding of what had occurred between them in Ukraine that had so significantly affected Michael. She said that she would be glad to tell her story and that I would be most welcome to meet her.

I flew to New York the following month.

Fortunately, our plane got up enough speed to become airborne before running out of runway space—one can never be certain that this will occur at our unique, mountaintop Charleston airport. At the end of the runway though is a cliff, so the plane will be thrust into the air in either case. It's just not a given that it will remain in the air after that.

After the short flight, I landed at LaGuardia. I took a taxi to Turtle Bay, and walked into the United Nations building for the first time and made my way to the Delegates Dining Room, where Dr. Iordanou said she would meet me at 1:30, feeling anxious because I was running about 10 minutes late.

When I entered the restaurant, I started looking around, making it obvious to anyone who cared that I had no idea where I was or what I was doing. I was therefore relieved when I saw an olive-skinned, stylishly dressed woman walking toward me. She was wearing a rust-colored dress, covered with buttons that looked like old coins and flashed a real smile, not the sort one puts on when meeting people one feels obligated to meet. As she got closer, I saw that she had deep dimples and emerald-colored eyes.

Making her way to the table, she moved with an elegant poise that seemed to pull the energy of the room toward herself. It wasn't an erotic energy exactly; it was more about dignity, grace, style—I'm straining to find the right words. One meets beautiful women and handsome men along life's way and they often light up a room. Dr. Iordanou did that but there was something else at work. It was not merely the fact that she was beautiful but that she radiated beauty; I mean that in the classic sense: beauty as a quality that precedes and supersedes the material through which it moves. All in all, she struck me as someone who had learned through experience how to restrain the power of her personal appearance, but this restraint added nobility to an already formidable charisma.

She selected a table at the edge of the room. Once seated, she asked the waiter to bring two glasses of agiorgitiko. I smiled, pretending to know what she was talking about. I don't drink much—Missionary Baptists claim not to do that and some of us actually don't. There was no way I was going to say all of that to Dr. Iordanou though, so I worried about how I was going to drink it. Fortunately, the glass was small and after taking a sip, I discovered that agiorgitiko was some sort of wine and is rather tasty.

She held up her glass and in words graced with a mixture of British and Greek influence said, "I have looked forward to this, Mr. Canterbury. I am grateful to have an opportunity to talk about Michael with someone connected to him."

I realized then that Dr. Iordanou was waiting for me to raise my glass. I did and she gently touched her glass to mine.

"I do wish I could have met with Michael," she continued. "I had so much I wanted to say to him face-to-face.

"I wrote him once. Then I followed up with a phone call. Michael was always polite. I could just tell he had no interest in speaking with me. I'm not certain why. He responded to my letter but his response was short—mostly apologizing for some offense he imagined he had committed against me. I thought his letter revealed a lonely, troubled, and sad heart, but perhaps that was a specific response to me. I had thought a phone conversation would help because I thought I could reassure him, tell him I remembered him fondly.

"He wasn't able to hear me.

"So," she continued with a sigh, "I do hope to learn something from you today about how Michael's life unfolded. Perhaps I can bring some closure to that chapter of my life."

After the waiter had arrived with our food then walked away, Dr. Iordanou closed her eyes for a moment and made the sign of the cross.

This religious act of piety, especially because it was done in such a public place, took me by surprise. Dr. Iordanou had impressed me as a cosmopolitan, urbane woman. It made me realize, for the first time I think, how, despite my profession of faith, I had learned to associate religion, especially public acts of piety, with ignorance, poverty, and powerlessness. Even though I considered myself a Christian, I had never imagined that religious belief and practice would be compatible with the sort of world in which Dr. Zoe Iordanou lived.

"Are you a believer, Mr. Canterbury?" she asked, as though reading my mind.

"Yes, I suppose so. I go to church," I said defensively.

"Well, earlier in life," she replied, "I was at war with faith —I still don't always get along with it, actually—it's just that time and experience, or perhaps my father's prayers, eroded my defenses. I may become one of those old women who keep all the churches open—when I get old, I mean!"

I started to say "Well, you hardly qualify as an old woman," but I couldn't figure a way for that to come out right. So, I just laughed, a bit nervously, I'm afraid.

"You know," she said, "when I lived in the Soviet Union, the government would always say that though there was freedom of religion, the only ones who still went to church were the old women. But people there who knew you well enough would say, 'Yes, but these can't be the same old women that were the only ones who still went to church fifty years ago! Somehow, the Soviet Union keeps coming up with new old women!'

"Anyway, we can hardly talk about Michael without some reference to religion!

"By the way, can we use our given names and drop the formalities? Michael would have hated this 'Mr. & Mrs., Doctor so-and-so' kind of talk."

I nodded by head in agreement and grunted "sure." Inwardly though, I was reluctant to address her so informally. I didn't mind her calling me Sam but I found it difficult to call her "Zoe." I realized that years before she had been a young student in Kiev who loved Michael. I saw glimpses of that younger woman in front of me. However, in the intervening years, that woman sitting across the table from me had become someone different, someone who evoked something akin to awe. (I'm probably oversharing, as they say.)

Anyway, I took another sip of agiorgitiko.

"Michael was an innocent person," Zoe said suddenly. "In some ways, he was more like a boy than a man. I don't say that to belittle him you understand. He was handsome enough, though not overly so. He had a quick but quirky intellect. His religion was sincere but tortured. I don't know, he just grew on me until I wanted him—that's the bottom line, as you Americans like to say.

"I didn't set out to seduce him! It was nothing like that. Despite my struggle with faith during those years, I respected Michael's vocation. I knew what being a priest was about. My father, who passed away last year, was a priest in Corfu, you see. But Michael wasn't a priest yet. Besides, we were young and . . ."

(There she was, Michael's young, playful lover. Then she quickly disappeared behind the mature, professional Dr. Iordanou.)

"At first," she continued, "I just enjoyed talking with Michael. That was what our relationship was all about— talking. I loved shocking him with passionate cries about global revolution and social justice. Mostly though, I enjoyed watching him trying to avoid the obvious—that we were a young man and woman for whom all that talk about politics and economics was a cover-up for what was really going on. A couple of times, his attempts to suppress this reality made him sweat, which made me laugh. I wasn't trying to play with his emotions, I just found the fact that he seemed unaware of his own struggle with me humorous and then increasingly endearing.

"So." She sighed. "As the weeks went by, I was fighting my own feelings for Michael and during that week he was in my dorm, I could no longer deny that I had fallen in love with him. That's why I went for broke. I was imagining having a life with him.

"I had no idea he would be so eaten up with guilt afterward. I tried to talk with him about it but he was always reluctant. It's like he had no words to express normal sexual life.

"Oh, from a Christian standpoint what we did was sinful—having sex, I mean. I know that. Still, all the guilt about love-making—it rather took me by surprise.

"One time after we had made love, Michael started asking for my forgiveness. God, that made me furious! I started crying and swearing at him. That made him more miserable. So, he held me and tried to console me, which soon resulted in us making love again!

"Later, lying in bed, Michael talked to me about how living in the Carpathians had made him homesick for his birth place. He told me stories about sick people in his country—the wealthiest nation in the world—without medical care, without easy access to education, the mistrust of his people in their government, and fear of just about anyone living outside the area in which he was raised.

"Maybe you are supposed to go back," I interrupted.

"As what?" he exploded.

"As a man of God, you, silly, silly man," I replied

"Lord, Zoe! Now I'm really some man-of-God, lying here after just having committed fornication!"

"Oh, get a life, Michael," I shouted. "Grow up! If you don't want to sleep with me, then get the hell out of my bed. I'm no Delilah and you're no Samson. We are just people. Maybe we made a mistake. If we did, then go to confession and put it behind you. But stop wallowing around in guilt like some little boy who just got caught jerking off looking at a girly magazine."

"Ok." He whispered. It's not you; it's me. I am kind of messed up about love and sex—all that kind of stuff—but I don't know how to get better."

"I kissed him on his forehead, knowing I had touched some very deep, raw nerve for which he had no words to describe. I got up, dressed, and made a cup of tea. We sat down at the table and had our tea in respectful and gentle silence.

"It was a weird week. I know it all sounds rather crazy and very immature. None of that matters. I have never been able to forget it."

"So, you would characterize your relationship with Michael as an affair?" I asked.

"Well, of course it was an affair," she shot back. "He was the first man I ever loved. Yes. It was a passionate and a beautiful affair. And it could have turned out differently—very differently!"

I was taken back. I thought she was angry with me, but I quickly realized was not the case.

"Please understand," she said, "that for years, my love for Michael had no closure. It kept me from getting on with my life. I finally told the story about me and Michael only last year, in confession, though I followed that up with a therapist later."

"Would you mind telling me about that?" I asked. "I mean, the parts of it that seem appropriate to you?"

"No, I don't mind," she said. "The story makes more sense each time I tell it and that helps me.

"Alexis Romanyuk, the monastic aspirant who went with Michael to Ukraine, serves a church not far from here. Unlike Michael, Father Alexis went on to become a priest.

"As I told you, I had finally written Michael—I needed closure to that season of my life—and he responded in graciously, but guarded ... I think he believed at first that I was trying to rekindle our affair, which was not the case. I was . . . I am, I should say, happily married.

"Anyway, in his response to my letter, Michael included Father Alexis's contact information. When I saw that St. Mary's Byzantine Catholic Church was less than a mile from where I lived, I decided to call him and arrange a meeting.

"When we talked, I asked if he would hear my confession. I thought he would be a safe and helpful person to do that—he had been so closely connected to my story . . . I knew I wouldn't have to explain the background as with another person.

"I told Father Alexis that Michael and I had been terrified, that it felt like the end of the world to us that week, and that we were so young. As I went on with the confession though, it came to me that Michael and I were both already melting down that night. We were both just like that damned power plant. I was losing my faith in communism. Michael was losing faith in his call to become a monk. Probably, neither of us understood that then. In retrospect, however, it seems clear.

"Since neither of us knew what to do with ourselves or with our future. That night we felt an insatiable hunger for comfort from one another. I told you already that I am an Orthodox Christian. I am the daughter of a priest, in fact. I know full well that what we did was not right but it was what it was. I wish I had the grace to say that I am sorry about it as my faith expects me to be, but I do not yet have the grace to honestly say that."

"May I ask you what led you back to Christian faith," I asked.

"Sure," she said. "I went back to Oxford to finish my undergraduate degree later the same year Michael and I...

"Well, in my last year at Oxford, I met a wonderful priest named Father Kallistos. He helped me recover my soul, mostly by listening to me ramble on about Marx, Jacques Lacan and others I thought could lead us to a new era of human progress. What a wonderful priest he was, Father Kallistos—I would like to tell you more about him sometime. He wrote one of the few truly great books about the history of Orthodoxy you might want to read.

"Anyway, by that time, Michael was living in London. So, I called him and arranged to meet at an Indian restaurant, near Harrods. For a few weeks, Michael was connected someway to a Church of England congregation located a few blacks from there.

"Neither of us intended to continue the relationship, at least as we had experienced it in Kiev. We had brought all of that to a friendly closure before he left Ukraine. We both wanted to keep that part of things closed; though, as I think you can see, I had some hope that perhaps we might find a healthier basis for a long-term relationship.

"Well, forget all of that. It's not important.

"To get back on point, I was planning to move to the University of Vienna, where I would enter graduate studies in international law. Michael, of course, was in his final weeks with the Redemptorists. That is what we talked about. We enjoyed a mostly uneventful but respectful lunch, followed by a walk over to the church he was attending. That was the last time I saw him.

"I do think I would have been interested in having a deeper relationship with Michael. I could see that he was in love with a woman in Pittsburgh though, and that was that. We wished each other well and went our separate ways.

"In the end, Michael didn't marry that woman either, I understand. Is that right?"

I nodded my head in agreement and she shook hers with a look of amazed incomprehension.

After the meeting with Zoe Iordanou, it dawned on me that I knew things about Michael's relationship with her that even he had not known. She had been in love with him! Obsessed with his own guilt, he had not understood that this incredible woman had been interested in forming a life with him. This filled me with a deep sadness for Michael. How could he not have known that he was being offered love that most people can only dream about?

We cannot know all Michael was thinking and feeling on July 17, 1986, as he flew on that old Aeroflot plane from Kiev to Frankfort. We only know that when the plane landed, he transferred to a Lufthansa flight to London, flying on to the United Kingdom to begin his final year with the Redemptorists.

As Michael landed at Heathrow, he was surely going through the shock of reentering the Western World. He had left behind the grey, sober life of what we now know was a dying Soviet Empire. He had no idea how things would turn out for him. His writings and talks with friends reveal that he believed his short affair with Zoe had exposed his lack of vocational grace for the Catholic priesthood. Indeed, Michael had by this time concluded that for most people, lifelong vows of celibacy and poverty were unhealthy, perhaps even pathological.

Nonetheless, his life was about to unfold in ways that would lead most people who knew him to believe he had taken those vows. He had not. He neither intended to remain single nor to embrace poverty. What he intended to do now was fulfill his commitment to the Redemptorists, return to Pittsburgh, confess to Sofiya what he had done in Ukraine, and then, if she would forgive his indiscretion, settle down to a life of marriage and family.

We can be reasonably certain that these were Michael's intentions.

19

CELTIC MADNESS
SAMUEL CANTERBURY

Michael met Rev. David Kildare at a secondhand London bookstore called Cup and Chaucer. Having newly arrived from Ukraine, Michael was wearing a cassock, which encouraged the American clergyman to approach him with inquiries about his work, nationality, and so forth. This led to tea and scones, a mutually satisfying discussion about Blake, Milton, and other possible (or imagined) Celtic influences on English literature.

Kildare had just returned from a private pilgrimage to Ireland in which he had attempted to visit places traditionally related to the early Irish saints: Patrick, Colmcille, Brendan, and Brigit. After a few days in London, he intended to travel north to Scotland where he would stay a few days on the Island of Iona, the place where, as he explained, St. Colmcille had established his missionary base for converting the Scots.

As we know from both Michael's later notes and interviews with Rev. Kildare, the conversation at the Cup and Chaucer included musings on the Glastonbury legends, which, in turn led to Blake's beloved poem and the hymn based on it. They were soon singing it together, a bit louder than what pleased the reserved proprietor.

> *And did those feet in ancient time*
> *Walk upon England's mountains green:*
> *And was the holy Lamb of God,*
> *On England's pleasant pastures seen!*

By the time they had gotten to "built Jerusalem in England's green & pleasant land," the two sounded like two drunks in an Irish pub.

In David Kildare, Michael had found a kindred soul, a lover of literature, a mystic, and a fellow Appalachian. At the time, Kildare pastored a church in Raleigh but was originally from Asheville, deep in the Appalachians. The two exchanged addresses and promised to stay in touch. Before leaving the store, Kildare pressed three books into Michael's hands: *Saving the Appearances*, by Owen Barfield; *St. Patrick's Confessions*; and *Reflections on Patrick's Lorica*, by Fr. Abbán Rúadhnait.

Meeting Kildare was momentous for Michael, who would thereafter root himself in what he came to believe were the ways of ancient Celtic Christians. This shift would lead to his decision not to take permanent vows in the Redemptorist order nor seek ordination in the Byzantine Catholic tradition. However, these changes of religious conviction also allowed Michael to join the two great spiritual currents of his life, bringing him a measure of peace from the religious tensions he had experienced during his previous years.

Sometime during his stay in the United Kingdom, Michael visited Glastonbury. He also spent three days in Keble College, Oxford for a three-way discussion between Byzantine Catholics, Anglicans, and Eastern Orthodox theologians. Michael was not an official participant—he lacked that level of theological sophistication—but he did take copious notes. Some of the comments made by Anglicans led him to believe that ancient Celtic Christianity had maintained living links with Egyptian and Syrian monks and had expressed a more Eastern form of the faith than that of other Western Christians.

We will leave to scholars to debate whether any of these things are true. What is important for us is that Michael found these emerging convictions electrifying. For the first time since leaving West Virginia, Michael began to think about returning to Appalachia. It is unlikely he expressed those sentiments to his fellow Redemptorists. He dropped hints in his letters to Sofiya though about his changing views and, in his correspondence with Kildare, stated those same views clearly and passionately. Some sort of page had turned in his mind about life and faith, which he had somehow linked to his understanding of ancient Celtic Christianity.

Several months later, Michael boarded the plane for Philadelphia. From there, he would fly on to Pittsburgh and began walking the path that would lead him to become Brother Michael, the Miracle Worker of Mingo County.

___

A CALL FROM HOME

On April 5, 1988, after being in Pittsburgh for less than a month, Michael Cooper received a letter from his Grandmomma Mullins. In this letter, the elderly woman expresses, in shaky, sometimes difficult to read handwriting, her affection for him. She says that she hopes to see him before her death and then, before she concludes the letter, shares a bit of news from home.

"I know you were fond of Inida Goins," Grandmomma Mullins writes. "I'm sorry to tell you she died last week from a drug overdose. She had been living for a couple of years with her mother and stepfather, in Sister Goins' old place, over yonder in Knoxville, Tennessee with that Indian character she took off with several years ago. He left her though. She had a sweet little boy, named Mickey. He has hair as red as you ever saw! I do think Inida tried to be a good mother to the boy. The drugs just got to her and the poor thing had gotten too broke down to resist. The Good Lord is merciful, and we know He will treat her kindly.

"Your Granddaddy did the service. Lots of people were there you would remember.

"I worry so much about our kids down here in Mingo County. They seem to have little to do other than listen to rock music, commit fornication, and take dope. I pray about that all the time. And now I worry about Inida's son, left all alone in the world with no one to care for him, poor thing!"

That night, Michael dreamed about a red headed young teenager calling for help. Michael would wake up in a sweat, only to fall back asleep to see that same face and hear that same voice. During the moments he was awake, he would pray for Inida's soul.

His prayers were deepened by his sense of guilt over the indifference he had felt for her during his years of absence from the mountains. He felt too a piercing regret for his banishment of her memory from his thoughts. His awareness of these internal realities provoked that peculiar form of homesickness that often afflicts mountain people living away from their land. He had often laughed about this affliction and denied its effect on him. That night he no longer laughed.

All these things are clear from his notes, made at the time and in the months later, about his return to West Virginia. He had gone for an interview at the Catholic high school where he had taught before leaving for Ukraine. His prospects for working there looked good for the fall but he needed to find work to sustain himself until then. He had been staying at St Paul of the Cross monastery since arriving from Ukraine but felt guilty about taking advantage of the monks' hospitality since he no longer believed he would be entering monastic life or even the Catholic priesthood.

Remembering Sofiya's reluctance to marry a priest, he had reason to hope that she would find this news to her liking. There was of course the matter of his affair with Zoe, which he had not yet revealed to Sofiya. On the Friday night after receiving his grandmother's letter, Michael and Sofiya went to dinner at Rennes, a new

Italian restaurant in East McKeesport. Afterward, they went to her apartment, where Michael talked both of marriage and of the events in Ukraine.

To his surprise, Sofiya did not seem exceptionally troubled by Michael's confession. She was kind and expressed her unreserved forgiveness. She was not, however, any more prepared to marry him than she had been three years before. Her response left him numb, knowing now for certain what he had long suspected.

Sofiya would never be his wife.

Over the next couple of weeks, it became increasingly apparent that the threads connecting him to life in Pittsburgh had unraveled. In the meantime, his longing for the home he had tried so hard to forget grew increasingly unbearable. Somewhere during those days, he decided to do what had once seemed unthinkable: he would return to Mingo County. In retrospect, it is possible to believe that this decision had been forming for some time. To his friends however, and apparently to himself, it came as a shock.

Michael knew he had one more piece of business to conclude though: he needed to see Father Maximus.

20

CONFESSION
SAMUEL CANTERBURY

M ichael wrote once in a letter that it can be difficult to explain the joy of confession to a person who has never confessed.

"It is not like people think," he said, "that someone with power to dispense or withhold grace stands between a naked soul and God. Confession is simply the movement of grace, the realization that one's personal transformation has begun."

Michael wanted to confess because he had, more than most, suffered from a damaged conscience. Overpowered early in life by well-meaning but toxic notions about ordinary human existence, puberty had expelled him from Eden and placed flaming swords to block his return. His tenuous adulthood thus had been hard earned and painstakingly maintained. Burdened by both real and imagined faults, confession offered Michael an assurance that he was beloved and welcomed by God and humanity, just as he was.

This was the reason Michael arranged to meet the

trusted old priest in a chapel made sacred not only by ecclesial usage but by his own previous encounters there with grace.

Entering the seminary chapel, Michael noticed that the old man standing in the front had grown visibly frail. It saddened him to know that the things he had come to confess would add more weight to those already stooped shoulders.

As in times past, Father Maximus stood before one of the two chairs in front of the iconostasis. The priest opened his arms to welcome the approaching penitent. Michael eagerly stepped into the embrace. The men expressed their joy for seeing the other and then sat down, entering, or so they believed, the Divine Presence that had moved to envelop them.

"Bring us out of prison that we may give thanks unto your name," Father Maximus began, reading from the small, tattered, leather book in his hand.

"My brother," Father Maximus said, "who may bring a charge against God's elect, since it is God who bids us come? Come boldly then to the throne of grace and make your petition known."

"I didn't waste any time," Michael wrote a few days later.

"I told Father Maximus about my affair with Zoe and why I had decided to not take final vows. I poured it all out—that I would not be entering the Redemptorist order, that I was returning to my mountain home, and that I was not priestly material.

"Father," I said. "I know that you believed in me and I truly do want to serve God. Unfortunately, I don't seem to have what it takes to serve God at that level. I'm so sorry to disappoint you."

Father Maximus was silent for the longest time. When he spoke, his voice was weaker than I remembered.

"Oh Michael." Father Maximus chuckled. "You are like a mule I heard about once that turned wild so that no one could get near it. One day, a new worker came to the farm who began setting out hay and water for the wild mule. After many months, as the worker was setting out hay one morning, he felt the mule nuzzling his sleeve. Naturally, the worker turned to touch the mule. However, the animal bolted at his touch. It didn't go far, just far enough to watch the worker from a distance. The wounded beast couldn't bring himself to trust the one who was feeding him."

I understood the metaphor and felt ashamed, not only of my sin but of my inability to accept assurances of forgiveness.

"I don't know how to change, Father," I said. "I have never really viewed God as loving or accepting."

"Well," Father Maximus replied, "you certainly don't change from obsessing over depravity and shamefulness. That only produces sorrow and despair; it is not real repentance. Wallowing around like that is nothing more than self-pity, the result of being disappointed in being a mortal.

"Real repentance—the Bible uses the word *metanoia* —as you know, describes a transformed mind. And that, my son, is something a human being cannot produce. A transformed mind must come to us as a gift. And that, dear Michael, requires someone willing to accept a gift instead of continually wallowing in melodramatic guilt!

"Now, how about talking to me about a few positive things that occurred on your trip?" he said.

I told Father Maximus about my discovery of St. Patrick and the early Irish Christians.

"Aha!" Father Maximus said. "Blessed Patrick understood something few church leaders know about now—the nature of the stoicheia—the network of ideas and values underneath our communities and nations—I think the English translation for it is 'elementary powers.' Anyway, St. Patrick understood that the stoicheia can become evil. When that happens, a community requires exorcism. That's what Patrick did in ancient Ireland. Unfortunately, you're about to learn this first hand!"

Turning around, Father Maximus opened an old metal box lying beside his chair.

"I'm going to give you something, Michael," he said as he opened the box.

As he pulled a leather strap from the box, I could see that attached to it was a very old, silver cross. Typical of Eastern Catholic or Orthodox design, it had the small bar at the top, upon which had been hung Pilate's mocking inscription "Jesus, King of the Jews," and on the bottom the bar to which Christ's feet had been nailed.

I was suddenly aware of the smell of incense, which having been so often burned in the chapel during worship had left a faint but always perceptible scent in the room. The smell had suddenly intensified. I turned to see who was burning it, put off by the fact that someone would interrupt our intimate, sacramental moment. Not seeing who it was, I turned back to give Father Maximus my attention.

He was now standing above me.

"Vasyl Velychkovsky blessed this cross," he said. "For years, before giving it to me, he wore it himself. Many people—and I am one of them—believe he was a saint. Anyway, when he gave this cross to me, he said that when I grew old, God would show me someone to whom I should give it. I had already decided you were the one before you left for Ukraine. I nearly gave it to you then. The moment was just not quite right. Now it is.

"I don't understand the road you have begun to walk, Michael. I have tried, but your path is now hidden from me. That means I have guided you as far as I can. I do know your journey will be arduous. You will face peril on every side in the work you are about to do. In times of danger, this cross will remind you that our Lord, his saints, and the holy angels are with you, helping you in the task you have been given."

"I don't know what you are saying, Father!" I protested. "I don't have any mission."

Smiling soberly, he lowered the cross over my head, motioned for me to stand, and then kissed me on both cheeks.

"We will not see one another on this earth again. Just know that I will pray for you every day and when, God willing, I graduate to that place where prayer is unceasing and unhindered, I will pray for you there. Now, my son, go in peace—until in God's own time we are reunited."

21

GOING HOME
SAMUEL CANTERBURY

A week later, Michael rode on a bus with a youth group from Holy Spirit Parish headed to a retreat just outside of Beckley, West Virginia. The driver made a stop in town at the bus station before going on to the retreat. After saying his goodbyes there, Michael loaded two suitcases, one full of clothes, the other one containing journals and books, on a Greyhound Bus bound for Logan.

Billy Joe Jerrell was waiting at the Logan terminal.

When Michael got off the bus, Billy Joe punched him affectionately on the shoulder.

"You ornery son of a gun!" he said. "You ain't hardly changed a bit!"

Michael grinned and went to pull his suitcases from the luggage holder under the bus and put them in the bed of Billy Joe's '98 Chevy pickup truck. From there, country roads took him home. Wordless memories filled the space between him and Billy Joe as they made their way to a world he had nearly forgotten.

Arriving in Verner, Michael embraced the tearful but speechless Lila Goins. He then walked into the same trailer he had fled so many years before. His first night home thus began as most seasons do, in darkness and solitude. The first day was spent in the metal cocoon that would shield him from the world as he worked his way through madness toward the yet unrevealed light.

Billy Joe, who saw Michael nearly every day during that time, recalls those two years fondly.

"When Michael first called from Pittsburgh t' tell us he wanted to move back to Mingo County, I was right happy about it," Billy Joe said.

"I always thought well of Michael. Of course, Lila always cared for 'im, 'specially now on account of him meanin' so much to Inida. Michael asked if we still had the old trailer out back because he wanted to use it for a few weeks. He wasn't sure his old house on his family property was good enough for him to live in. I agreed because I had been by there a few weeks before and didn't think it was much to count. Anyway, our trailer was still here. We'd kept it closed up all right 'gainst the elements, which is about all I could say for it. I told Michael it would need a lot of work but that he was right welcome to use it."

Collecting his thoughts as he scratched his head, Billy Joe continued.

"A few days after he got here, he went and seen for hisself that the old house over at his place wasn't in good enough shape to use. That's how Michael ended up living in the trailer for right near two years.

"Lookin' back, I don't know what I would have done

without him. He worked like a dog. I can't do much of anything anymore you know, arthritis and such.

"But Michael repaired our fences, mowed the grass, painted the house—I can't tell you all he done. I can tell you it wasn't long before this old place looked kept and presentable. And I couldn't believe what he did to that old trailer. He cleaned it up, covered the walls with some thin wood paneling he found in his Granddaddy's shed, put up a few religious pictures and such. When he got done with it, well, it felt like you were walking into someplace real nice. He made it a bit spooky-feeling, but not in a bad way, if you know what I mean.

"Every morning before daybreak, he did his prayers. I know that because I could see the little light from his candles. If I went down there during that time I would hear 'im singin' 'is prayers. I asked him about it and he explained he was a singin' Psalms from the Bible— I never heard the likes of anything like that 'round here. He burnt incense too. You could smell it clean out here in the yard.

"Tell you the truth, I liked goin' down there to listen to him singin' his prayers. Course, he didn't know I was there outside. Hearin' him sing that a way calmed my nerves for the whole day."

"There was some weird stuff too," Billy Joe continued.

"I could see that in some ways Michael just wasn't normal. Like, a while after bein' back in Verner, the way he hurt his hands. He hurt 'em real bad. I thought he done it on the old barbwire fence out back he had been helpin' me take down. But even though his hands were bleedin' considerably, he wouldn't go to the doctor. That was probably on account of him not havin' money for a doctor. Anyway, Lila made him put salve on his hands and wrapped them up in some clean pieces of an old pillowcase she ripped up.. She said Michael's hands were bleedin' pretty bad when she did it.

"He got some better bandages after a few days. A few weeks later though, when I saw that he still had the bandages on his hands, I asked him about it.

"'Michael,' I said, "ain't your hands got no better?'"

'They're okay," he said. "Don't worry about it."

"When I asked him about it again later, he told me he didn't want to talk no more about it. He seemed right embarrassed about his hands. It was the darndest thing. I never made no sense of it.

"Right before that, he had gone on for some weeks without eatin' anything. I know he wasn't eatin' 'cause even though he loved Lila's cornbread and came over to eat it with Mickey a couple times a week, he didn't come over none during that time. He got real thin too! It worried me but I didn't say nothing. I think that's how he hurt his hands. He ripped open his hands on something because he got too wore out to pay attention to what he was doing. That's probably why he got so embarrassed about hurtin' hisself.

"After he hurt his hands though, he started eatin'. He just never took off the bandages. I never saw him without his hands all wrapped up after that.

"Isn't that kind of crazy?

"You know something else what's strange?" Billy Joe continued. "Michael didn't drink none after he came back from Pittsburgh. Funny thing was, he didn't mind others a drinkin'. Round here, religious people give you Hell for havin' a beer. Get's on my nerves! But when my friends came over for a few beers, Michael would join right in. He told stories and old jokes and such. He just wouldn't drink. One night, Brady Mullins, Michael's second cousin, asked him what had happened, seein' that before he left for Pittsburgh he would sometimes put back a beer or two. Michael didn't get mad at Brady. He just laughed.

"'Well, gentlemen,' he said, 'I misused this particular gift of God's good creation. Unfortunately, that's not the only one I have misused. So, I won't join in with you that way. But I ain't no party pooper. Y'all just help yourself; it doesn't bother me none.'

"Michael didn't judge nobody but himself. He was awfully tough on himself.

"Like I said, he acted kind of crazy sometimes. But he wasn't really crazy. No sir! For instance, he had a real knack for helpin' people who were sad or upset. Take Lila for instance.

"She wasn't ever right after Inida died. For the longest time, she didn't even talk. I mean, she wouldn't say nothing. She didn't have anybody around here that cared for her much after her mom died. People said some awful things about her years ago and never took them back. She took all that in stride. But when Inida was gone . . . Well, that might neigh did her in.

"The night Michael came back from Pittsburgh, Lila hugged him and cried. She might have called his name— I forget . . . I believe she did. But she wouldn't talk, even then. Michael would sit with her for two or three hours at a time though, out there on the porch. He would tell her old stories from his childhood and things about his trip overseas. She listened but wouldn't say nothing back. Then one morning, Michael told me that he wanted to take Lila to the graveyard to visit Inida's grave. I didn't think she would go, but when Michael asked her she just followed him right on out to the car.

"They were gone for right some time.

"When they came back, I saw that Lila had been a cryin' but I didn't ask any questions. She went on to bed early that night. Then, the next morning, she came into where I was sitting and asked if I wanted some coffee. I could hardly believe it, but I acted like that was the most normal thing in the world. I told her I would love a cup. Well sir, she fixed me that coffee, poured some for herself, and then remarked about how it looked like we would have an early fall. She acted like it was perfectly normal for her to talk, even though she had not said more than a dozen words for over two years.

"Lila never talked as much as she had before Inida died. But after that day with Michael, she talked with me almost every day.

"Once, I asked her what had happened out there at the graveyard. She walked over to where I was, kissed me on the head, and smiled. I knew then she would never tell me. But that was all right. She had found herself and we had several more good years together.

"Now one thing special about Michael," Billy Joe suddenly added, "was his effect on Inida's boy Mickey. Michael would light up like a Christmas tree around him.

Mickey was already getting to be a teenager, when most boys don't show much respect for older people. It didn't matter: Mickey loved Michael and Michael felt that same way about him. I sometimes watched them working together cutting grass and they would look like that had been together their whole life. That was a wonderful thing."

Six months after his return to Mingo County, Michael finally expressed some of his own thoughts about returning home.

————

M.J. COOPER

Coming back to Mingo County has been a strange delight. I had imagined Mingo County might have changed and of course it has, at least somewhat. What I didn't realize is that the man who returned to Mingo County was not the same person as the boy who left it. I have all that boy's memories, but neither my physical nor my inner eyes see quite the same things that he did.

The day I left for Pittsburgh, I thought I was escaping the world of my childhood, leaving behind the craziness and tragedies of the mountains. The truth is, no one ever escapes their past. The past must be welcomed into a bigger and more informed world. If we don't do that, the past metastasizes into bitter repressed memories or perhaps even worse, decays into the sweet-smelling putrefaction we call nostalgia.

In Pittsburgh and Ukraine, I discovered that I could

neither repress nor sentimentalize my past. Nor could I escape my own self. During those years, I tried on a half a dozen selves I created from my fantasies: I was by times an anarchist, an impassioned Mountain Man standing up for a unique and noble culture against unappreciating snobs, a suitor wanting to settle down with the love of his life and make family—each of these masks, that is what the word 'person' originally meant after all—was false only in the sense that it disclosed merely a glimpse of the unique human being behind it. I wore those masks because I had not yet formed a face.

In his greatest novel, C.S. Lewis asked, "How can we see God face-to-face until we have faces?"

How indeed? Did I have a face? Was I yet a person, able to see and be seen by other persons? Was I ready to face the world with my real face instead of peering out through the mask I had made to hide my face?

These are not only important questions but, or so it seems to me, among the most important things of one's life.

So it was not nostalgia that pushed me back to Mingo County. I knew full well the spirits of the mountain cannot be overcome by mere men. Mountain life consists of bursts of joy among crushing defeats. It ends with one's ultimate surrender. I do think I returned home to make a difference, but I had no illusions about exorcising the darkness from the mountains. I hardly dared believe I could cast out the darkness within myself.

What I knew was that I had used Zoe and made myself unworthy of Sofiyia. Sofiya had been kind, but she wasn't going to marry a would-be man of God who took advantage of women supposedly in his spiritual care.

Then there was Inida. I had used her as a sedative, a way to calm myself from trauma. I then pushed down all my memories of her in a bitter forgiveness I could not bring myself to acknowledge. But even after all these years, Inida is to me like the sheer force of nature. The memories of my times with her have haunted my nights. God knows that is true.

My penitence for having misused these women is this life without companionship. I can at least hope to not inflict my physical desires on another innocent woman as I pray for the ones I have misused.

For the first few months after returning to Mingo County, I did what I knew to do: I sang the Psalms each morning and evening. I worked with my hands to bring order and beauty into the world around me. I tried to bless my friends with a joyful countenance and acts of service. Then, on Ash Wednesday that first year home, I began the Lenten fast in hopes of "cleansing the doors of my perception" as Blake put it.

Each day of Lent, I began by praying Saint Patrick's Lorca, "I arise this day with a mighty power." I would then give thanks for the glass of water I drank, and start my work day. I did the various chores I had set out for myself, stopping only to recite various portions of Patrick's prayer, such as "I am made strong by the hardness of rock," or "I am made strong by the fierceness of wind." Other phrases from that prayer would spring to mind as I encountered various elements, plants, and animals throughout the day.

On the third Tuesday of Lent, shortly before dawn, I was on the back acres of the Goins' property when I fell to my knees, crying out the words "Christ above me, Christ beneath me, Christ on my right hand, Christ on my left," and so on. Suddenly, I was seized by a great force so that the natural world faded away. Finally, I saw nothing except for a blinding light. Soon, the light formed into strange shapes—circles and spirals, multi-colored paisley-looking images moving in slow hypnotic patterns.

That's when I first felt the pain in my hands.

At first, I thought I had gone blind. Afraid to make my way back to the trailer because of the danger of falling from the cliffs should I take the wrong path, I decided to just sit there praying and waiting for whatever God had in store for me. Then, gradually I realized that my vision was returning. It was nearly noon before I started walking back to the trailer, still not understanding what had just occurred.

I thought that perhaps I had experienced some sort of stroke or seizure and, upon falling, had tried to brace my fall by holding out my hands. "They must have been cut on sharp rocks," I thought. Whatever happened, my hands were killing me. I also felt disoriented and alone.

That night is when the terrible nightmares began that would last nearly a month. I dreamed of floods, explosions, and trials in which I was convicted for unknown crimes by unknown people. Sometimes, I dreamed I was walking to my execution, only to awaken, trembling, and covered in sweat.

The nightmares ended the week before Pentecost. In

the last one, I dreamed I had been tied to a tree and left alone. A great serpent was coming toward me with its huge mouth open. It stopped just inches from my face when it heard what I also was hearing—the strumming of a mandolin and an old man's voice croaking, "I've anchored my soul in the haven of rest."

That next morning, I awoke from that dream and I shouted out the words, "I arise this day with a mighty power!" And, finally, it was so.

I had found that haven my Granddaddy had sang about. I had peace at the center of my soul and was no longer afraid—of anything.

I also knew I was not supposed to remain secluded from life, obsessed by my own brokenness. I was called to descend from the mountain and make a difference in the part of the world I had been placed in.

I knew I was no St. Patrick, but then again, neither was he—at least at first. Patrick was a humble, marginally-educated man who just decided to bless the difficult environment he had been brutally dragged into.

I didn't yet know what I would do or how I would do it. I just knew I was called to leave this place of retreat and plunge into life. And so, that's what I did.

22

HOUSES OF HEALING
SAMUEL CANTERBURY

Two and a half years after his return to West Virginia, Michael combined funds from the sale of his family property in Verner with gifts from two unknown donors and bought twelve acres just outside of Man, on which were an old farmhouse and a barn. That is where he founded St. Patrick's Healing House.

He and a group of friends from various twelve-step groups around the area began working to convert the barn into a chapel. They used the house as a meeting place for recovery groups. He moved into three rooms on the first floor of that house and converted two of the upstairs rooms into a library. The kitchen-dining area was remodeled to host groups of 20-30 people.

Michael began leading discussion groups about scripture, catechism, and life skills such as financial management. He also arranged for GED instruction and college prep information. These groups resulted in perhaps as many as a hundred people from the Buffalo

Creek communities obtaining high school diploma equivalents, and dozens of others entering distance-learning college courses over the next five years.

One of the most interesting things about St. Patrick's was the chapel. Michael had enlisted folk artists from the area to paint the walls with biblical characters as they perceived them. The only thing he personally insisted on was that they place an inscription above the entrance: *I Arise Today With A Mighty Power*. On one side of this phrase was a wild goose, and on the other, a woven-like scrollwork in the form of a triangle. At the front of the chapel, just behind the altar, was a painting of a lamb carrying a banner over its shoulder upon which was a cross.

The launch of St. Patrick's Healing House, by a person who seemed to come out of nowhere, was more mysterious to the people of Man and the Buffalo Creek communities than it would have otherwise appeared, simply because its founder was a native of the area. Had he been an outsider, the center would have been ignored by most people for several years until it either closed or its founder had passed the unofficial initiation process required for inclusion in the life of the community. However, the fact that this rehab/educational center, which was somehow loosely connected to a church and was led by a survivor of the flood of '73, left the people of the area to believe they might cautiously trust the intentions of both the center and its founder.

Early participants added to this confidence by sharing their stories of care and healing with others. People began to realize that no story was too shameful, nor any addiction too entrenched to keep the suffering away from this new source of hope.

From the beginning of his mission, Michael made it clear that he had no patience with the fierce anti-intellectualism common to mountain religion. At the same time, he would react furiously against caricatures of the area's indigenous spiritual life.

Once, according to one of the people who attended AA meetings at St. Patrick's, a pastor of a 'respectable' denomination decided to poke some fun at one of the Buffalo Creek Communities.

"Maybe instead of meeting down here each week to commiserate about our dysfunctional lives, we should just go up to that Holy Roller meeting in Riley and get zapped by that preacher woman!" the clergyman said with a laugh.

"It wouldn't hurt you any, Roy," Michael retorted. "I don't know a single soul up there in that church that doesn't have enough sense to stay away from the titty bars over in Logan that you find so fascinating! Maybe you could learn something about humility and chastity from those folks that you enjoy callin' holy rollers! Besides, I don't see how fallin' down and shoutin' out for God's help hurts anybody any, and I don't know why goin' to your boring church would be much of an improvement!"

Even though Michael had no patience with any sort of religious class system and always defended the area's folk religion, he nonetheless emphasized the importance of getting a good education and developing one's social skills.

"Last thing poor people need around here is more ignorance or any more ugly," he often said. "I can't see how not knowing anything about biology, history, or literature ever helped anybody become holy."

Michael became known for healing people. That is not so exceptional, of course. Indeed, in southern West Virginia it would have seemed strange for a Christian leader not to pray for the sick. He personally met with a constant stream of individuals who came for prayer and sent anointed pieces of cloth to those who couldn't get to him. In the meantime, he discovered which doctors, dentists, and other medical workers were willing to work on a sliding scale for those without adequate resources. After praying for someone, he would often send them to these medical practitioners.

As the years went by, Michael was spending hours of each day praying and counseling with needy people. Some began to tell stories about how much they had been helped, and so word began to spread about how Michael's prayers were effective, perhaps even miraculous.

Michael's protests against these rumors added to the growing mystique because people began to say that Brother Michael not only possessed supernatural powers but was humble, like Jesus. Michael deliberately resisted these attempts to build up his ministry around personal charisma or reports of supernatural powers.

When leading prayer or communion, Michael followed a revised liturgy, like those used by Episcopalians and Lutherans. However, if the worshippers decided to sing the sorts of songs familiar to mountain people, Michael not only allowed it but usually joined in. If the singing went on a while, or if people got a bit enthusiastic, he never seemed to mind. If the services went on longer than he had planned, he just let it go. Worship services would last as long as they lasted; those who didn't want to stay could excuse themselves whenever they pleased.

Unfortunately, his growing reputation for healing and other supposedly supernatural phenomena did nothing to endear him to other religious leaders. Both those from traditional denominations and those from the innumerable sects and independent churches throughout Southern West Virginia became increasingly suspicious. Some began saying he was a charlatan, others that he was creating a cult, yet others that he was some sort of Catholic secret agent.

Although he rarely talked about it, Michael carried an ordination of a small but legally recognized denomination: The Charismatic Orthodox Church of North America. Sometime during the two years he had lived on the Goins' property, Michael had been ordained first a deacon and then a priest in this offshoot of the Episcopal Church. It was, incidentally, the same group to which Rev. David Kildare belonged. Unfortunately, I found the leaders of this group reluctant to talk about Michael. The infamous *Star* article had something to do with this evidently—the church leaders I talked with certainly found that article embarrassing—though as far as I could see, the article did not mention the group.

Kildare, who moved to Atlanta, Georgia sometime after Michael's passing, was friendly and helpful but he offered little information about the group itself. It felt to me that like Michael, Kildare viewed his denomination more as a support system, as a tangible connection to the broader Christian world, than as any sort of spiritual home. At any rate, from what I have been able to gather, Kildare and Michael were anomalies in the group that ordained them; mystics in a denomination largely populated by Anglophiles who admire order, reason, and pageantry far more than transcendent experience or the journey toward personal sanctification.

Nevertheless, Michael took his membership in the group seriously and sometimes expressed his gratitude for the bishops and other priests of this small denomination that had made a place for him.

Despite the denominational affiliation though, this man, whom people around Buffalo Creek increasingly called "Brother Michael," seemed destined to not fully fit in anywhere. Furthermore, the media was about to make it even more difficult for him to feel at home, even in these mountains where his ancestors had settled before the American Revolution.

23
MAD DOG
SAMUEL CANTERBURY

James Earl Callahan, the Logan County sheriff, was born in 1950, in Delbarton, a tiny town in Mingo County. He attended Burch Middle School. Halfway through the eleventh grade, he was suspended for breaking a classmate's arm with a tire iron. He never bothered to return.

This event was something of a watershed in Callahan's life because he would have done the boy he had bullied even more damage had the coach not intervened. Callahan had not submitted peacefully, however. Indeed, he had swung at the coach, swearing about how he would "fight his way through the whole damned faculty" if necessary.

The coach had responded by putting Callahan in a chokehold while yelling, "Boy, if you're gonna act like a mad dog, I'll be obliged to treat you like one!"

After Callahan had calmed down, the coach said, "Now, why don't you take two weeks off, Callahan? You can use that time to think about how to control yourself."

Callahan then swaggered off the field, proud now of the nickname that would follow him on to Vietnam and then to the jobs he had with the Mingo, Wyoming, and Logan County police departments after his discharge. Later, when he ran for Logan County sheriff, the posters and local television all carried the slogan, "MAD DOG CALLAHAN: FIGHTING FOR LAW AND ORDER IN LOGAN COUNTY."

Like most people in Logan County, the sheriff didn't feel any need to pay much attention to Michael Cooper, at least at first. Mountain towns are full of preachers, healers, and prophets who huff and puff in churches made up of a handful of neighbors and relatives. Their stream-of-consciousness word salad draws upon Bible stories, local situations, real and imagined issues and events, and personal experiences of life to weave their tiny congregations into shared states of terrorized euphoria.

These preachers can be amusing or boring, but the best ones are master story tellers with a shamanistic skill that fascinates the listeners. Listeners who rarely expect anything like what people outside the region would think of as information. The sheriff lacked the ability to articulate such a depiction of mountain preaching; nonetheless, he understood the general concept.

The last book of the Bible contains a line that says, "Blessed is he who hears and understands," and then goes on to mystify and perplex. Many readers, far from dismissing the book as something beyond comprehension, delve deeper into the text, experiencing the awe and wonder of word intoxication without anything resembling rational explanation.

Two thousand years of reading has resulted in neither an agreed upon interpretation nor a dismissal of the book's significance. Even the likes of D. H. Lawrence have tried their hand at wrestling rational significance out of the tapestry of its sacred images.

That's what listening to mountain preaching is like. It doesn't make sense, but it moves you all the same. It is an art form whose words point to something different than the sermons of other traditions.

As far as Mad Dog Callahan was concerned, Michael Cooper was simply one of these mountain men, possessed of a type of madness that should be respected but not taken seriously. For his part, the sheriff also represented a long and unique Appalachian tradition— jurisprudence and law enforcement as artful performance, full of passionate declarations about justice and peace not intended for literal interpretation.

Accordingly, the sheriff forgave all the drunk drivers, turned a blind eye to moonshiners and meth makers, and never stuck his nose into issues of domestic violence; but, by God, he intended to keep the peace. He had campaigned on the slogan 'Law and order for Logan County,' and was determined to maintain the order he had inherited with the full force of the law he represented.

When Callahan discovered that Michael had gone over his head in the Gerald Humphries case, he hit the roof.

Humphries was a buddy from back in Delbarton and had given the sheriff a generous cut of his various cash-only businesses. Callahan was convinced, indeed had formed his opinion on the solid, respectable word of Humphries himself, that the man's poor niece was "a frustrated nymphomaniac." She had, the sheriff said at the diner, "seduced half of her ninth-grade class and was, believe me, no model of chastity, if you know what I mean."

"Humphries niece," the sheriff said when Michael confronted him with the evidence, "was a pathological liar.

"She bruised herself on purpose and then got an abortion to cover up her roll in the hay with God knows which high school football player. She then blamed her poor uncle, biting the hand that fed her!"

Callahan had taken the signed reports Michael and this niece had filled out "for his files" and assumed that would be the end of the matter. That would have been the case had Michael been any other preacher in Logan County.

Unfortunately for Callahan, Michael had lost his fear of snakes years before. That's why, on his way back to Man, Michael mailed copies of the reports to the Hiding Place, an abuse shelter in Charleston. He attached a note with the reports to Wynonna Grisham, the shelter's director, asking for her advice about how to secure justice for a fifteen-year-old incest victim who had come to him for help. The day Michael's letter arrived, Grisham was on her way to lunch with Jeffries Hardt, FBI, assigned at the time to investigate systemic government corruption in the southern counties of West Virginia.

The following Monday, Sheriff Mad Dog Callahan, defender of law and order in Logan County, received a routine, friendly inquiry from the bureau, asking if he had any information on one Gerald Humphries, who had been accused in 'an anonymous tip,' of abuse of minors. Callahan assured agent Hardt that although there had been rumors, he had determined there was nothing substantive to investigate and had therefore not felt the need to create a formal file about the matter.

"Now should the bureau wish to forward any concrete information, well by God the FBI can count on the full cooperation with the Logan County Sheriff's office!" Callahan said.

That was how Sheriff Callahan determined Michael Cooper was a threat to the order and peace of Logan County. It was one thing to warn people about hell, hold a lit torch under one's face, or prance around the front of a church with a rattlesnake. It was another thing altogether to question the judgement of the county sheriff, especially based on the word of a simple-minded girl barely out of puberty.

As the battered women, drug addicts, and other marginal miscreants continued making their way to St. Patrick's Healing House, the accusations against the sheriff's golfing buddies and fellow country club members increased. Callahan—realizing that a simple "bless your heart," followed by a quick spit of tobacco juice, would not put an end to the complaints—grew increasingly anxious.

The sheriff was clever and crafty, but he was not wise or even intelligent. When confronted by a person without fear or someone with a measure of understanding about how to advance a rival narrative, he began to brood about how to rid himself of the unsettling new voice disrupting his domain, as he knew no other way to address the threat.

It would not be long before the sheriff would have some surprising allies in this quest.

24

BROTHER MICHAEL, MIRACLE WORKER

SAMUEL CANTERBURY

In February 1987, *The Speculator*, a supermarket tabloid, ran a front-page article that would soon generate serious controversy for Michael and his ministry to Southern West Virginia.

The headline read:

MINGO COUNTY MIRACLE WORKER

Supernatural Phenomena Surround Mystery Priest Deep in Appalachian Coal Country

The writer was William Thomas Terrell, author of several articles about alien artifacts at Roswell, scientific breakthroughs that will lead to human immortality, and other similarly sensational topics.

The Mingo Miracle Worker article consisted of interviews with people from Buffalo Creek who claimed to have witnessed supernatural occurrences connected to Michael Cooper.

The lead story centered on Mrs. Maple Toney, of

Kistler, West Virginia. She claimed that her two-story house had been haunted since the great flood of 1972. Alongside the text was a picture of her house, complete with ominous shadows of tree limbs etched into its white wooden face. Superimposed on this picture was one of Michael Cooper, hair and beard flying in the wind, eyes flashing like someone possessed.

The picture, I discovered, was a gag. One of the members of a twelve-step group had asked Michael to pose for a picture. Michael responded at first by striking this crazy posture and only later allowing the man to take a legit picture. The crazy one though was hung on the wall at the center, where countless people saw it over several months, knowing that it was intended to poke well-meaning fun at the founder's expense. That is where Terrell found the picture and, realizing its potential for his sensational article, simply swiped it.

The article begins with quotes from Mrs. Toney.

"Every night as we were trying to get to sleep, we would hear groans and cries. It was like they were coming from the air! Sometimes, things would come flying right off the wall or turn upside down—that sort of stuff. It was so scary! We dreaded going to bed! Once, my little granddaughter woke up screaming because she saw a ghost woman, soaking wet, standing in the door-way. When I went to check on her, the floor around the door to her bedroom was covered with water! That's when I became as scared as she was!

"We knew we had to do something. We had heard of Brother Michael, over in Man and decided to call him the next day. Can you believe that he came over that very evening! He went right to work too, as soon as he got here. He was wearing some sort of wide ribbon around his neck which hung down past his waist. It had an angel on each side. Between the ribbon with the two angels was the oddest cross I'd ever seen—like two or three crosses all put together, with a picture of Jesus hanging on it.

"Michael went through the house praying, sprinkling water on stuff, reading things out of a book—the Bible, I guess. He sang songs to weird melodies which he said were Bible verses. It took him about an hour to go all through the house. He wouldn't take money; said if I had some biscuits with honey or jam and would add a cup of coffee to go with it, that would be all the payment he needed.

"There never were no more ghosts or noises after that! It's been peaceful ever since."

Another story was about a man suffering from black lung.

"Couldn't get no air at night," the man said. "Somebody told me to call that preacher fellow over at Man—originally from up the road a bit, in Mingo County, they said. So, I called him. I figured it couldn't hurt; the doctors sure weren't doing much for me.

"He came here hisself and just talked for a while—told me stories about his folk workin' down in the mines, stuff like that. Before he left, he hung a cross over my head and smeared something on my forehead, right over my eyes. Then he asked me if I had noticed that I was already breathing better. I hadn't been paying any attention to it, but by golly, he was right! Now the he had mentioned it I realized that I wasn't havin' much trouble breathing.

"Ain't that something?"

"Brother Michael told me that if I was havin' trouble at night to put that cross around my neck, close my eyes, and hold on to it as I said the Lord's Prayer. That's what I've done and it always seems to help.

"He also told me to keep goin' to the doctor, which I have. I don't tell the doctor about Brother Michael. I just tell him I have been feeling better lately."

There were a few other stories in the article about holy oil, water getting sprinkled on things that needed exorcised, and so forth. The overall impression of the article was that Michael was some sort of Appalachian shaman who used Christian language to mystify needy people.

Several people I interviewed insisted that Michael found the *Speculator* article embarrassing. He didn't write anything about it in his journals. Fortunately, he did reference it in a letter to Sofiya.

"There was an article about me in one of those papers one finds when checking out of supermarkets," he writes.

"Whoever wrote it took advantage of a nice lady who lives in one of the towns affected by the '72 flood. She had been traumatized like the rest of us, but evidently, she didn't get any sort of professional help. Anyway, she found it increasingly difficult to sleep in her house. Since it had been built on higher ground than most of the other homes, it survived the flood. However, she watched from her porch as debris, including a few dead bodies, was being carried away by the water. The experience naturally left her anxious.

"I took my time blessing the house and carried it out with exaggerated ceremony, thinking it would give her a way to process and reframe her painful memories. When I finished, I told her not to worry anymore, that her house was blessed and that nothing evil could now touch her or her family.

"How the tabloid writer discovered the story is beyond me, and what he made of it demonstrates a creative imagination that could be put to a more profitable use in film. Anyway, the article resulted in a constant stream of visitors, phone calls, and letters. People keep coming for prayer, exorcism, and other kinds of miraculous intervention. Most of these requests are from poor people without material resources. The needs they describe, even the psycho-somatic ones, are very real and I do what I can to comfort them.

"These needy people are too desperate to exercise healthy skepticism, and I don't feel bad at them. What bothers me are the religious leaders and some of the wealthy people around here who find this grasping for hope amusing. Nearly every week, someone pokes fun at me in some public place. They ask me to do things like bless a lottery ticket or heal their baldness. I always laugh with them.

"I take no offense at this mostly good-natured humor. However, in some cases, underneath what presents as good-natured fun is really a disdain for suffering people, people who have their entire lives, put up with daily deprivation and a sense of personal powerlessness. Most of these deprivations are the products of a purposefully designed social structure crafted to hide the consequences of unrestrained greed and power on the part of those who control our region.

"The truth of the matter is, if I really was a 'miracle worker,' I would do a whole lot more than exorcise spirits from old houses. I would bring in food and shelter, clinics and hospitals, and, perhaps most of all, good schools—the kinds of things that might exorcise the real ghosts of Southern West Virginia—poverty, illness, and ignorance.

"Hopefully all is well with you. My best to Rwanna, by the way."

As to the question of whether miraculous cures or supernatural phenomena were truly features of Brother Michael's final years, we must conclude that the answer lies in the eye of the beholder. Michael never made such claims for himself. In fact, he generally offered natural explanations for the stories told about him. At the same time, those stories abound. Some are difficult to explain, especially those from people who describe themselves as naturally skeptical. One such story came from a man who knew Michael when he was a student in Pittsburgh.

Dear Mr. Canterbury,

Please excuse the tardy response to your letter dated August 13. To tell you the truth, it provoked many memories I found both delightful and disturbing. So, I needed to think about how to respond.

As you mentioned, I served as catechist in this diocese for about six years. That was the time and setting for my relationship with Michael Cooper. Father Anastasia had asked me to give this young student from Carnegie Mellon special attention because, our priest believed, Michael showed potential for the diaconate, perhaps even for the priesthood. That's why I arranged to meet him at one of the sandwich shops near the university.

It was early spring and still a bit chilly here in Pittsburgh but I remember Michael was wearing only a light sweater when he sat down and ordered a coffee. I was worried he might be cold.

I was aware though of something I noticed each time I met him: his gray blue eyes that seemed to pierce into one's thoughts. It unnerved me. Don't get me wrong, Michael was courteous and respectful, though self-conscious and perhaps a bit neurotic. Nonetheless, I always thought he was the one doing the interrogating. It never seemed to matter that I was supposedly his teacher.

Our catechism lessons, which began soon after our meeting and lasted for several months, were uneventful. Well, except for two things. First, Michael asked rather challenging questions about the Trinity. I had to do some research to answer them. Secondly, was his an audacious claim that I had a mole on the inside of my left thigh that was about to turn malignant. He blurted that out one day after catechism.

Since I did indeed have a mole on my left thigh— something he would have had no way to have known, I was rather disturbed. He was aware of my discomfort and told me not to worry. He assured me that the mole had not yet turned cancerous but that I should visit a dermatologist soon to have it checked out. This bizarre experience shook me up. I thought it about it quite a bit over the next several weeks.

Unfortunately, by the time I saw a doctor, the mole had indeed turned cancerous. Although the doctors were able to remove it, I was left with a deep scar. That has been many years ago. I have had no further problems with skin cancer.

Obviously, one doesn't forget experiences like that. The truth is, Michael's intervention saved my life. Whether that constitutes a miracle depends on one's view of reality—another one of Michael's favorite subjects.

Through the years, I have put the incident with Michael down to one of those mysterious hints that there may be more at work in the universe than what we usually see and understand. There is a beautiful line from Shakespeare about that very thing which I have long ago forgotten. Engineers tend to forget such things!

One thing more: I suspect this strange story had something to do with my subsequent calling into the diaconate. Michael's mysterious warning reawakened the wonder of my faith.

I hope that helps. If I can be of any further help in your investigation, please don't hesitate to ask.

Sincerely,
    Father Cyril

25

THE POWERS THAT BE
SAMUEL CANTERBURY

In June of 1994, Shane Collins, grateful for his dramatic recovery from crack addiction, offered Michael a long-term lease on a property located in downtown Logan, for $1.00 a year.

Mr. Collins' hope was that Brother Michael would use this property on Bridge Street to open a branch of St. Patrick's Healing House. Michael accepted the offer. He began working there three days a week, spending the nights in a backroom that contained a cot and a desk. Soon, a steady stream of people were visiting Michael in Logan just as they had in Man.

The Logan center operated similarly as the one in Man, with programs focused on addiction recovery, education, health care, and spiritual instruction. Over the following months, volunteers built a makeshift chapel and meeting rooms within the century-old building to accommodate this work.

Brother Michael, much like country and state law enforcement, declared war on drugs. Unlike secular authorities however, Michael never declared a war on drug addicts. Painted on the back wall of the chapel in the Logan center was the words which expressed his view about recovery as a form of exorcism: *"They Who Sat In Darkness Have Seen a Great Light."*

Michael saw drug addicts as victims and poisoners and believed he had access to a power that could overcome darkness.

Whether that was true or not, the poor and drug addicted believed it and poured into the centers he had founded in search for deliverance. Today, hundreds of people throughout Logan and Mingo trace their journey out of drug dependency and poverty to an inspiring evening at St. Patrick's. Michael's work has made an immediate and deep impression in Southern West Virginia because hope became available to those who had been utterly without resources.

It is hard to understand why this did not make everyone happy.

The truth is though, there is functionality in every dysfunction, a way of operating within chaos that often benefits the few even as it disables the many. Although the recovery movement often brings increased health and hope to the disadvantaged, it sometimes threatens those who through comparison to their addicted neighbors have seemed smarter, holier, or more mature than the ones through whom the dysfunction has been more overtly manifested.

An old Spanish proverb says that in the village of the blind, the one-eyed man becomes king. Or, to put the principle in less proverbial terms, when the family drunk suddenly gets well, the cruelty and deception of the other family members quickly become visible. When this occurs, you can be sure that some will blame those who have turned on the light rather than acknowledge the sickness of their soul.

At any rate, as the stories of healing and deliverance increased, a web of influential people, both in government and in the religious community, began unifying around a growing distrust and disdain of Brother Michael. As with most webs, this web was spun and maintained by a spider, and her name was Sadie McCormick.

"Sadie McCormick was nobody to mess with," said Dr. Joe Welsby, former pastor of the McFarlin Methodist Church in Man, West Virginia.

"When she was younger, she was a mover and shaker over at Nighbert United Methodist in Logan," he continued. "Then she joined up with some religious women who traveled around the country to meet famous preachers. After that, she turned into a crusader for righteousness in Logan County. This calling required her to expose people she viewed as secret deviants, miscreants, or God help us—Darwinists. After the *Speculator* article, she added Brother Michael to her list.

"No, I didn't put that quite right. Sadie didn't just put Michael *on* her list, she moved him clean up to the top! Michael Cooper represented everything Sadie McCormick thought spiritually wrong with Southern West Virginia and so she made it her business to bring him down.

"She started calling people, writing letters to the

paper, holding meetings all over the county—and in surrounding counties to boot. She just built a fire under her behind about what she called Michael's 'demonic influence;' that and her hints about Michael being gay.

'How could he not be gay?' she said. 'Him being unmarried, working with all those young men, never seen flirting with a woman . . .'

"She would say things like that and then raise one eyebrow without finishing the sentence.

"Lord, that woman was a piece of work.

I had asked Dr. Welsbey to help me make sense of why so many church leaders in Logan County responded to Michael's work the way they did. Once he started talking about Sadie, he could not seem to stop.

"Sadie would not have become as much of a pain if she had not been constantly playing bridge and heading up charity drives. If you ask me, her husband, George, was delighted to throw some money at her social causes to keep her out of his hair. Unfortunately, that charitable work helped her form relationships with pastor's wives, country club members, coal mining officials—just about anyone who held any kind of ecclesial, social, corporate, or political power in Southern West Virginia. She used all those connections to stir up trouble for Michael.

"I'll tell you a funny story. Fred Saunders pastored over at Nighbert for several years. He told me that when Sadie stopped coming to his church because it was not spiritual enough, it was the best birthday present anyone had ever given him. She had made his life a living hell you see, constantly stirring up gossip, strife—as soon as one cause had settled down, she was cooking up a new one! The woman had more drive for meanness than I ever saw in a person.

"Anyway, Fred came over here one Sunday afternoon after church and said, 'Joe, I want a glass of wine, a big glass—or maybe two. That harpy's gonna drive me straight to the nut house at Spencer before she's done!'

"So, Fred was probably glad to see her move out of his church and find some new enemies.

"Anyway, we all knew that poor Michael didn't have a chance. The truth is, a lot of people around here thought of Michael as a bit awkward, unsocial, and distant. People up the hollers didn't see him that way, but those who mattered here in Logan and over in Mingo County certainly did. In their eyes, Michael was upsetting things by giving a voice to the sort of folk Sadie and her friends wanted to forget. In their world, those who mattered knew how to make money. If you didn't know how to do that, it was evidence that the Good Lord had not seen fit to advance your cause."

"But Dr. Welsby," I interjected, "wasn't she intrigued with all the reports of unusual phenomenon connected to Brother Michael?"

"Oh, all the hullabaloo about miracles positively enraged Sadie," he said. "She saw it as proof of Michael's connection to demonic powers. After that stupid article in the *Speculator*, she worked even harder to get religious leaders in Southern West Virginia fired up against this 'wolf in sheep's clothing,' as she called him.

"You must understand, Sam, that even though Sadie got excited about television preachers, faith healers, and all of that, what she had in mind was the rich ones on television. She had no use for poor people around here who took that stuff seriously. She wanted charismatic experience considerably more refined than what the holy rollers up Buffalo Creek offered. And Lord—any connection with Catholicism was certainly not a part of any future she envisioned for a redeemed Logan County. To Sadie, Michael was a holy roller, hillbilly, Catholic Frankenstein. He brought together everything she despised.

"Michael ignored Sadie. He thought that she would respond to his kindness and patience. He was naïve about that. He tried several times to meet with her face-to-face, but she always refused.

"Unfortunately for Michael, Sadie was intelligent, charming, and socially connected. That's why her crusade became increasingly convincing to those who mattered. She didn't intend to stop until he was out of the picture.

"I think if I would have been Michael, I would have hired a hit man to take her out. Hit men aren't that hard to find in Logan County! Of course, had I done that I would have lost my pension with the Methodist Church and couldn't have retired over here in Greenbrier County! My wife sure wouldn't have been happy about that.

"Also, I never claimed to be as saintly a person as Michael Cooper, and believe me, that is a considerable understatement."

26

LIGHTING THE FUSE
SAMUEL CANTERBURY

Despite the growing opposition, or perhaps even because of it, Michael Cooper remained aloof from the political and social life of Southern West Virginia. Because the churches of Southern West Virginia were being increasingly drawn into local and national politics, Michael's detachment raised suspicions on all sides. Regardless, he endorsed no candidate, worked for no political party, and ignored all invitations to formal dinners where such things were promoted. He remained busy hosting twelve step groups, praying for the sick, and facilitating discussions; doing, in other words, those things he believed helped people help themselves.

One notable exception was a letter he wrote to the *Charleston Gazette*. It was published as an op-ed piece in a Sunday edition in late April 1996 as a response to a series of articles about the role of religion in West Virginia. (As a point of self-disclosure, I was one of the writers for this series.)

Michael pulled out the stops in this letter, hitting several issues that he clearly intended to hit as hard as he could. Unfortunately, this fired up some old enemies and made several new ones.

I have decided to quote the entire letter in hopes that the reader will sense its intensity and perhaps understand the fury it provoked.

I want to thank the Charleston Gazette for its recent articles on the religious life of Southern West Virginia. Every day, I work with church leaders who give themselves to care for the people of this state, and your acknowledgment of their service has been encouraging.

Religion has suppressed, if not eliminated, many grosser forms of vice that have plagued our region. Few influences have been as effective as religion in confronting such evils as incest, addiction, and violence. Furthermore, the most effective kinds of religion in this regard have been the sort that grip individuals and sometimes entire communities at the emotional level. That is why I am not among those who disdain our native-grown expressions of Christian faith.

Christianity, both here and elsewhere, encourages and organizes the care of the sick and dying. It helps lift the heavy burdens of those permanently or temporarily disadvantaged and, in general, raises the quality of a people's moral and ethical life. The collection and distribution of food and clothing throughout the counties of Southern West Virginia by various Christian groups is an example.

No honest atheist, much less a believer, will minimize these benefits of religious life.

That said, believers rarely acknowledge religion's darker side which, in my opinion, honest men and women must do.

Historically, it has been too easy to use religion to stir up our darker passions, leading to wars against people of other religions and, at times, even against those of the same religion. Thankfully, we have rarely experienced that here, at least in its darker and more violent forms. What we do see in our state is a subtler (but no less destructive) effect of religious life: the willful and conscious embrace of ignorance as a form of piety.

This misuse of mystical experience as an escape from (or even a suppression of) knowledge affects learning much as attaching an anchor to a swimmer's foot affects swimming.

Mountain religious culture tends to harbor a disdain for any kind of knowledge that lacks an immediate, practical utility. In other words, we tend to appreciate knowing how to repair a car but do not appreciate the study of physics, neurology, or literature. Unfortunately, religion, through what it ignores and through what it promotes, plays a part in this suppression of civilized life.

In our state, religious people are rarely interested even in the history of their own religion or the intricacies of their own text. They are often much less interested in what they regard as secular subjects. Certainly, most professing Christians will try to avoid stealing, sleeping with someone else's spouse, or murdering anyone. However, this basic moral and ethical code rarely matures to include serious opinions about medical ethics, class stratification, or the dignity of work. Furthermore, this superficial religious life is not merely the passive result of disinterest in such things; it is the active result of a belief that Christians should not care about them. Thus, even though Holy Scripture constantly addresses education, personal moral development, social justice, and vocational life, many popular forms of Christianity deliberately suppress interest in such things.

These faults of religious life in Southern West Virginia constitute what generations of Christians called "sins of omission." As the old English prayer puts it, these are "the things we have left undone."

As for our "sins of *commission*," those "things we have done that we should not have done," I will mention only this: our obsession with end-of-time themes that rob our children of curiosity for those subjects that require years of discipline to understand or for fields of knowledge that our church leaders find suspicious. Naturally, if the universe is soon to be destroyed, what possible purpose is there for making any plans for one's future?

Unfortunately, this "know-nothing" strand of religious life keeps entrenching in our part of the nation. It will lead, I predict, to a further inability to govern ourselves. When uneducated people become afraid of the world because they feel disinvited to sources of knowledge or, are led by leaders they trust to be fearful of knowledge, they elect tyrants to think for them and to protect them. That is the reality of many of our churches and will soon be the reality of our political life as well. When religion becomes toxic, the poison seeps into every facet of community life. This is especially true of an area like ours in which religion is so influential.

The most serious component of toxic religion is the way it cooperates with and defends political corruption. When a religious leader, especially one from a financially disadvantaged background, meets at a country club with a county clerk, a political party boss, or a judge, the aim of the meeting is usually to at least silence and, if possible, make a religious leader complicit in the graft, violence, and fraud that plagues our state. The various expressions of Christian faith, which might otherwise offer a moral counterbalance to the secular powers of society, find themselves instead cooperating with the darkness.

Taken together, these toxic features of our religious life have combined to discredit funding for our schools, libraries, and social programs. They have empowered and emboldened the petty little Ahabs and Herods that rule our Southern counties. In these ways, a deficient and thoughtless form of Christianity is being deceived into defending and maintaining the structures of poverty and ignorance it was founded to destroy. And, most damning of all, many of our popular expressions of Christianity find themselves actively subverting the Gospel of Christ.

Rev. Michael Cooper
St. Patrick's House of Healing
Logan, West Virginia

Michael's letter hit a nerve.

Within days, television and radio preachers were commenting on it, which naturally resulted in more readers. One of the loudest voices was that of Brother Oliver Wayne, pastor of the Overflowing Life Assembly in Charleston and host of the television show, *Overcoming Life*.

Wayne came from a similar background as Michael Cooper. Wayne however, had successfully repackaged himself in the mold of the contemporary Charismatic movement. At Overcoming Life Assembly, people had little concern with sin and sanctification but focused instead on Biblical passages related to prosperity and health. They talked about being 'the head and not the tail,' and 'forgetting those things that are behind.'

Wayne was a superb story teller who could keep a crowd spellbound with his 'down-home' demeanor and self-deprecating remarks about having never been to "cemetery—I mean seminary," or, "I know a little Greek; he owns a restaurant over in Kanawha City," and other such banalities that never failed to amuse and delight. He was a master of directing a conversation away from topics that might reveal his ignorance about the world outside his own religious community.

Wayne's television program consisted of contemporary Christian music performed by local artists, followed by calls from listeners with questions about spiritual matters. Wayne, who evidently did not read the newspaper, learned of Michael's letter from one of these listeners, who proceeded to read a few lines of it over the air. This is the portion she read:

"Naturally, if the universe is soon to be destroyed, what possible purpose is there for making any plans for one's future? Unfortunately, this 'know-nothing' strand of religious life keeps entrenching in our part of the nation and will lead, I predict, to a further erosion of our ability to govern ourselves. When ignorant people become afraid of the world, they elect tyrants to think for them and protect them. That is what we are already doing in many of our churches and will soon be doing in our political lives as well."

Wayne's immediate response was rather lame. However, by the next day, it was evident that he had read and reread the piece. In fact, Wayne spent an hour, not so much attacking the piece, which he only half-heartedly attempted, but by attacking what he called "this would-be New-age false prophet who is himself a fulfillment of Christ's prophesy about the end of times."

Listening to these old recordings, it occurred to me that Wayne was probably more defensive about the learned tone of Michael's letter than by the content, which he seems to have only superficially grasped. Also, the letter threatened Wayne's economic interests.

Wayne had just released a new book—offered free to "those donors giving $30.00 or more to the support of this broadcast"—entitled: *Understanding God's Calendar: Fifteen Prophetic Realities that Prove we are in the Last Days*.

With the charge about obsessing over the end of time continuing a religious pathology, Michael had fired a shot over the bow of Wayne's boat. For his part, Wayne, who despite his 'aw shucks' demeanor was known to possess both a thin skin and a hot temper, was furious. Furthermore, the remarks about religious compromise with political powers came the same week Wayne had appeared on stage with a candidate for the United States Congress. A picture of this event had been blown up to banner size and placed inside the church vestibule. Underneath were the words: "Let's Send a Man from God's House to the People's House!"

Wayne also felt he had to respond to Michael because he had heard that several people in his own church had made the trip to Logan for prayer. Even more egregious, several recovery groups had sprung up in Charleston served by facilitators trained at the St. Patrick's Centers in Logan and Man. In fact, Wayne's own daughter-in-law, Camellia, had joined one of these groups. It was there she had found the courage to press her husband into confronting his parents about several family issues.

After Wayne's program on May 4, 1994, Sadie McCormick made a trip to Charleston to meet with the locally famous television preacher. In this meeting, Wayne evidently promised to pass along her concerns about "irregularities in the St. Patrick's Healing Centers" to the State Auditor, with whom he had breakfast twice a month at the capitol building. Meanwhile, the attacks continued from Wayne's pulpit on Sunday and on his daily television program.

After the first week, the attacks were rarely pointed at Michael personally, though the innuendos were obvious. (It is thought that the church's lawyer had given the preacher some advice about that.) However, Wayne's warnings about New Age influence in the twelve-step program, demons appearing as angels of light, and the ever-effective accusations about "undercover Jesuits who were at this very moment infiltrating our mountain countries" alarmed many listeners.

Meanwhile, the listening audience of Wayne's daily television program drastically increased. Best of all, donors, interested in obtaining Wayne's informative book about the end of time lined up to make contributions.

Someone had made hundreds of copies of the old *Speculator* article in the meantime, and one Sunday morning decided to distribute them to worshippers at Overcoming Life Assembly while they were walking from the parking lot into the church. Ushers tried to stop the people distributing these papers but the church attenders, angry about the ushers' heavy-handed approach, began asking for stacks of them to share with their friends. Wayne felt compelled to address this matter publicly, which resulted in an increased demand for copies of the article around the city. The old issue began popping up around town in convenient stores, which added further fuel to the fire.

Because of the unexpected publicity, the healing centers in Man and Logan were swamped by calls from all over the state for prayer and information about dealing with addiction. The Fall sessions at both the Man and Logan Centers were packed to capacity, placing a strain on the volunteer networks that sustained these programs.

Michael, who was of course at the very center of this controversy, seemed only slightly aware of it and only marginally interested in knowing more about it. He rarely watched Christian television and seemed unimpressed with Wayne, but most of his disinterest was probably the result of his heavy schedule and passionate commitment to his work.

That would all change by late Fall.

The Tuesday night after Thanksgiving, 1996, Woody Samuelson was driving a couple of men home from a twelve-step meeting. On a whim, Mickey Goins decided to ride with them. When they saw flashing blue lights behind them, Woody stopped the car and then waited for the officer to approach him. When the officer asked him to get out of the car, he complied. He had just followed the officer to the side of his vehicle and had begun pulling his wallet out of his back pocket when one of the men riding in the car opened the back door, jumped out, and began running toward the woods. Mickey then jumped out of the car and ran after the man, pleading for him to come back.

Meanwhile, the officer had run to the front of the car, shouting for the man to stop. When he did not, the officer pulled out his gun. Mickey stepped in front of the officer at that point, with the likely intention of pleading with the officer not to shoot the man Mickey knew to be suffering from paranoia. The other two men in the car claimed the officer began to curse and then said, "OK then, carrot top! We'll do it your way!" The officer denies this and nothing of the sort appears in the official record of the incident.

Whatever was or was not said, the officer shot the boy in the stomach, then calmly returned to the patrol car and called for an ambulance, which arrived fifteen minutes later. Upon arriving, the paramedics shook their heads, loaded Mickey Goins' lifeless body in the ambulance, and then drove away.

Woody was taken into custody but released later that night. The two men who had been in the car had, by that time, walked back into town to St. Patrick's Healing House.

Michael was in Man at the time and didn't get the call until nearly midnight. When he did, he headed immediately to Logan and was, in fact, the one who formally identified Mickey's body. Billy Joe was in Beckley at the time, visiting family, and could not be reached for several hours.

In the following days, Michael descended into darkness. What appeared to be dangerous and silent depression alarmed the volunteers in Logan and Man. A few of them even feared that Michael might harm himself and debated whether they should ask for him to be admitted to a mental health facility for his own protection. These were well meaning and reasonable concerns but were thoroughly mistaken. Michael was not thinking about harming himself, though that was a story that emerged after what happened later in the year. What Michael was doing was planning how to turn up the heat.

Michelle Lazarus was one of those who witnessed Michael's growing resolve to act. At the time, she worked as a server at The Hot Spot, a decades-old restaurant most folk in Logan called simply "the diner."

"I was working at the Cafe the day Brother Michael came in," says Lazarus. "He pronounced doom on everybody connected to drug dealing, which, in his opinion, included the city and the county government."

"The sheriff had been sitting there for better than an hour," she continued. "I remember because I was watching the clock. The sheriff never tipped anybody, you see and would hold a table for as long as it suited him. He didn't care a hoot about how that affected us.

"A couple of the Pierce boys were sitting there with the sheriff, just telling jokes and shooting the breeze when Brother Michael came in. It was still pretty cold that March, but he didn't have on much of a coat. I remember that.

"He just burst through the door without saying anything to anybody. That wasn't like him, so I knew something was up. He headed straight to the booth where the sheriff and his owners were sitting.

"Brother Michael's eyes were on fire, and I thought to myself, 'Something bad is about to happen.' I certainly wasn't wrong about that! Anyhow, Brother Michael stood in front of their booth for the longest time before saying anything. He just stared like he was daring them to talk. When he finally spoke, what he said came out slow and stern—like when you're talking to a child that has done something bad.

"'Gentlemen,' he said, 'I've got a message for you and all your friends. Your little kingdom is coming down. You've got sixty days to make things right with God and with the people of this county. After that, judgment's coming.'

"God! I've never been so afraid in my life. I thought either Michael was gonna pull out a gun and shoot the sheriff or the sheriff was gonna shoot him. Even though it was just the sheriff and the two Pierce boys facing Brother Michael, it felt like some kind of a war was about to start in that diner with hundreds of people on both sides. My entire body broke out in a sweat! I could see that the sheriff and Pierce boys were afraid too. They didn't say anything at first. They seemed paralyzed.

"After a while, the sheriff found his voice.

"'Michael,' he said, 'everybody knows you're real upset about the Goins boy. Hell, everybody liked him. But he had a hard life and he made some wrong choices. Anyhow, we can't bring him back.

"'And by the way,' the Sheriff continued, 'you need to stop railing against coal companies and surface mining. I don't know where you learned all that environmentalist crap—those tree hugging creeps never worked a day in their lives, pampered little pussies that graduate from schools with ivy crawlin' up the walls—what do they know about work, real work? Coal is king around here and I mean to defend it. I might be the prince of coal! So, you need to just sit yourself down and have a cup of coffee.'

"Mad Dog pushed the salt shaker to the end of the table after he said that, like a dog pissing at the edge of a field to mark his territory.

"But Michael didn't sit down. He kept on a talking. And it was obvious that he was the one in control. After all, it was the sheriff who was sitting down!

"'You and your gang of thugs killed that boy,' Michael said. 'Fact is, you've killed lots of people. You steal, you harass people—you oppress this county like it belongs to you. But that's all about to come to an end.'

"'Whoah,' the sheriff replied. 'I can tolerate you being upset about the boy. I'll roll with that. But you can't start accusing people like you're doing. Besides, you're threatening people and I can take you in for that.'

"'You can take me anywhere you please,' Michael replied. 'This isn't about me. And I ain't threatenin'; I'm prophesyin.' There's a difference between those two things, something you're about to discover. So you better listen up. You've got thirty days. I'm not responsible for what happens after that.'

"When he had said his piece, Brother Michael walked out like he had come in; back straight, eyes a glowin', and peacefully fierce, like a lion resting on a rock might watch a man without a weapon.

"No one said anything for several seconds. It was Bud Pierce that broke the silence. 'Looks like we got us a crazy preacher on our hands, Sheriff. Crazy preachers do stupid things; they ain't no different that way than anyone else.'

"'Ahh, Michael?' the Sheriff replied. 'He's harmless. I knew his folks over in Mingo County, up Spice Holler.

They were all talk. Not a one of them worth owl bait. Snake handlers, most of 'em. He's just upset about the Goin's boy. Folks back in Mingo County say the boy was his. Maybe it was; the boy's momma sure was hot to trot. She wouldn't have minded to bed down a preacher.

"'Don't worry about Michael. He'll calm down directly.'"

27

THE SERPENT'S REVENGE

SAMUEL CANTERBURY

There seems to be no way of knowing what exactly occurred on May 26.

The healing centers were busy preparing for the Pentecost celebrations planned for the weekend. For the first few days of that week, no one seems to have thought to check on Michael's whereabouts. He was last seen alive Sunday afternoon in Man, at a dinner honoring two women from Buffalo Creek. One had earned a bachelor's degree and another one who had finished an MA program. All three had earned their GED at the Healing Center.

Afterward, Michael indicated he'd be spending the night at the Logan center. He left about 9:30.

What we know is that sometime late Sunday night, Michael Cooper and three unknown persons opened a rarely used door to the cellar under the Bridge Street property. All four of them walked down the first few steps, but then about halfway down, Michael fell, or was pushed, to the bottom of the stairs. At that point, a dozen large timber rattlers were tossed either on top of Michael or beside him. He was almost immediately bitten by several of them.

Michael's body was not found until Thursday afternoon. A recovery group facilitator looking for chairs opened the cellar door because he thought it led to a closet. He nearly fell down the stairs before he found the light switch. As soon as he did, he saw the body lying on the floor below and began calling for help.

That is what we know from the investigation. We do not know who accompanied Michael Cooper to the cellar or why they were there in the first place. At the time of this writing, the investigation continues. There is hope that in time to come we will learn more. Meanwhile, we have the voices of those who were involved in the case, one of the most interesting being that of James Cleaver, assistant to the county coroner.

My interview with Mr. Cleaver was one of the most upsetting couple of hours of my life. I needed to capture the essence of his experience with the autopsy. However, I found myself becoming too emotionally involved in his account to write anything. Weeks later, when I knew I had to get something down on paper, I took several days to listen to the recording and wrote the following:

"It was a hot August day, Mr. Canterbury," Mr. Cleaver began.

"Brother Michael's body had been down in that cellar for days. I don't mean to be gross but those kinds of conditions make for a real mess. And God Almighty, it was a mess!

"We already knew about the snakes before we went

—a dozen or so large, eastern diamondbacks! Just hearin' about them gave me the creeps. Meanwhile, the sheriff had been sayin' Brother Michael had gone crazy, that he had been raised in a snake-handlin' church over in Mingo County. Which, for all I know, he may have been! But Lord, everybody 'round here knows somebody that goes to that kind of church. We all know them people ain't crazy. I wouldn't have anything to do with it myself, but the folk I know that go to a snake-handling church don't handle no snakes unless they're in a church service. To think someone would tote a dozen big snakes down into a dark cellar by himself—there weren't no box or nothin' you see—somebody would've had to carry all them dammed snakes loose! Nobody does anything as stupid as that.

"The forestry people had removed the snakes, but the body was still layin' on the moist dirt. It was all swollen and disfigured by the snakebites and, of course, the decomposition. But the darndest thing about it was the body didn't stink! I don't mean to say that it wasn't as bad as I had expected, in some ways it was, but what I mean is . . .

"Jesus, I've never had . . .

"Well sir, it was kind of like rose and clove, just not as sweet . . . I just never smelled nothing like that before."

The Logan County Coroner's assistant was working hard to keep his composure.

"Damn, I hate this," Mr. Cleaver said, spitting out the words as if disgusted with himself. He then continued.

"What I'm trying to say Sam, is that I don't have no

category for what happened—not just that one day down in that cellar but in the days afterward.

"For one thing, that smell didn't go away after I left the cellar. It followed me on to my car and then into my house. My wife and kids smelled it. For weeks, it was like that. All sorts of people asked me what the smell was, but I didn't know then and don't know now. And I didn't want to talk about it.

"There was all kind of weirdness when we carried the body over for the autopsy too. For one thing, the county was expecting us to find evidence of suicide, which we didn't, though we tried. That was several weeks before the sheriff and the Pierce boys all got arrested in that FBI sting, you see. Anyway, the best we could do for the county was to make a statement for the papers about the results having been 'inconclusive; not definitively allowing us to rule out suicide'—that kind of double-talking political crap.

"And another thing: we unwrapped the bandage-like stuff Brother Michael kept on his hands. What we found underneath were the weirdest bruises I'd ever seen. I mean, his hands were hurt. It just wasn't due to anything anyone had done to him. It wasn't like he had cut himself or anything. The damned snakes couldn't have gotten through the bandages either. I don't know . . . the whole mess just creeped me out and it still does. I don't think I'll ever be the same.

"Take for instance—I haven't smoked a cigarette since that morning in the cellar when we were a pickin' up the body. I mean, I went into the cellar puffin' away on a Lucky Strike, like I had been doin' ever since junior high school. But I don't even know whether I finished that cigarette or not, or where it went if I didn't finish it. All I know is that it was several days before I noticed I hadn't been smoking. When I remembered that I ought to have been smoking, I felt plumb disgusted even by the thought of doing it. It was like it would be a crime to interfere with that other smell that had attached itself to me.

"I don't smell that fragrance much anymore; just catch a whiff of it every few months or so. But I still don't want no cigarette."

Billy Joe's retelling of the events surrounding the funeral and burial were also challenging to put into words. The best way to communicate what he said is to simply quote him:

"When the police were going through Michael's belongings, they found a letter in his desk. Evidently, he had kept it there so we would know what to do in the case of his death. The police gave that to me because my name was the one Michael had written on the envelope.

"The letter said that in the event of his death, we should call the bishop, who, as it turned out, lives up in Philadelphia. So, we called to tell him we were planning a funeral for early the next week. We had to give time for the coroner's office to do their work, the police investigation and all that, you see.

"Later in the day, the bishop called back to tell us that unfortunately he would be unable to attend the service but was sending a priest from Columbus, Ohio.

"When the fellow from Columbus showed up, he immediately started telling us what we could and could not do at the funeral. We couldn't have the kind of music people sing around here, for example. His idea seemed to be that he should read some words out of a book, get things over with as soon as possible, and then get out of here. He also made sure to inform us about all his titles and accomplishments, which impressed us about as much as finding a doorbell on a tombstone.

"Well sir, as you can imagine, the funeral was as dry as a popcorn fart! The priest went ahead and read his prayers like he was solving algebra problems for a high school teacher. He walked around all high and mighty, like he had a 2x4 up his batootie, and it just didn't please anybody down here. Not at all. I bet all of three people went forward to receive communion, which didn't seem to bother the priest any.

"I don't know what they teach preachers like that up in Ohio. I've only been there a couple times myself, and I probably shouldn't say this but I'd just as soon live down in Hell with my back broke as live up there!

"Of course, it was a right good drive over to Mingo County to the graveside. I had the preacher with me because I wasn't sure he'd be able to find his own way back out. He expected, just as we all did, that the graveside service wouldn't take much time. But when we turned that bend over near Spice Holler—the one right before the old Mullins Cemetery—we saw cars parked on both sides of the road, all over the grass. There must've been 70 of them! The license plates told us that the people were from Georgia, North Carolina, Tennessee and Kentucky—I had no idea, and I still don't exactly, how all those people got the word about the graveside service, or why it was so important to them to be there.

"I found out later that folks over in Mingo County had heard the story that the sheriff had first put out. He wanted people to think that Michael had gone crazy and had carried those snakes down into the cellar for some kind of private snake handling service. People knew that something was wrong with that story! Still, the way mountain people interpreted it was that Michael had been persecuted on account of his upbringing. Far as they were concerned, his death had returned him to the fold. That's why in their mind, they needed to come to bury one of their own. They figured he was someone who had died from being snake bit while he was a prayin'. Folks from those kind of churches don't mind travelin' hundreds of miles, you see, to attend the funeral of somebody who's been bitten by a snake thataway.

"Well, the priest commenced to carry out the service just like he had planned. He opened his book. He read a Psalm. He said a prayer. It was all just as formal and uninteresting as he knew how to make it—which was something I could tell he was good at.

Meanwhile, the folk who had come in those cars had been standin' around waitin' for the priest to get done. When they heard him say amen, they started gatherin' round the grave. Nobody knew what they intended to do. We could just tell they had something up their sleeve by that intense look on their faces.

"It didn't take long before some woman started hollerin' in a way that could've awakened the dead, a hollerin' out the first words of a song folk around here sometimes sing at funerals.

> *"'Ain't no grave gonna hold my body down;'*
> *ain't no grave going to hold my body*
> *down.*
> *When I hear the trumpets sound, gonna get*
> *up out of the ground;*
> *Ain't no grave can hold my body down.'*

"Soon, they were all singin' at the top of their lungs in the weird kind of harmony that shakes a man's soul loose from hisself. They went on and on like that. When they finished that first song, it was obvious they weren't done yet 'cause they all started singin'.

> *"'I'm a child of the King, yes I am, Yes I am.*
> *I'm a child of the King, yes I am.'*

"I knew then we were in for it then because I've heard that song sung before and I recollected it had right near 600 verses. That ain't much of an exaggeration either!

"By this time there must've been 15 tambourines and God knows how many guitars. People were clappin' and singin,' and at one point they stopped singing for a few minutes while some guy in the back spoke in tongues. It raised the hair up on the back of my neck!

"It went on that way for an hour or more. I don't remember all the songs. I just recall them a singin' *I'm a*

Holiness Child because they got all right worked up with that one!

"About forty minutes into this graveside service, I looked over at that poor Ohio preacher. Ain't no other way to put it; he was plumb terrified. A twistin' first this way and then that a way, constantly tryin' to see if our car was still blocked, which it was. The guys from Logan had made sure of that!

"I told the Ohio preacher that the snakes were about to come out and that him being a man of God and all, it wouldn't be proper for him not to participate. It was a lie of course, and I hope the good Lord will forgive me for it; but I just couldn't help myself. Lord, that man was plumb miserable!

"Anyhow, after the undertakers had buried Michael's body, and all those folks were singing the 30th verse of some song I can't recall, a blue mist came from nowhere and settled over everybody.

"I swear to God that's what happened. There ain't no pictures of it and nobody's going to believe me, but everybody out there that day saw it just the same. Not only did we see it, we smelled it. I don't know what it was, and I figure somebody over in Charleston will give you a perfectly natural explanation. All I know is the people around that grave went stark raving nuts.

"I'm a mountain man. I've lived around this kind of stuff my whole life. Sometimes I think it's fake. Sometimes I don't. I've never really made up my mind about it. All I can tell you standin' here right now is that something happened out there on the mountain that I don't have no explanation for."

Two years after the events Billy Joe Jarrell described, I was putting the finishing touches this manuscript. I decided to go Mingo County and visit Brother Michael's grave. On an autumn, late-afternoon, I read aloud the transcript of the interview with Billy Joe, imagining the scene he had described. After I finished, I stared at Brother Michael's tombstone and meditated on the inscription: *He Shall Wipe Away Every Tear From Their Eyes.*

I saw then that the stone was taunting the darkness; that the brutalized corpse beneath it was a guarantee of the ultimate defeat of everything that oppressed and exploited our majestic hills and a promise of final liberation for the people of God who live in them.

28

A FINAL WORD
SAMUEL CANTERBURY

I originally planned to end the book with that. However, something happened after I wrote it that I knew needed to be added.

The day I finished the book, I had prepared a hard copy and put it in a box to send to the publisher. Since I was going to the post office anyway, I took a notice with me that I had received from the post office a couple of days before.

The notice was about a package that was being held for me at the post office. It said that I should bring a valid form of identification to claim it. The strange thing about it was that it was addressed to "St. Patrick's Healing House, c/o Samuel Canterbury, Montgomery Director."

Of course, there is no such thing as a center like that in Montgomery and so I am not the director of anything!

Elsie Wells was working at the post office that day and she was the one who weighed the box containing the manuscript, and had me sign the forms for sending it certified mail. After we had done all of that, I paid and then handed her the notice I had received.

After typing my driver's license number into the computer, she went into a back room, and then returned with a box about the size of a book, which is what I assumed it contained.

"Sam, do you know anything about this package?" she asked.

I told her I didn't.

"It doesn't happen very often, but sometimes a package will get lost for a while," she said. "I've never seen one lost this long though. It's taken nearly three years to get here. All this time it has been sent from place to place for some reason. It originally came from somewhere near Pikeville, Kentucky, but there's no return address on it. There's just this one scribbled word I'm trying to make out. Is that an "M" at the beginning of the word? I think it is. If so, it says 'Mullins.' Do you know anyone over there by that name?"

"Not really," I replied, feeling the same strange chill I had felt when all this business started.

I didn't want to open the package there at the post office. I was afraid of what I might find. But when I got home, I sat on my couch and placed it on the coffee table in front of me. I used a pocketknife to carefully open it up. Inside was a Russian-style metal cross attached to a leather cord.

As soon as I saw that cross, I was aware of an overpowering fragrance.

Lois had come in while I was opening the package and was standing in the doorway watching. I could tell

that she had started to ask, "What did you get this time?"
And I could hear from the tone of her voice that she was
intending to add something sarcastically humorous. But
she never got that far.

She was crying.

"My God, Sam! What's that smell?" she asked.

I looked up and saw she was beaming, like someone
in love. She had also run out of words.

All I could find to say back was, "I don't know, Lois. It
smells like God."

ALSO BY DAN SCOTT

FAITH IN THE AGE OF AI

Artificial Intelligence, decoding the human genome, links between mind and computer... All these things that were once science fiction, are now quickly—and *absolutely*—becoming science *fact*.

The world is understandably worried. Fortunately, this isn't the first time humanity has faced such uncertainty.

In Faith in the Age of AI, pastor, scholar, and counselor Dan Scott invites you to learn what revered early writers—from Plato to St. Paul, and Laozi to C.S. Lewis—have already said about faith in the age of Artificial Intelligence.